When scandal and an ambitious prosecutor wreck talented chef Scarlett Ross's life and she learns of a grandmother she never knew she had, she flees the notoriety to pay an anonymous visit to Sweetgrass Springs, Texas, a town kept alive only by her grandmother's determination and carried on the strong shoulders of sexy Texas cowboy Ian McLaren. There she is surprised to discover a yearning to sink roots deep in the Texas Hill Country—but she is terrified that the secrets she's hiding will endanger everyone she's come to love.

Texas Roots

Texas Heroes:
The Gallaghers of Sweetgrass Springs
Book One

Jean Brashear

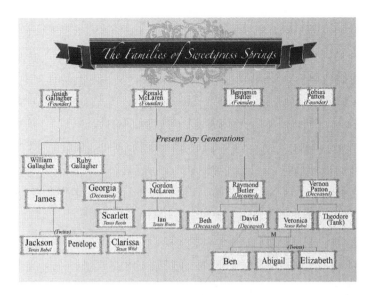

The Families of Sweetgrass Springs

Josiah Gallagher *(Founder)* — Ronald McLaren *(Founder)* — Benjamin Butler *(Founder)* — Tobias Patton *(Founder)*

Present Day Generations

- William Gallagher — Ruby Gallagher
- James
- Georgia *(Deceased)*
- Gordon McLaren
- Raymond Butler *(Deceased)*
- Vernon Patton *(Deceased)*
- Scarlett *Texas Roots*
- Ian *Texas Roots*
- Beth *(Deceased)*
- David *(Deceased)*
- Veronica *Texas Rebel*
- Theodore *(Tank)*

(Twins)

- Jackson *Texas Rebel* — Penelope — Clarissa *Texas Wild*

M

(Twins)

- Ben — Abigail — Elizabeth

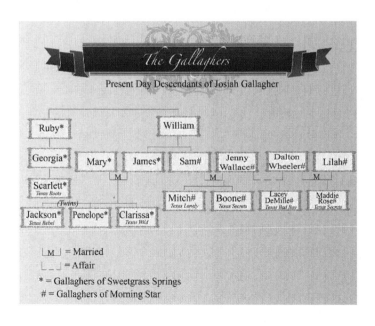

The Gallaghers

Present Day Descendants of Josiah Gallagher

- Ruby*
- William
- Georgia*
- Mary* — James* — Sam# — Jenny Wallace# — Dalton Wheeler# — Lilah#
- Scarlett* *Texas Roots*

M

- Mitch# *Texas Lonely* — Boone# *Texas Secrets* — Lacey DeMille# *Texas Bad Boy* — Maddie Rose# *Texas Secrets*

(Twins)

- Jackson* *Texas Rebel* — Penelope* — Clarissa* *Texas Wild*

⌊M⌋ = Married

⌊_ _⌋ = Affair

* = Gallaghers of Sweetgrass Springs

\# = Gallaghers of Morning Star

The Legend of
Sweetgrass Springs

L ost and alone and dying, thirsty and days without food, the wounded soldier fell from his half-dead horse only yards from life-giving water. His horse nickered at the scent, and the soldier gathered one last effort to belly his way to the edge of the spring.

But there he faltered. Bleeding from shoulder and thigh, he felt the darkness close in on him and sorrowed for his men, for the battle he would lose, for the fight he would not finish. In his last seconds of life, he wished for the love he would never find.

Rest, a lovely, musical voice said.

He managed to drag his eyes open once more.

And gazed upon the face of the most beautiful woman he'd ever seen.

And perhaps the saddest. Her eyes were midnight blue and filled with a terrible grief as she lifted a hand toward him.

I am dying, he thought. *I will never know her.*

But the woman smiled and tenderly caressed his face as she cradled his head and brought life-giving water to his lips.

You will live, she said. *Be at peace. Let the spring heal you.*

Around him the air went soft, the water slid down his throat like a blessing. His battered body relaxed, and the pain receded.

Sleep, she said. *I will watch over you.*

He complied, his eyes heavy. His injuries were too severe; he knew he could not live. But though he would not wake up, he was one of the fortunate, to have an angel escort him into the afterlife. *Thank you*, he managed with his last breath.

Wake. All is well.

The soldier opened his eyes, surprised to feel soft grass beneath him, trees whispering overhead. From nearby, he heard the bubbling music of the spring.

Then he saw her, his angel. *Where am I? Is this heaven?*

Her lips curved, but her eyes were again midnight dark with sorrow. *You are still of this world.*

Who are you? he asked. *Why are you sad?*

She searched his eyes. *Will you stay with me?*

I would like nothing more, but I cannot. I must return to my men.

She turned her face away, and he felt her grief as his own.

I'll come back. When the battle is over and I am done, I will come back to you.

You won't. A terrible acceptance filled her gaze. *I will never have love. Once I was mortal like you, and I was loved, but I turned away from it. From him, my one true love. He was beloved of The Fates, and they cursed me to wait. I cannot leave this place.*

Wait for what?

It doesn't matter, she said sadly. *You must go. They always go.*

I'll come back. I'll set you free. Tell me how, and I'll do it.

She stared into him for a long time, then shook her head. *There's only one way.*

What is it? he asked eagerly, rising strong and well again, already searching for his horse to ride away.

She watched him in silence. Made herself invisible because she knew.

Where did you go? he called out, searching the clearing, striding to the spring to peer into its depths. When he didn't see her, with a heavy heart he mounted, but for a moment he lingered. *I'll come back, I promise. You can tell me then. I'm sorry, but my men need me, and I have to go. I will return for you.*

He wouldn't, she knew. They never did. She'd brought her eternal loneliness on herself, and she was losing hope.

So she watched him ride away after one last look.

Only love can set me free, she whispered softly.

Love strong enough to stay.

Prologue

Each night her café was open—which was every day but Sunday—Ruby Gallagher declared a twenty-minute recess she called halftime. Coming not long before sunset, halftime wasn't actually the midpoint of a day that began at four every morning, but it was her recess and she'd by golly call it what she wanted.

Climbing the stairs to the cupola on top of the court-house—all three stories of it—was a whole lot harder at seventy-one than it had been when she'd first declared halftime the year her daughter ran away. Ruby figured she was still on her feet all day and into the night because, well, she stayed on her feet. Didn't sit on her fanny watching soaps all day or whatever foolishness passed for retirement. She had no desire to be idle.

Her work wasn't done.

She stared out the arch that was her picture window to the glory of the Texas Hill Country, the rolling peaks, the gnarled mushroom shapes of the live oak trees, the ribbon of water fed by Sweetgrass Spring that curved through the center of the town that was the spring's namesake.

She was weary to her bones, not that she'd ever say so to anyone but herself. Discouraged, too, though that was something else she wouldn't breathe to a soul. There was a note coming due on this decrepit old courthouse she'd purchased several years back after the county commissioners had decided to move the county seat to a bigger town. Lacking its center, Sweetgrass had been dying ever since, and she couldn't stand to watch its demise.

She'd been determined to start reviving her hometown by not letting this grand old limestone building fall to wrack and ruin. She'd had high hopes for putting Sweetgrass back on the map the way it once had been, back when everyone in the county came to town to do their business.

These days, Ruby's Café was about all the business that still existed.

And she was fast running out of options.

But as she gazed out at these hills that had been a grant to her Gallagher forebears and the three other founding families, all veterans of the Texas Revolution, the sacred charge she'd felt since she was knee-high to a grasshopper stirred inside her.

Fifteen hundred sixty-seven folks still called Sweetgrass their home, even if few of their children stayed on. How could she let it die on her watch?

She just couldn't, that was all. Nor could she abandon The Lady, the spirit of the spring, waiting so long for her lost love. Others thought her only a legend, but Ruby felt her presence. Felt in her bones the sorrow and the loneliness.

Sometimes even heard her voice. *Stay.*

Love strong enough to stay.

It wasn't only in hopes that her daughter would return that Ruby had never left Sweetgrass. She'd been hearing The Lady since she was young, had a few times seen her sad, pretty face.

I've stayed, Ruby thought. *But so many others have gone, and you're still caught here, aren't you? We're a pair, aren't we?*

A pitiful pair, she sometimes thought. Two fools who couldn't pack up and go and just...forget.

She glanced up at the evening star as it appeared.

Star light, star bright
First star I've seen tonight
I wish I may, I wish I might
Have this wish I wish tonight.

Her eyes scanned the darkened buildings below, save only the bright lights of Ruby's, the faint glow from her aunt Margie's house just behind it—her house now.

She'd lost a child but she still had a town to mother.

Please, she wished with everything in her, *don't let me fail in this, too.*

Chapter One

What had possessed her mother to keep Sweetgrass Springs a secret for thirty-two years? To tell her that they had no family?

Scarlett Ross pressed the accelerator and tried to think about that mystery instead of the fear that tangled beneath her breastbone: would she be safe there?

No one knew about the town—she herself had not until two weeks ago. She hoped she'd been careful enough in her hasty exit from New York—she'd certainly never expected to find herself in a situation like this. She had bought a throwaway cell phone—not that she had anyone to call after the scandal—and the car was not registered in her name. She hadn't had any use for a car in Manhattan, so she'd never owned one.

The District Attorney would be furious, of course. He wanted her on hand in case her testimony would make the difference. How that could be, when she'd known nothing about her boyfriend Andre's illegal activities until she'd wound up in handcuffs, she hadn't a clue.

But that didn't seem to matter to a DA running for reelection, determined to take down a very bad man named Viktor Kostov. Kostov, she'd learned, was suspected in a variety of crimes both here and in his native Bulgaria, and the DA would use anything that might possibly help him. He didn't want to believe in her innocence. Blind ambition, yes—that she was guilty of. Being too trusting—check. Ridiculous optimism? That, too.

What seems too good to be true usually is, she'd always been told—but she'd wanted her chance so badly. She was a talented chef, but there were plenty like her in New York, so when she'd been offered a shot at headlining in a high-end restaurant, she'd jumped on it with both feet.

Damn you, Andre.

She crested the last hill, the tiny town a small diamond of light cushioned in flocked green velvet as the smudged violet of night stole over the Texas Hill Country. January here was far kinder than in New York. While the grass was a flaxen hue and some trees were only bare trunks and branches, many were still green.

The road curved left, right, left again, while Sweetgrass Springs winked in and out of view. Dead tired from the long drive fleeing the wreckage of her life in Manhattan, Scarlett longed for a meal and a bed. Best she'd been able to tell from the limited information available online, however, only the meal would be available in this town of fifteen hundred sixty-seven. The nearest motel was an hour back the way she'd come, but after running full-speed halfway across the country, Scarlett couldn't bear to wait another night to find out if she, in fact, was not alone in this world, after all.

She had nowhere else to go. Her career was in ruins and the media hounded her every step, screaming for juicy details of her affair with a drug lord. For two years she'd been a meteor on the rise in the only city that mattered…and now she was a star in a tragedy. A farce, except that a cop had died in the raid.

She wasn't a criminal…but she was criminally stupid, no question. How could she not have seen? How could she have blithely accepted Andre's assurances that it was his love for her that made him want to showcase her talents in the gem of a restaurant into which she'd put her heart and soul?

Instead, Mirelle had been simply a front for illegal activities that had gone on under her nose. And she'd never once, in the whole two years, suspected. Never wanted to look. She'd simply been grateful for the focus, the distraction from her grief. His offer had come right after she'd lost her only family, and she'd boxed up her mother's effects without a look. Instead of immediately leaving for parts unknown as her mother had always done when things got crazy, she'd tried something radical: she'd planned to stay in one place. She'd been too devastated to think straight, had been ripe pickings for Andre's machinations.

She'd been grateful, so grateful for the rescue. She'd lost her only compass in a life spent on the move, and she'd welcomed the chaos and endless work that allowed her not to think. The solace of someone who cared.

Except Andre hadn't really cared, had he? She'd been a dupe, and she'd walked into his trap with gratitude, playing her part to perfection.

The velvet-lined trap had sprung just when her future seemed brightest, when she was at last emerging from grief and loneliness.

Only to wind up in handcuffs, with her picture on the front page of the newspaper and featured on the evening newscast. Andre had escaped scot-free, no doubt on some tropical island drinking mai tais with a new idiot, while she stood holding the bag because he'd put her name on the more damaging documents.

And she'd thought him so sweet to both bankroll the venture and give her Mirelle.

She'd been trapped in New York for twelve days while the District Attorney had bled her brain dry, then she'd been freed under the stipulation that she'd testify against Andre and his cohorts—should they ever be found. On one of many sleepless nights, wandering the apartment filled with hated memories of Andre, in desperation she'd dragged out a box of her mother's things. There, in her mother's girlhood diary, a stunned Scarlett had discovered family. In Texas, of all places, one of the few states she and her mother had not lived.

A grandmother, still alive, from what little Scarlett could determine…a treasure she'd longed for all her life. Why Georgia Ross had never spoken one word of Sweetgrass Springs or family was reason for caution, certainly, but Scarlett had decided that once she had her life back together, she would seek the answers she craved to the riddle of her mother's past.

Then came a late night visit from two very scary men. She woke up with a knife to her throat and cold, flat shark's eyes staring into hers. If her drunken neighbors hadn't chosen that moment to erupt into another screaming battle and the lady across the hall hadn't yelled out that she was calling the cops…

Scarlett shivered at the memory of the harsh whisper warning her that they would be back, that testifying would mean her life. She'd tried to tell him that she knew nothing useful, but he'd only pressed the knife a little harder and said in that odd accent that she was a loose end Kostov wouldn't tolerate.

Then they'd vanished as quickly as they'd come.

In a panic, she'd thrown clothes into a suitcase, grabbed the box of mementos and was gone within a few hours.

Texas had been the only place she could think of to go. To pay a visit to the grandmother she'd never known existed and to buy herself a few days to think what to do next.

She had nowhere else to go. No options.

Okay, she still had her skills, and there might be some corner of the world where no one read the headlines. Truth to tell, New York only thought of itself as the center of the universe—there were other foodie towns like Santa Fe or San Francisco, other places where her skills could take her. Where the confidence she'd once had in spades could land her a new position.

If only she weren't so tired. So scared.

What if her grandmother wanted nothing to do with her? Why had her mother kept her family a secret? A million things could be wrong, so many ways this could go bad.

She was alone as never before in her life. Until two years ago, there had always been her mother. They had moved often, yes, but they were a team, they were solid. As long as they'd had each other, they needed little more.

How Scarlett missed her.

In Georgia's place remained only a mystery.

Who was her mother? Why did she leave here and never say one word to Scarlett about this place, when they had always been so close? Why did Scarlett have to find out about it when she could ask no questions? Was there some reason she should stay away, too? Her mother had been footloose but not foolish.

It was only a meal. A chance to reconnoiter. She didn't have to say anything to a soul.

The road ran alongside a ribbon of water, and a little further she could see it wind through the town next to a three-story courthouse that formed one corner of the town square, most of the buildings dark and closed, only a handful of them taller than one story. It was surely the tiniest town she'd ever seen.

She rounded the corner, and one building spilled out light in welcome. Ruby's Café. Owned by one Ruby Gallagher.

The grandmother Scarlett had never known existed.

Scarlett sucked in a deep breath for courage. She'd been the new kid countless times.

But her mother had always had her back.

Nonsense. I'll be okay. I'm a grown woman. It won't matter if she can't love me.

Chapter Two

"Whatever happened to Shania Twain?"

Ruby kept one eye on the hamburger she was grilling and jostled the basket of fries turning golden as she answered her waitress. "To tell the truth, Jeanette, I hadn't missed the girl until you asked." She lifted the handle and parked the fries to drain as she flipped the meat. "But when I get time, I'll be sure to worry."

Jeanette sailed right on past the sarcasm. "She married someone butt-ugly, like Loretta Lynn and her Mooney, I could swear it." She stacked plated orders up and down both arms and whisked them away to a table with the grace of a ballerina.

Ruby spared a second to watch, then shifted her gaze to the new girl, so young, wiping down a table. Brenda—if that was her real name, which Ruby severely doubted—kept her head down as she scrubbed circles on the formica surface. Her facial bruises had faded, but she moved as though her clothing hid others.

"She'll never make it as a waitress, you know that." Jeanette was back to grab a coffeepot. "Why you persist in filling your house with hard-luck cases I will never know. Oh, crap—" Jeanette was off like a shot as Brenda ignored the group of four who had just arrived.

Jeanette was right, of course, but the girl needed help. Dollars to donuts she was pregnant, and almost certainly she was on the run. Ruby understood only too well how it was to be pregnant and single, though she'd have dared the devil himself to raise a hand to her back then.

She had space enough, didn't she? She would have rattled around in the old two-story monstrosity that had belonged to her great-aunt, but it made a fine boarding house. She didn't mind a bit sharing it with those less fortunate. And hadn't another lost soul named Henry turned out to be aces at bussing tables and helping with cleanup?

"We're gonna run out of the coconut cream pie. Chocolate's already down to one piece," Jeanette muttered. "That table's gonna order it, I just know, and then Ian will be flat out of luck if he shows up."

Ruby stemmed a sigh. She did not have it in her to make one single more pie each morning. "Ian McLaren doesn't show up once a week, at that. He's too busy trying to keep his daddy from realizing that they're all but losing the ranch."

Jeanette's expression turned wistful. "The man works too hard, and his daddy doesn't appreciate what Ian gives up."

Jeanette wasn't exactly unbiased where Ian was concerned. She'd had a crush on Ian since both of them were in high school.

The bell on the door clapped against the glass again. Ruby peered over the pass-through to see if Brenda would rise to the occasion.

All the young woman did was flinch and turn away.

A single woman entered, petite, mounds of curly black hair and clothes that screamed *City*. For a second, that hair took her back. Georgia's hair had been like that, a lush profusion of midnight curls falling past her shoulders.

Would she ever quit missing her child? And wasn't she the fool for still holding out hope?

The woman glanced around the room, and Ruby tried to see it through her eyes: red vinyl booths, unmatched dinette tables and chairs, counter stools that creaked in protest as they spun.

Ruby couldn't be worrying about that. She returned her attention to the grilled cheese that was just the right golden, the shrimp basket ready to plate.

"Jeanette?"

A big sigh. "I'm on it."

Jeanette would complain, yes, but Ruby knew she would take care of everything without supervision.

Meanwhile she had folks to feed.

"Whatcha want to drink, hon?" The tall blond waitress set down a basket with biscuits in it.

Scarlett scanned the menu in vain for anything that wasn't fried. "Um, iced tea?"

"Sweet or unsweetened?"

Sweet tea. Scarlett and her mother had lived in various parts of North Carolina for a couple of years, Atlanta for one. She hadn't had sweet tea since. "Sweet."

"Know what you want? Like to hear about the special?"

"Sure." Though Scarlett had little hope for it.

Just then a grizzled cowboy walked past her booth and popped the waitress on the behind. Scarlett's eyes went wide, and she stiffened.

The waitress just laughed and dimpled. "Harley Sykes, what would your wife say?"

"Melba ain't here, now is she?"

The waitress's head cocked at a flirty angle. "You just get along now. Nothing here for you, hound dog."

He slapped one hand on his chest. "You're breakin' my heart, Jeanette. Draggin' it right through the dust."

"I'd hate to have to break your head if that hand strays again." But she was grinning as he left.

Men. A hot rush of loathing suffused Scarlett. "You don't

have to put up with that, you know."

The waitress he'd called Jeanette turned around. "What?"

"Him. He has no right to treat you like that."

The woman rolled her eyes. "Oh, hon, Harley is harmless. He just likes to flirt a little. Melba would peel the hide off him, and furthermore, he's all talk. He loves that woman to distraction. So, like I was saying, the special is meat loaf with mashed potatoes and gravy and a salad or green beans. Hold your horses, Shirley," she said, looking past Scarlett. "I'll get your coffee in a second. Take your time, hon. I'll bring your tea." And with that, she was off, leaving Scarlett still sorting out who she was talking to.

The salad was probably iceberg lettuce with one wedge of cardboard tomato, the green beans likely turned to mush by hours of cooking. Scarlett could nearly weep over the thought of the culinary wasteland she'd entered.

She shouldn't expect more, however. The interior was worn, though its Fifties diner look possessed a shabby charm. She had landed square in small-town America, complete with red vinyl booths, an odd assortment of tubular aluminum tables and chairs, the spring-loaded stainless steel napkin holders and even small jukeboxes in the booths. The walls sported historical photographs that appeared to be of this town in earlier incarnations. She was dying to peruse them to see if the faces of the bearded men and women in long dresses bore any resemblance to her own, but every table and booth was filled with patrons.

Nothing was new here, but even as a stranger, she felt the warmth. She cast a quick glance back toward the kitchen, wondering if her grandmother was around, but she couldn't see past the high ledge. Then hunger got the better of her, and she reached for one of the biscuits, disdaining to top it with the little pack of margarine spread, the very sight of which made her shudder. She popped a corner in her mouth.

The flavor hit. Faintly sweet, nearly falling apart, and

possibly the best bread she'd tasted in forever. Simple, filling—Scarlett barely stopped herself from gobbling and consoled herself with the notion that if the meal were inedible, she could happily dine on these.

"Here you go." An old-style curvy diner glass was set on the table before her, a battered iced tea spoon sticking out of the top. "Where you from, hon?" But Jeanette wasn't looking at her, she was frowning toward a younger woman whose head was down, refusing eye contact with those she served. "I swear to goodness, Ruby, you have gone too far this time," she muttered. "Brenda—" she called out but had to repeat herself. The girl's head jerked around, terror taking over her features. "Your order's ready. Can't you hear the bell?"

"Is she here?" Scarlett asked. "Ruby, I mean."

"You know her?"

"No—that is, I just…I heard about the place a few towns back."

"Really? Well, I'm not surprised. Folks come from all around to eat Ruby's cooking. Not that she has any business working as hard as she does at her age." She gestured with the coffee pot in her hand. "Want more biscuits, hon? Good, aren't they?"

"They're amazing. Ruby's recipe?"

A nod. "Woman gets here every morning at four to make a new batch."

"And she's been here all day?"

"Sure has. Kitchen's closed for a bit before supper, but she doesn't go far. She lives nearby, anyway. Don't know what keeps her going. When I'm seventy-one, you can bet your bottom dollar I'm not gonna be on my feet."

Scarlett could only imagine. Restaurant work, in any capacity, was murder on legs and feet and backs and to be doing it at seventy-one…

"You still need more time?"

Scarlett snapped from her musing. "I'll try the special.

With green beans," she added, though once she would have sneered at it, as would her trendy clientele. Meat loaf was stepchild cuisine, comfort food that no restaurateur with any pride would think of serving.

But she wasn't in New York anymore. And she could use some comfort.

When her meal arrived, Scarlett studied it with an expert's eye. Humble white pottery, old and scarred. Silverware that barely qualified for the term. The meat loaf was thick and steaming, and surprisingly smelled quite good. Mashed potatoes, a huge portion—real potatoes, not dehydrated flakes—topped with gravy that was thicker than she'd like but also fragrant and not lumpy. The green beans, though predictably overcooked, occupied their own little bowl, bits of onion and bacon swimming in the juices with them.

The first bite explained why the place was crowded with more bodies than the town looked big enough to hold. Plain fare it might be, but every bite met the definition of comfort food. True home cooking. Scarlett stopped for a second, realizing that it was made by a grandmother's hands.

Her grandmother's hands. A grandmother was a luxury she'd envied others. The closest she'd ever come to family besides her mother was an absentee father she'd never met. All Georgia would say about him was that Scarlett was the only worthwhile thing to come from a six-week marriage in Florida one sweltering summer.

Whoever Scarlett's father had been besides some stranger whose last name was Ross, Georgia had more than made up for his lack of interest. Georgia's love had surrounded Scarlett every hour of her life—but why would she have wanted to deny that other family existed?

Don't think anymore. Just eat. You still have to find a place to stay tonight. Long drive ahead.

Scarlett glanced once more toward the kitchen. For a second she thought she glimpsed the top of a head with black hair, but surely Ruby's would be gray by now.

The cowed waitress dropped a plate just then. The skinny blonde, Jeanette, rolled her eyes and shook her head. A young man in his twenties hurried over to help pick up the pieces.

Then out of the kitchen came a woman built so much like Scarlett herself—black hair included—that all Scarlett could do was stare with hungry eyes as the older woman soothed the girl, held off the skinny blonde with a glare and patted the boy's shoulder, all while scanning the room and indicating without a word that people should just go on with their business.

When Scarlett continued to stare, safe in the assumed anonymity she was so used to in New York where eye contact was a mortal sin, the older woman's gaze moved over her and past—then whipped back to her.

For a second, for several, Scarlett held her breath, wondering what the woman who might be her grandmother saw. Could she tell the relationship? The woman's hair wasn't curly like Scarlett's and her mother's, but it was black like theirs. Georgia had been statuesque and curvy, but this woman was small like Scarlett, though she didn't resemble a prepubescent boy the way Scarlett did.

When the girl began to cry, the older woman's attention snapped away like a rubber band. As she led the girl back into the kitchen, Scarlett felt the loss herself.

Come back, she wanted to say. *Or let me come in.*

But they were strangers, and Scarlett didn't know why. Until she understood what had made Georgia leave and never return, why she'd never spoken a word about this place or this woman, she would bide her time. The café was busy—no time for a family reunion even if she received a welcome, which she wasn't counting on.

Besides, she didn't like the idea of meeting her grandmother under a cloud of disgrace. Maybe her grandmother wouldn't believe in her innocence, either. She had to think about how to approach this woman, and fatigue was pulling at her. She had miles to drive before she could rest.

But she wanted just one more glimpse of the woman who, however much she'd doubted it up until the last few minutes, seemed very likely to be her grandmother.

Maybe she would have dessert.

Two amazing cups of coffee and one mouth-watering piece of coconut cream pie later, Scarlett finally stirred herself to go. The day had been long, and she was weary. The fifty miles back to a motel seemed like four hundred.

And she was more aware than ever that she was lonely. Fear and humiliation had propelled her out of Manhattan, and she'd welcomed how the days of driving had soothed her ragged emotions and given her a chance to breathe. Beyond the threat that had sent her running, she'd been surprised at the relief of escaping not only the hounding of the press but the pressure cooker of the constant striving for visibility in a city that lived and died by fame and glory.

But tonight, watching the good-natured teasing, even the petty bickering between the tall, skinny Jeanette and the spunky small woman who'd only poked her head from the kitchen once more, Scarlett was painfully aware that she had no one. Really no one, not even the staffs at various restaurants she'd tried to make into a family to substitute for her own. Her life had been a constant pulling up of roots, that and work and more work. The longest she'd been in one place before Manhattan had been to attend culinary school—but even then, she'd traveled to Paris for an internship.

She recognized the dynamic at Ruby's—these people were the kind of clan often found in the restaurant world, a cadre made up of individuals who worked long hours under killer stress and constant demand, trying to satisfy one of life's most basic needs: sustenance. Yet what she was witnessing was more, somehow, and all she could credit was the size of the town. Every dining establishment with any success had its regulars, but in the city the ties began and ended at the front door, for the most part.

Tonight she'd seen people who'd known one another's fathers and grandfathers, childhood companions whose kids were now growing up together, from what she'd overheard. For Scarlett, who'd seldom attended the same school two years in a row, the concept was nearly beyond imagination.

"Want me to top that off, hon?"

Scarlett came to herself suddenly and realized that around her, the sounds of closing down for the night could be heard. "Oh—no, sorry. I—I'll go. How much is it?"

Sympathetic gray eyes met hers. "You never said where you were from."

"Here and there." Scarlett grabbed her purse and stood.

"Where you headed?"

A part of Scarlett wanted to bristle. Strangers didn't ask those questions where she'd been. They didn't meet your eyes or extend sympathy with theirs. "I'm not sure," she surprised herself by responding.

A faint frown. "It's getting late. Where did you plan to stay?"

Scarlett couldn't help casting a quick glance toward the kitchen, toward the sound of the older woman's voice. What had she thought would happen when she found her grandmother? Why hadn't she at least introduced herself?

In her life of constant moving, there were two main ways of dealing with being the new kid in school. One was to be good at forming connections quickly; the other was to sit back and—knowing you'd move again soon—not even try. Scarlett had always chosen the latter, and she did so now. "I'll be stopping in Fredericksburg. I'd better get underway."

She picked up the paper ticket and nearly gasped at the price. The bill for a full meal and dessert wouldn't have covered the smallest appetizer at her last place. Quickly she calculated a generous tip, then doubled it for hogging the booth all night. She wasn't flush with extra money, but she knew how hard waitressing was. She'd done her share. "Would you please tell the cook that the meal was wonderful?" She took a deep breath and forced herself to ask, "Was that her, Ruby, the small woman with the black hair?"

"That's her, in the flesh. Want to tell her yourself?" Jeanette turned as if to summon Ruby.

Scarlett was shocked to feel her eyes fill. Quickly she turned her head away. "No—I, uh, I really have to go." Scarlett began to walk to the door.

"You come back anytime, you hear?" the waitress called. "Breakfast here will really stick to your ribs, and you look like you could use some feeding up."

Scarlett felt the woman's eyes boring into her back as she slipped outside. She wanted, more than she could say, to try that breakfast. Longed to meet the only family she had left in the world.

She would have, gladly, if she'd still been the celebrated, up-and-coming young chef.

But she was in disgrace now. She had trouble snapping at her ankles.

Old habits died hard, and for now, Scarlett would run away.

Chapter Three

S carlett wasn't in the mood for the radio, but she was sleepier than was safe, despite all the coffee she'd consumed.

The wheel jerked in her hands. The car surged toward the ditch at the side of the road. She wrestled the car back straight while frantically looking for a safe place to stop.

What she found wasn't great, out on a very dark road with trees looming like bony-fingered branches in a horror flick.

For a couple of minutes, she simply sat inside and tried to stop shaking.

And fought not to weep.

Why? She wasn't normally the weeping type. She didn't know that woman back at the cafe. For all she knew, her mother had very good reasons to stay away.

But she felt so lost. She didn't know what to do. Where to go. Maybe Kostov would be satisfied that she was gone—but what if he sent his thugs after her? What if she hadn't covered her trail well enough? And though the DA had said it could be months before any trial, how would he react to knowing she was gone?

She wanted to just…give up.

But she'd never been a quitter. Time to figure out the next step.

In the middle of this sparse population, should she even bother trying 9-1-1? She wasn't hurt, so doing so would be overkill. Why hadn't she joined Triple A? One glance at her cell phone killed that notion, even if she had. No bars…okay, maybe a half of one.

Sweetgrass Springs was, what, about five miles back? She could walk five miles, surely—in New York, she walked all the time. Everyone did.

But it was night. And so very dark out there.

She saw no sign of habitation anywhere, so the notion of help any closer than Sweetgrass Springs was out. She had no idea what was wrong with her car—how many years had it been since she'd even driven one? In the city, you didn't need one.

With a steadying breath, she gripped the handle. *You've walked all over Manhattan, all hours of the night. You can do this.* Operating on the rip-off-the-bandage-fast theory, she forced herself into the night.

She gravitated toward the headlights. The front left tire looked all right. The hood wasn't steaming, but she couldn't see to open it. Was there a flashlight in the trunk? The tiny one on her keychain was halogen, so it shone brightly at close range, but there was a lot of dark out there, once you got past the hood.

On the passenger side, she got her answer.

Flat tire. Oh, boy. Not once in her life had she changed one.

But that's what they made owner's manuals for, right? Scarlett shivered in the rising wind and gratefully sought the warmer interior of the car.

Fifteen minutes later and several degrees warmer, she emerged. First she popped the trunk open and moved her belongings to the back seat, thankful she was traveling light. She donned her coat and changed into boots. With gloves on her hands and jeans covering her legs, she was as armored as possible against what might be crawling around in the darkness.

Though if she spent any time thinking about snakes, she'd never get through this.

After checking the manual again, she located the mat in the trunk and peeled it back, then unscrewed the big winged

nut holding down a sort of cardboard cover. Beneath it—
shazaam!—lay the spare tire and pieces of what the instructions assured her was the jack.

If only she had the faintest notion how to assemble it.

She removed the metal components and shivered again.
She'd packed a set of long johns, but she wasn't eager to
spend time removing boots or stripping off jeans. Activity
would warm her. *Keep moving.*

Next the tire, which was determined not to leave its cocoon. She was strong for her size from years of hauling
around big pots, but never had she cursed her small stature
more. The thing weighed a ton, and it was wedged in there so
tightly she couldn't get it to budge. She'd go to the next step,
then come back to the stupid spare.

Nothing went better after that. Jacking up the car was a
nightmare, and trying to loosen what the book called lug nuts
simply wasn't happening. Cold and scared and frustrated,
Scarlett forced herself to think hard about the alternative:
walking back to Sweetgrass Springs. But the town had been
deserted except for Ruby's, which was now closed. Did she
want to meet her grandmother by waking her up, banging on
the door to her house, even if she could find it?

Too tired to think straight, she decided the best course
was to get back in the car and take a short nap, then see if that
would help. She'd lock every door, but even so, the very
notion was creepy—but what choice did she have?

Think, blast it. There's an answer here, you just can't see it. Fatigue was making her thick-headed. A nap, then, just a short
one. She'd figure this out.

Scarlett crawled into the car and locked every door. Then
she lay down on the seat and made herself as small and
unnoticeable as possible.

And wished she knew how to pray.

No wonder her mother had left. The back end of nowhere was not where Scarlett belonged.

Chapter Four

Just past dawn, Ian McLaren rose from his haunches, crumbling the clumps of dirt in his hand as he stared across acres drenched in his family's blood and toil. Legs spread and solidly planted on the ground that had belonged to McLarens for one hundred seventy-six years, Ian wondered if he would be the last of his line able to claim it.

He held the remaining bits to his nose and drew in the scent of earth that was the foundation of his existence. Not for him would be the wanderlust of his boyhood buddy Mackey or the rebellion of his best friend Jackson Gallagher, banished at eighteen and never heard from again. The Double Bar M Ranch was Ian's future. His blood and bone…his heritage. Stewardship of this place was what he'd been groomed for all his life.

And every last bit of it might be gone for good, if something didn't change, if he didn't find the answers his dad Gordon would accept. He had a degree in agribusiness from Texas Tech and had formulated a plan he thought might work.

But Gordon McLaren wouldn't bend. Wouldn't accept that change was inevitable, and he was still the owner of the Double Bar M. Ian's plans would involve borrowing money, anathema to his dad's Scots blood. Gordon had always sold his calves at the market barn in Johnson City and had not needed to borrow money to replace his cows or do improvements for many years. He could quote chapter and verse on the pitfalls, citing examples like the neighbor who was forced to sell because he'd wasted all that money on cross-fencing his land to do some new intensive rotational grazing program—then the drought had hit and the bank had called the note.

He turned deaf ears to Ian's ideas about raising organic beef, about setting up his own small organic feedlot to supply the enormous appetite of Austin and San Antonio restaurants and high-end groceries. That his dad could put other local people to work if he'd expand further into an organic packing plant went right past Gordon's rock-hard head. If only his dad had listened to him, they could have been positioned to own those extra 1200 acres to the west to add to their 2500. Instead, six attorneys from Houston would be hunting there twice a year.

Yes, the Double Bar M possessed deep waters, fertile valley floor soil, sweet green grass that allowed the raising of cattle few other spreads could afford. Two dry years were behind them, though, and another ahead if the weathermen were to be believed. The ranch account books, which Ian had taken over after his dad's stroke, no longer were plump with commas and zeroes. He'd stripped the ranch staff to a skeleton, was doing his dad's work and his own, yet the evidence was indisputable.

Something had to give.

There were options to Ian's plan, of course—the place would sell for a princely sum to rich city folks whose first step would likely be to abandon the simple stone ranch house built by Ian's great-great-grandfather. Instead they'd build some monstrous mansion on top of the ridge, with its breath-stealing views of the Hill Country, but his dad would never have to worry about money again, and Ian himself could go anywhere he wanted.

But Ian loved his father, and Gordon's pride had been damaged enough. That he couldn't take his active role any longer grated on Gordon, and Ian wouldn't be part of sacrificing one more bit of his father's pride.

He could turn the place into an exotic game ranch and entertain hunters, but Ian wasn't much on company, nor was his dad, not since Ian's mother had left them when Ian was small. Somehow, during her whirlwind romance with a cowboy, his city sophisticate mother had misunderstood Gordon's quiet nature and his intense connection to his land. Desperate when she realized there would not be frequent vacations or trips to fancy restaurants or art galleries, she'd made a half-hearted attempt to take Ian with her. When Gordon had flat refused to let his son leave, Ian's mother had abandoned them both, her only legacy bitter resentment and a lifelong distrust of footloose women.

Ian let the last grains of earth drift through his fingers and strode toward the main barn. From this part of the ranch, he could faintly hear the river. He turned his face in that direction, more than a little tempted to seek out the refuge he always found on its banks, but before he took one step, he shook his head. He had no time for idleness.

Not if he was going to save the Double Bar M.

Something cracked against the window, and Scarlett bolted awake, screaming.

A man's tall frame loomed in the car window.

Kostov's man.

She scuttled into the corner of the back seat. "I have a gun," she shouted. "I'm calling the cops!" In the dim light of pre-dawn, she prayed he couldn't see that she was unarmed and her phone wouldn't work.

"Lady…" said a decidedly Texas drawl. Dark brows snapped together while empty hands rose from the man's sides, palms out. "I'm not going to hurt you. Just stopped to see if I could help."

The slow smooth baritone took her fear down a notch. She shook her head to clear it. She'd tossed half the night. "I'm fine. Go away."

"Need help changing that flat?"

Oh, crap. She'd forgotten. She peered closer. Even in dawn's light, he looked nothing like the men who'd threatened her in New York.

This one was no brute. He was gorgeous. Broad shoulders filled out a denim shirt to a mouth-watering degree. The ball cap on his head covered shaggy hair curling up a little around the edge.

Golden brown eyes studied hers. "Would you open the window so we can talk? I can't hear you."

Uh-uh, no way. She scrabbled around for her purse, for her pepper spray.

He was already headed around the front of the car.

"Stop! Don't move!"

He looked askance at her and continued on his way. At the right front, he stopped. Broke into a grin that didn't seem remotely dangerous.

But she was a long way from anything familiar. "Step away."

"What?"

"STEP. AWAY."

He exhaled. "Would you please roll down the window? I'll keep my hands out to the side if that will make you feel better."

She couldn't lower the windows from the back seat, but he only seemed exasperated, not dangerous.

And he was trying to help.

She opened the door a crack. "Stay back." Maybe he wasn't from Kostov, but he could be a serial killer. Not all of them were ugly.

"Why?"

"So I can come out and look."

He rolled his eyes. "You're worried about me, when what you should be worrying about are the critters."

"What critters?" She glanced around but saw nothing.

"You probably think you're safe with pepper spray, right?" A pitying look. "Rattlers don't much care about pepper spray. Or scorpions, for that matter."

Scorpions. Snakes. Maybe she'd just stay right where she was—but there was still that flat tire. "Stand over there," she ordered. "By your pickup."

"Because I couldn't cross the distance and jump you before you could say *boo*?" He shook his head. "You're from New York, huh?"

"What makes you say that?"

"Your license plates?"

Oh. Right. She would never see him again, but still caution reared its head. "I'm not from anywhere, really."

"Everyone's from somewhere. You don't have a Yankee accent."

"I don't have any accent."

He frowned and glanced at the sky. "Listen, I've got stock to dose. Get a move on if you're coming."

Stock to dose—what on earth did that mean? "So go. I'll be fine."

"Uh-huh." He gave the tire a pointed look. "A gentleman doesn't leave a lady stranded. Anyway, this jack setup is pathetic."

"You're too annoying to be a serial killer," she muttered, shoving the back door open and jumping out.

As she approached him, she noted the difference in their heights, the powerful frame. His jeans were worn, his boots were scuffed. He looked as though he'd been formed by this land, rugged and handsome.

And he was trying unsuccessfully to hide a grin.

That did it. "The jack works just fine. And I am not help-less. Maybe I've never changed a tire, but any idiot can read a book. Yes, it took me a while, but I figured out where the jack was and got it out. It took forever, but I raised the car. I just couldn't get the, the—whatchamacallits, the little things, off."

"Lug nuts?"

"Right. Lug nuts. And stop smirking."

"I would never smirk."

She narrowed her eyes at him. He only grinned again, and this time she noticed a dimple in his left cheek, an oddity on that square-jawed, rugged face. "I simply needed to rest because I'd driven all day. I feel much stronger now."

"Uh-huh. Well, how 'bout you save all that strength for driving, then." He whistled one piercing note, and through the window of his enormous, beat-up black pickup leaped a dog, a big one, who came charging straight for her.

She backed up against her car. Stifled a scream.

"Blue—" the man shouted. "Sit!"

The dog plopped on his butt right in front of her.

"Um…good boy?" She didn't take her eye off the dog. "Is he—shouldn't he be over there with you?"

"He won't move a muscle unless I say so."

"But…what do I do?"

The dog cocked his head. His coat was a shaggy patch-work of tan and gray and white. His eyes were weird, light and ghostly.

"You could let him sniff your hand."

"I don't think so." She fisted both hands and drew them high on her chest.

The dog whined softly, and his butt wiggled. He had a short tail that seemed to be wagging. But still… "I think you should call him."

"Why?" In seconds, the car was jacked up twice as high as she'd managed. "Pop the trunk," he ordered, "then come around here and let's see what you can do."

She inched to the side but didn't look away. To her relief, the dog didn't move. She reached inside the driver's door and released the latch on the trunk, then eased toward the rear, away from the dog.

"You can walk around wherever you want to. Blue doesn't bite."

"You sure? He's big."

"Not that big. You're just little. He's an Australian shepherd. He herds things, he doesn't attack them."

"Oh." She thought for a second about holding out her hand to the animal but decided to save that. Instead she scooted around to where the man hunkered. Though she was freezing, he'd rolled up his sleeves. His forearms were ropy with muscle.

Not that she was going to notice. "The car is up really high. Is that safe?"

"What's not safe is it not being level. A car can fall off a jack and do some damage. Give me your hand."

Gingerly she extended hers.

His forehead wrinkled as he perused her palms. "You need gloves or you'll get blisters."

"My hands are strong."

"Of course they are." His tone made his doubts clear. With impressive ease, back muscles flexing beneath his well-worn shirt in a way that made her mouth water, he removed the lug nuts, one by one, and laid them inside the hubcap. Then he wrenched off the tire and dropped it to the side, where it landed with a thud.

"I'll get the spare," Scarlett said.

"Best let me. You could hurt yourself."

She huffed and hurried toward the trunk. Men out here were as Neanderthal as she'd feared. She'd never let her size hold her back. She reached inside and unscrewed the bolt holding the spare. She had to pull hard, but at last it came free. She lifted it, gritting her teeth as she had to drag it over the edge, bracing it against her stomach.

Once out, the weight of it staggered her, but sheer pride had her holding on instead of dropping it completely. She righted it and began to roll it around the car, frowning as she spotted the black smear across her shirt.

But she'd done it, hadn't she?

He watched her but didn't interfere, and she liked him a little better for that. She came to stop in front of him, daring him with a look to make fun of her efforts.

He simply nodded to her. "Thanks." She rested her hands on her hips and worked not to let the exertion show. If the dimple winked a time or two, at least he didn't point out how much she'd struggled.

When he lifted the tire in one hand and swung it toward the wheel, she tried not to hate him.

"Want to tighten these?" he asked.

She looked at him with new respect. "I would."

He moved back and let her in front of him. "Tighten all of them as much as you can, then we'll let the jack down and go around one more time. You don't want one coming loose. That's real dangerous."

She was intensely aware of his nearness, and she had to concentrate hard to shut him out and focus only on the exertion. When she'd gone all the way around and put her back into every one, she glanced over her shoulder. When he nodded, she felt a real sense of accomplishment.

"Now let down the jack slowly until the tire is resting on the ground."

She complied.

"Okay, now see if you can tighten them any more."

She did, but she could only get two of them to tighten further. She looked back at him again. "You could probably do better."

He shrugged. "Only because I probably outweigh you by a hundred pounds. You did good."

The sense of pride was a welcome change from the last several weeks. Still, she handed him the tire tool. "I don't want to be foolish."

They exchanged positions, and he did indeed manage to tighten all of them.

While she tried not to notice his seriously fine behind in those jeans.

"Remember how to take the jack apart?"

She wrested her attention back to the car. "I think so." Okay, she didn't remember completely, but she began, anyway. She might be going a long way from here, and she couldn't be certain she wouldn't need to do this again. After she took it apart more swiftly than she'd assembled it, she picked it up and smiled as she stood.

He towered over her, all male and muscle, but she didn't feel cautious about his size anymore. "Thank you."

"You needed to learn. You're smart, just…small." He smiled back, killer gorgeous. "But banty roosters are small, and they're as fierce as any big one." He nodded. "Now for the real trick—repacking that tiny trunk."

She sighed. "Too true. Not much room for error."

He grabbed the tire and followed her around. "No reason to repack this tire. You don't want to be driving around without a spare. You can either follow me out to my place and I'll fix it, or we can take it into town and let Jonas repair it while we eat breakfast at Ruby's."

"I can't ask you to do more. How much do I owe you?"

"Owe me?" He seemed perplexed. "For helping you? Nothing. That's what neighbors do."

"I'm a total stranger."

"It's just how we are, New York."

She thought about Jeanette last night, asking if she had a place to stay. "I guess so." Just then her stomach growled.

"Best breakfast in Texas just a few miles that way." He pointed back toward Sweetgrass Springs.

Last night she'd considered returning, hadn't she? Anyway, she desperately needed to pee, and there was no way, after hearing about scorpions and snakes, she was playing nature girl. She wasn't ready to mention that she'd been there already, though. "How far?"

"Follow me," he said. "Heck, I'll even buy you breakfast. Just to be neighborly." He pulled off his cap and ran a hand through hair the color of aged whisky, a rich brown sun-streaked with gold.

"I should buy yours. Anyway, I thought you were dosing stock—whatever that means."

"It means just what it sounds like. I'm giving them doses of various medications—" The dimple flashed again. "–in various places."

She was not going to ask.

"But first, I'm eating breakfast. I've been working since before dawn, and I'm hungry." He swept out an arm. "After you, New York."

"I have a name."

"And that would be?"

"Scarlett."

One eyebrow rose. "As in *Gone with the Wind*?"

"Unfortunately." She shrugged. "My mother said Scarlett was a survivor. That despite her mistakes with men, she endured and that was something to remember."

"So what's your middle name?"

"I don't know you that well."

He burst out laughing. "Then I'll have to make up my own. I'm Ian, by the way. Ian McLaren." He held out a hand, and she took it. "Pretty strong grip for a girl," he observed.

"I'm tougher than I look."

"I noticed." His eyes lit. "Well, let's saddle up. I got bacon and eggs calling my name." He slapped the side of one thigh and headed for his truck, dog at his heels.

She watched those long legs eat up the ground.

After a minute, she climbed into her own car and followed.

Ian only let himself look back once. The last thing he needed in his life was one more complication. His dad, the ranch...he had enough on his plate.

Anyway, she had the figure of a twelve-year-old boy. If he was going to make time for a woman in his life, it sure wouldn't be one who barely qualified and had a sizable chip on her shoulder to boot.

Though she did have one sweet little backside, he had to admit. And big blue eyes a man could fall into.

Forget it. He was running late, thanks to New York back there, and he'd be working 'til dark-thirty as it was. He ought to just skip Ruby's and grab some jerky at the gas station.

But he had his mouth all set for some of Ruby's biscuits, so no way would he let New York ruin that for him. He punched the accelerator but couldn't resist one glance in the rear view mirror.

And there she was, in that silly foreign job that would barely hold a set of his boots, much less a saddle or a sack of feed.

He whipped his gaze from the mirror and focused on the town cropping up ahead. "I shouldn't have invited her," he said aloud. He should sit at the counter at Ruby's and grab a quick meal, then be on his way. "Right, Blue?" He stopped in front of Ruby's and shoved the truck in Park. Beside him, Blue whined. "Yeah, yeah...I'll remember the bacon." Ian reached over and absently rubbed the dog's head.

Ruby heard Jeanette enter through the front door and wondered what on earth she'd do without the girl. Woman, really—Jeanette had been with Ruby since high school, and that was, what, nearly fifteen years ago?

Jeanette needed to leave Sweetgrass Springs and see the world, but lordy, how Ruby hoped she wouldn't. She wasn't sure how much longer she could be on her feet all day, but at least with Jeanette around, she didn't have to ramrod everything else. Yes, they butted heads from time to time, but that was necessary to ensure that Jeanette and everyone else here knew that Ruby was still paying attention, still determined that no one ever got a bad meal at Ruby's Café.

But she sure did wish Jeanette could cook.

Not that she didn't love feeding people, because she did—it was only that her feet were screaming by midmorning, her right hip never quit aching and her fingers were losing some of their grip.

She was getting old—shoot, who was she kidding? She was already old.

And Sweetgrass Springs was dying. Ruby's was the only part of it that didn't have one foot in the grave already.

Jeanette rounded the corner.

"Get the—"

"Coffee started," Jeanette completed. "Yeah, yeah…don't I know every blessed move we make, inside and out?" she muttered.

Ruby's gaze followed her. She was all too aware that Jeanette had never intended to stay here, had only taken the job to save up money for college, but somehow one year had turned into the next, and Jeanette was still around. Still hoping for—

The front door opened, and Jeanette didn't even need to turn. "How's it going, Raymond?"

"Fair to middlin'," said one of their regulars.

"Raymond's here," she called out to Ruby.

"Already got it goin'," snapped Ruby. "Like I don't know who just walked in." The man ate the same thing every morning of the world—oatmeal with butter and sugar, two eggs, bacon and buttered toast—heavy on the butter—with exactly two cups of coffee, no more, no less. The miracle was that Raymond Benefield remained skinny as a rail, despite the caloric intake of a longshoreman.

Jeanette frowned at her tone, and Ruby knew she should apologize. She was just so blasted tired. Some of that was from being her age and having made thousands of chicken-fried steaks and flipped a million or so pancakes.

But most of it had to do with the sleepless night she'd had, wrestling over the call from the bank over in Fredericksburg about the note on the abandoned courthouse building.

As if she were likely to forget.

A fool's errand, it seemed, buying the history-filled building, but she just couldn't let the past die. Her forebears had recorded the deeds that had created Sweetgrass Springs there. Records of births and deaths and marriages...maybe they were on computers now, but once they'd been contained in big leather-bound ledgers Ruby was still trying to get custody of for the museum she wanted as part of a center for tourism that would make Sweetgrass Springs hum again.

She was a foolish old woman who was beating a dead horse, and her arm was so tired she was ready to give up.

Except somehow she just couldn't, blasted cockeyed optimist that she'd always been.

Her great-nephew Jackson would give her the money to pay it off—he was always asking what he could do to help her—but she would never ask. She was the only soul in Sweetgrass Springs who knew whether he was dead or alive—not that half the folks here wouldn't still gladly see him dead—and she couldn't give up hope that someday he'd return. It wouldn't be fair to use his money to save the town that had cast him out.

Sure he'd gotten richer than Croesus with his video game empire and he had a real fancy lifestyle up there in Seattle, but every time they spoke, she could hear his longing for Sweetgrass, however much he would deny it.

He missed this place. His best friend Ian. Missed his sisters, his twin Penelope and their kid sister Rissa.

And, though he would never say it, he missed Veronica, the Juliet to his Romeo. Ruby was almost certain she was the only one besides the two of them who knew about their young love. Veronica's father would have killed Jackson if he'd known.

The bell rang again, and she knew without looking that it was Arnie.

Hadn't she just seen the old fool snoring away two hours ago?

"Hey, Arnie," Jeanette greeted and went on pouring Raymond's coffee at the oval table reserved for the regulars. Every chair was spoken for, and woe betide the fool or stranger who plopped down in one of them. Even if one of the morning coffee bunch was absent, a given person's seat could only be used by that individual.

Raymond's chair was at the far end on the north side of the table.

"It's a lovely day out there, Jeanette." Every day was lovely in Arnie Howard's estimation.

Silly darned old man had proposed to her again last night. Ruby shook her head and started his breakfast.

"Mornin', sweetheart," he called out.

Ruby slammed a skillet onto the stove instead of answering.

"Somebody got up on the wrong side of the bed," Jeanette stage-whispered as though Ruby couldn't hear her.

"I, uh, I wouldn't know," Arnie replied.

"Uh-huh," Jeanette responded, likely rolling her eyes.

It was not the town's business whether or not Ruby wanted to get married, no matter how often Arnie proposed. He'd made a habit of it for eighteen years now, ever since his wife Lurlene passed on, but Ruby had survived having and losing a child with no partner, had built a business all by herself and she would be dadgummed if she would take on all the trouble and aggravation a man could cause, at this late date.

She was an independent woman. She'd die that way.

Jeanette kept on going, as though Ruby didn't have two perfectly good ears and couldn't stand on tiptoe to see them clearly over the pass-through if she wanted to bad enough.

A quick lift to her toes showed Jeanette patting Arnie's hand while she poured him coffee. "Just one of those days, I guess."

"She's not feeling so good lately," he said quietly. "Her bad hip is acting up. But I didn't say that."

Jeanette made a zipping motion across her lips. "She should have retired five years ago, but—"

He nodded. "What would this town do without Ruby's? I know you don't much like to cook, but something's got to give."

"I don't have the touch, even if I wanted to."

"Order up!" Ruby hit the bell extra hard. She was not a subject to be gossiped over.

The chime on the door rang again. Out of the corner of her eye, Ruby spotted the real reason Jeanette wouldn't leave Sweetgrass Springs entering the café.

But Ian McLaren had never really seen Jeanette, not the way she wanted him to.

He nodded as he entered. "Hey, Jeanette."

"Your stool's warmed up and ready. Coffee's hot." She lifted the pot.

But he didn't approach. Instead, he remained by the door and peered out a window. "I'll be there in a second."

His tone was odd. Odder still when he pulled off his cap and finger-combed his hair, since Ian had no vanity about his looks, though he had every right to. He was surely one of God's finest specimens of manhood on this earth.

And one of the best men, to boot.

Suddenly he straightened, then pushed the door open.

And who should walk through but the woman Ruby had glimpsed here last night? She'd been too busy to pay much attention, but Jeanette had been full of speculation about why the clearly out of place woman would be here and hang around so long.

Just then the woman pushed her hair back from her forehead in a gesture Ruby had seen untold times.

And Ruby couldn't breathe.

The long, curly black hair was indeed very much like Georgia's.

And her petite build resembled Ruby's own.

The room spun.

Ruby lost her balance, and the skillet tilted. Grease splashed over the edge and onto the burner. Flames shot high, grease spattering her hand.

She gasped. Dropped the cast-iron skillet.

The floor rushed up to meet her.

Scarlett was removing her coat when she heard the yelp of pain from the kitchen. The crash.

The waitress named Jeanette called out, "Ruby? You okay?"

A sudden flame flared high behind the pass-through, and Ian charged toward the kitchen. He grabbed the fire extinguisher off the wall, aiming toward the stove.

"Wait—" Scarlett dropped her purse and coat and shoved past him, then grabbed an empty pan and covered the flame, which immediately went out. "You shoot that thing into a kitchen fire, and she'll be shut down for the rest of the day."

The kitchen was suddenly filled with people all talking at the same time. Scarlett ignored them and crouched next to Ruby. "Don't move. I only see a burn on your arm. Did it splash anywhere else?" She spoke without looking up. "Somebody hand me my purse."

The quiet, skittish waitress produced it from where Scarlett had dropped it.

"Thank you. Is there a first aid kit?"

The young woman nodded and hurried to a set of shelves.

Scarlett rummaged inside her purse and produced a small spray bottle she was never without.

"What is that?" Jeanette demanded from above her. "What are you doing?"

"What needs to be done." Scarlett sprayed the ointment over the burn, about three inches long and one inch wide. "It's a burn treatment."

Ian crouched on the other side, a worried older man beside him. "Ruby? Where else are you hurt besides your arm?"

"Sweetheart?" the old man asked. "Honey, wake up."

Sweetheart? Could this man be her grandfather? But Mama's diary had said she didn't know who her father was.

The old woman stirred. Her eyelids fluttered.

The young man who'd been bussing tables the night before keened and rocked himself. "Are you okay, Ruby? Please be okay." He wrung his hands over and over.

Scarlett glanced up at Ian.

"What do you need?" he asked.

"I guess it's too much to expect there to be a medical facility in town?"

Ian nodded. "Yes, but the county EMS is available." He pulled out his cell and handed it to the old man, who had tears in his eyes. "Arnie," he said gently. "If you'd call for an ambulance—"

"No ambulance." At last Ruby spoke.

"Sweetheart, we don't know how bad you're hurt," Arnie protested.

"Not the first kitchen burn I ever had," she groused. "Won't be the last. Hand me my burn goo, Jeanette." She tried to rise.

"Whoa there, Ruby," Ian said. "Lie still for a minute. You took a fall, too. Let's make sure nothing is broken."

"I've already treated it. The burn is only first degree," Scarlett said. "But you need to be looked over anyway."

Eyes as blue as her own snapped to hers. "Who are you?"

Scarlett wondered if that was hope she saw there. She hesitated, afraid of what she would learn once she revealed her identity. This woman had a sharp tongue—had she driven Scarlett's mother away? Why hadn't she tried to find them? Would she care?

At this low point in her life, Scarlett wasn't sure how much more rejection she could take.

Oh, get over yourself. She had a sharp tongue of her own, and she was no weakling. "I'm Scarlett Ross. My mother's name was Georgia." She heard the entire group gasp, but she only had eyes for the woman in front of her. "I think I'm your granddaughter."

Chapter Five

R uby blinked. Blinked again, and her eyes filled. "Was? My baby girl is…"

My baby girl. That was not a term for a child who was unloved. The mystery deepened.

Scarlett's chest tightened. She could only manage a nod.

"When?" Ruby shoved up to sitting and winced.

"Two years ago."

Ruby sagged.

"Please—" Scarlett found her voice. "Are you sure you should be sitting up? Let's wait for the ambulance."

"Help me up, girl." Ruby curled her legs beneath her, drawing her injured arm close to her chest.

"Not yet," Scarlett said firmly. "We need to see what else is hurt."

"Ian, you get me up, you hear? I have breakfast to cook. Arnie, get that hangdog look off your face. I'm nowhere near—" Her voice cracked, but she shook her head fiercely. "I'm not dead yet."

"Sweetheart…" The poor man was clearly at a loss.

"I'll help you up," Scarlett offered. "After you tell me where else you're hurting."

"I'm old. Something always hurts." Her gaze narrowed. "A bossy little thing, aren't you, girl?"

"My name is Scarlett. And I'm no bossier than you."

The older woman's lips twitched.

Scarlett fought a smile, then looked at Ian. "Let's get her up slowly. Jeanette, will you make everyone back up?"

"You heard her. Move back. Give Ruby some air," he ordered.

As Ruby gained her feet, the group crowded into the kitchen cheered. Scarlett kept a hand on Ruby's good arm, and she noticed that Ian didn't release his grip on Ruby's waist.

"See? Good as new." Cradling her injured arm, Ruby took one step, but she swayed.

"Henry—" Ian ordered. "Bring a chair in here."

"I don't need an ambulance," Ruby snapped. Then her shoulders sank. "But I guess the café is closed for the day." She settled in the chair the young man provided.

"It doesn't have to be," Scarlett said, accepting the first aid kit the timid young waitress proffered. She selected gauze, covering the burn loosely.

"No one here can cook, hon," Jeanette said.

"I can." Ruby's gaze swiveled to hers, and Scarlett nodded. "I'm a chef, trained in Paris. I had my own—" Scarlett clamped her mouth shut before she ruined everything.

"So why would you want to be here and sully your fancy hands in this place?" Jeanette sneered.

"So I can help my grandmother," Scarlett snapped, but the very word made her heart flutter. She forced herself to calm down. "I can handle bacon and eggs, I promise."

Ian was frowning at her. Ruby was studying her carefully.

"Have it your way." She started to rise, then remembered that her flat wasn't yet fixed. Never mind—she'd get another spare along the way.

Then Arnie, of all people, spoke up. "It was my breakfast that went up in flames. I'm game."

Everyone chuckled. Except Ruby, the only one whose reaction mattered.

"Fine. I don't stay where I'm not wanted." Scarlett turned on her heel.

"Slow down, New York," Ian said.

"My name is Scarlett."

"All right. Don't get in a huff." He glanced at Jeannette. "She's offering to help Ruby. Anybody else here got a better offer?"

"Wouldn't kill folks for us to close for one day." The waitress folded her arms.

"Hush, girl," Ruby ordered. At last she nodded to Scarlett. "I appreciate your offer, I do. I'd be grateful for the help. I'll just stay and watch until I'm sure my customers will be taken care of."

Scarlett arched one eyebrow. "No, you won't. You'll be going to the doctor."

"In a pig's eye," Ruby said. She turned to the assemblage. "All right, everybody. Show's over." As everyone but Ian and Arnie scattered, she gave Scarlett a long perusal. "Well, now. Let's see what you can do."

Ian was still studying her, clearly not sold, either.

Scarlett took the challenge. "Give me your apron." She held out a hand.

"Not just yet. I'll keep mine on for now. Henry—" Ruby called out. "Get the girl her own apron."

Scarlett took a look around at all of them. "Somebody bring Ruby another chair to put her feet up on, then everyone out of the kitchen."

Ian took his sweet time before responding. He might be one fine-looking man, but his attitude could use some work. He practically bristled with protectiveness for Ruby.

But at last he nodded. "Come on, Arnie. Let's see what the city girl can do."

Arnie hesitated.

"Shoo now," Ruby said. "You all leave me alone and quit hovering. It's only a scorch."

Scarlett had her doubts that Ruby was as hale and hearty as she wanted to seem, but she would keep an eye on her.

From the reactions of the others, it was clear she wouldn't be the only one.

After the crowd cleared, she did a quick scan of the small kitchen. The setup was basic—grill with burners to one side, fryer to the other. Behind her, prep table and sink, dishwasher and another deep sink on the side wall. Beneath the pass-through in front of her was a shelf with plates and bowls, above it was a wheel with clips, orders attached, covering half the surface.

"That's not all the orders. If it's for a regular, I already know what they want. Like Ian. He'll need to be on his way. He's late already. He takes bacon, hash browns, biscuits and three eggs over easy."

Of course, it would be the White Knight she'd have to cook for first. "After Arnie." She accepted the apron Henry retrieved for her. "Thank you, Henry. I'm Scarlett."

He blushed to the roots of his hair. "Yes, ma'am."

Since he couldn't be much more than five years younger than her, the *ma'am* felt weird, but she didn't quibble. "So what do you do here, Henry?" Beginning to make the neat fold she preferred at her waist, she suddenly realized that she didn't need it, that the apron, unlike most, actually fit her without being tucked.

"I fetch things, mostly. Clean up the tables after folks leave. What do you need me to do?"

"What does Arnie eat?"

He rattled it off, and she scanned the supplies.

"Arnie doesn't do a blasted thing all day," Ruby complained. "Ian works harder than any ten men. He should go first. You sure you—"

Scarlett faced her. "I promise you I know what I'm doing. Give me a chance to help."

"Folks around here aren't used to waiting. I run a tight ship."

"So do I. Don't you dare get up."

"We're shorthanded. That's how I ran into trouble."

"I can manage. Sit."

"You are one bossy bit of goods, aren't you?" Pain chased over Ruby's features then.

"You ought to see the doctor."

"Maybe later."

"You could have sprained something."

"I've been worse."

Finally Scarlett stopped arguing. The likely way to settle Ruby down was to get to work. "Henry, would you please ask Arnie if he's okay with waiting until after I fix Ian's breakfast?"

"I am." Arnie appeared from around the doorway where he'd apparently been hovering.

"Get out of my kitchen!" Ruby snapped.

Scarlett met the older man's gaze and shrugged.

He smiled at her and winked. "The woman adores me. Can't keep her hands off me."

"Well, I never—" Ruby huffed.

Scarlett laughed as she laid bacon strips on the grill, added a helping of grated potatoes to brown—

"That's not enough," Ruby interrupted. "Ian's a hard-working man. He needs a good-sized batch. Double that. And give him six strips, not four. Three biscuits to start."

Wow. Amazing the man wasn't round as a barrel instead of lean and ripped and hot. Scarlett added the bacon, doubled the hash browns, then twirled the wheel to see what was on the upcoming orders while she waited to start his eggs. She watched the pace at which the bacon cooked and calculated when to start the eggs. As soon as she'd flipped first the potatoes, then the strips, she took three eggs and cracked them onto the grill one handed. She glanced around for paper towels to drain the bacon on.

"What are you looking for?"

She told Ruby, who pursed her lips. "I don't drain it extra.

Folks who get enough exercise don't have to worry about cholesterol. Just put them on the plate."

O-o-kay. That threw off her timing, but Scarlett flipped the eggs, plated the hash browns and bacon, then retrieved the eggs and added biscuits with only a small shudder for Ian's arteries.

She dinged the bell and handed the plate to Jeanette, who eyed it suspiciously, then sniffed. "Hash browns could be more done, but no time now. People are waiting." She huffed off.

Behind her, Ruby snickered. "Don't mind her. She thinks nothing's good enough for Ian. Not that he notices."

Scarlett took a second to glance toward where the man in question was seated at the counter. He looked at his plate, then up at her with raised brows as if he were surprised.

Scarlett glared at him, then returned to work.

About twenty minutes and countless orders later, Ian finished his meal, rose and made his way into the kitchen. "I guess you were right, New York. Nobody's died yet."

She spared him only a jaundiced glance.

"Get out of the kitchen," she and Ruby said as one.

He glanced from one to the other. "I will, after I convince Ruby to go see a doctor with me."

Ruby harrumphed. "Just a little scorch mark, a few aches. I don't need someone poking and prodding at me. You go on now, Ian."

"I'll walk you out." There was an edge to Jeanette's voice when she turned back to Scarlett. "Then you and me got work to do."

Scarlett watched her go, her hand possessively on Ian's arm. She scanned the dining room and knew the waitress was right. The tables and booths continued to be filled with new arrivals. Farmers and ranchers had been replaced by a scattering of men in suits, clutches of women and what appeared to be truck drivers. "Where on earth do they all come from?" she muttered.

"People drive for miles to eat here," Henry said from behind her. "All the way from San Antonio, even."

"Amazing."

"Ruby's a really good cook." He blushed again. "You're doing fine, though. Nobody's complaining except that you're slow."

Her eyes widened with insult. She'd never—*never*—been called slow. If she couldn't keep up with a woman in her seventies, then—

She plated two orders and slapped the bell.

Her competitive streak, never far from the surface, had her hands moving faster.

Ian pulled out his wallet to pay for a breakfast that wasn't Ruby's but was surprisingly good. He ate the same thing so often he already knew the total and left it, along with his tip, on the counter by the cash register.

Not exactly the breakfast he'd planned with New York, but it was just as well, he was certain.

Ruby's granddaughter? For real? He shook his head at the notion. Ruby had been alone forever. It was common knowledge around here that she had once had a child, but that daughter had left years ago, when he was a little kid.

"You have a good day, you hear?" Jeanette leaned in, continued under her breath. "You just gonna go and leave her here with Ruby?"

"Who? New York?"

"She could be anybody," Jeanette whispered furiously. "Maybe she's a con artist out to swindle Ruby of her life savings."

Ian glanced back toward the kitchen. He could just catch

the top of New York's head and occasionally the eyes. "She's built just like Ruby, got black hair."

"Ruby's hair color comes straight from a bottle."

"So what am I supposed to do? Ruby seems fine with her."

"You brought her here. She would have been long gone."

"What does that mean?"

"She was here last night. Stayed for hours."

"Casing the joint?"

"Don't you dare grin, Ian McLaren. Ruby deserves better than to be taken advantage of by some big-city hustler."

"Her?" Ian frowned as he glanced once more at the petite woman who looked, well, not harmless exactly, but definitely not sinister. "What does Ruby have that anyone would want? She's like everyone else around here, just hanging on."

"Do I look like I know? But that woman is your responsibility."

"She is not—" Then he sighed. She was, though. Jeanette was right. The city girl had been on her way out of town when he'd taken pity on her and invited her to breakfast. Okay, maybe not pity. It wasn't as though Sweetgrass Springs was exactly overrun with beautiful women and yes, he'd yielded to the temptation of a new face with new stories. A glimpse of the outside world he'd never get to travel.

"All right." He exhaled. "No idea what I can do, but I'll have a word with her."

"You forget something, Ian? Because I know you're not going to try again to drag me off to some sawbones."

Scarlett glanced up at Ruby's voice, then quickly turned her attention back to the grill.

"I was just going to have a chat with New—with Scarlett."

She glanced over. "You'll have to make it quick. I'm a little busy, in case you hadn't noticed."

"Ian, you know I don't cotton to folks getting in the way in my kitchen," Ruby complained. "Don't you distract her. She's just now getting up to speed."

Scarlett glared. "I'll have you know I am right on top of these orders. Nobody's going hungry." She flipped pancakes and spoke without looking up. "What do you need?"

"What are your plans?"

"Excuse me?" That got her attention. "What do you mean?"

He shrugged and moved closer. Kept his voice low, so only she could hear over the sound of the grill vent. "It's nice of you to help out Ruby and all, but weren't you headed out of town earlier? Your car was pointed in the other direction, and Jeanette says you were already here last night."

Her hand stilled on the spatula. Just as quickly she realized one pancake was getting too dark. Swiftly she took care of it. "I'm simply helping out. Can we discuss this later?"

"I won't be around later. I'm behind enough as it is."

She cocked her head. "And my plans are your business because…?"

His eyes narrowed. "Because we take care of each other around here. Ruby's important to me and to everyone else in town."

Her jaw dropped. "And, what, you think I'm somehow here to take advantage of her?" She plated the pancakes and bacon and rang the bell. "Thanks a lot. What part of *I think you're my grandmother* did you not understand?"

"Look, you're a stranger here, and I'm just asking what your intentions are. Ruby is the heart and soul of this town."

For a second, the reality of her life crashed into the nice distraction she'd had going. Nothing soothed her like cooking, and she'd gotten lost in the comfort of focusing on food, of feeding people.

And she'd forgotten that she didn't belong.

Anywhere.

"Want to run me out of town on a rail, Marshall Dillon?"

"Of course not, I just—"

"Don't trust me with Ruby. My own grandmother."

"You said you think. You don't know that for sure, and neither do we. Nobody ever heard of you."

"Who died and made you God?"

"What's going on over there?" Ruby started to rise. "Ian, what is it?"

Their furious whispers had attracted her attention. Scarlett glared at him. Spoke to Ruby. "Nothing. Ian was just leaving." She jutted her chin at him and dared him to interfere. "Thank you again for changing my tire."

He glared right back. "You're welcome." He turned to Ruby. "I'll be back for supper and to see how you're doing. I still think you ought to go get checked. I could drive you over to Johnson City."

"Oh, pish." Ruby waved off his concern. "I'll be a little sore tomorrow, but that burn spray of hers works just dandy. Mine's better of course, but this will do in a pinch. Don't you worry one bit." She patted his cheek. "You go on now. I know you've got a full day ahead."

He glanced back at Scarlett while speaking to Ruby. "You give me a call if you need anything, you hear? And I will be back to check up. I'll bring her tire when I come."

"Ian McLaren, you cannot take care of every soul in this town. I'll be fine, and so will my granddaughter."

Scarlett tore her angry gaze from Ian's, yanked out of her fury over his clear threat by the words she never dreamed she'd hear in her entire life.

My granddaughter. So Ruby believed what Scarlett had found so astonishing. She smiled at the older woman. "My grandmother is right." She did an inner dance at being able to use those words right back. "We will be more than fine. No need to concern yourself at all."

He arched one eyebrow at her, making his skepticism clear.

Then he turned his attention back to Ruby. "Getting out would do Dad good. See you at supper. You get some rest, okay? Take advantage of having the help. Go take a nap."

"And leave someone else alone in my kitchen? You know better than that. Go on now. We'll see you this evening. Tell your daddy I'll make him a cobbler."

"You should be resting."

"You should be minding your own business." Ruby squeezed his arm and sent him off.

He glanced back at Scarlett.

She proffered a smug smile. *Ha! Mind your own business indeed.*

Ian's cell phone rang. He unsnapped the holster and retrieved it. "This is Ian."

"Boss? We got a problem." The Double Bar M's longtime foreman Billy.

"What is it?"

"Fence is down in the southwest pasture, a hundred-yard stretch."

The pasture the cattle were in right now as he let the others rest. "How many got out?"

"Twenty-four head, best I can tell."

Ian didn't groan, but he wanted to. "Twenty-four. On Tank's land."

"Yep. We're on it. Just thought you'd want to know."

"I promised Veronica I'd stop by first thing, and I'm already behind." The widow of one of his oldest friends would understand if he cancelled, but she was struggling already, with three kids to raise and no insurance money after David's untimely death. "I'll get there as quick as I can."

He disconnected. As if the day hadn't already started off wrong, now he had to talk to the childhood foe who still bore a grudge. Tank Patton wasn't as bad as his old man had been, but the acorn didn't fall too far from the tree. Tank was a bully—worse, a bully who wore a badge. He had hated Ian and his buddies, David Butler and Jackson Gallagher, since they were kids. Then when Randall Mackey had moved to town in sixth grade and become the final member of what the town called The Four Horseman of the Apocalypse—first for the constant trouble they got into, then when they were an unbeatable combination on the football field and basketball court—Tank's hatred had only grown.

That Tank's sister Veronica had married David had never set well with him, though David had tried hard to extend the family ties. Ian didn't exactly blame Tank—it couldn't have been easy growing up with a mean drunk and a mother who wouldn't protect her kids from him. But along the way, Tank had come to resemble the old man who had made his own life hell.

He'd be ticked off at anybody's cattle trespassing on his land, but for them to be Ian's…well, he'd probably shoot them on sight.

Yet again, Ian wished their destinies hadn't been so closely linked at the formation of Sweetgrass Springs, but both his forebear and Tank's had fought together in the Texas Revolution and had been awarded land as compensation. Josiah Gallagher, Ronald McLaren, Benjamin Butler and Tobias Patton had each contributed a corner of their land to form what was now Sweetgrass Springs. That was a noble history, but it was the deed restriction they'd made—that none of the original town acreage could be sold without agreement of the majority of surviving founding family members residing in Sweetgrass Springs—that rankled Ian and complicated Ian's hopes for the future of Sweetgrass.

Jackson Gallagher was gone, banished by his father at eighteen. David Butler had died last year, leaving a son barely a teenager and two small girls. Veronica Butler had been a Patton and thus a founding family member, but she had her hands full after David's death. Jackson's sister Rissa was preoccupied with keeping the Gallagher ranch from going under.

So the fate of this town rested primarily in the hands of Ian and a man who was more resistant to change than Ian's dad and who hated Ian for reasons he'd never really understood.

He punched Tank's number into his phone.

"Patton."

"Tank, it's Ian."

"What do you want?"

"My fence is down. Some of my cattle are on your place. My men are rounding them up, and I'm headed there now."

"They better not tear up my pasture."

Which you're not using, Ian thought but didn't say. "We'll get them out as quick as we can. I have no idea what happened to the fence." The shared fence that only he bothered to take care of.

But he didn't say that, either.

"They better be out of there before I get back."

Another rancher would have offered help. But this was Tank.

"They will be. See you." *Unless I get lucky.*

"I'll be checking tonight. Anything's damaged, you'll be hearing from me."

"Understood." Ian disconnected and restricted himself to tossing the phone onto the dash since he couldn't throw something at Tank's head.

Chapter Six

Ian pulled into the drive of Butler's Blooms, the flower farm Veronica was trying to keep functioning without David and, best he could tell, going without sleep to do it. He huffed out a breath to rid himself of Tank's malice before he had to talk to the only worthwhile member of the Patton family.

He spotted her leaving one of the four greenhouses he'd helped David build, juggling four buckets of blooms. He rushed to help her.

"Mornin'."

"Good morning," she replied with a tired smile.

A few years back, Veronica had had the notion to turn her green thumb into a sideline business, and she and David had discovered that flowers were a much better return on the money than growing vegetables. Now, nearly five years later, the sideline had become their main source of income. They'd still raised the cattle for their own beef and a few cow-calf pairs to sell every year, plus they had hens for eggs and their own vegetable garden. They'd both been working hard, but they'd been surviving quite well, with business growing all the time.

Until David had died when his tractor had accidentally jumped into gear when he was clearing a limb from the shredder and had run him over, leaving Veronica to juggle everything plus three grieving children, all by herself.

She'd lost too much weight, and she always looked weary.

And this was the slow season.

Veronica couldn't keep things going indefinitely, not at this rate. She didn't talk about it, but Ian was pretty sure they'd taken out a loan to build the last two greenhouses and buy some equipment not long before David died.

He helped her as often as he could, but it wasn't enough.

And this morning he had cows to round up.

"Bad morning?" he heard her ask.

He set the buckets in the back of the beat-up van she used for deliveries. "I've seen worse. How are you?"

She smiled—she always smiled—but it wasn't reflected in her eyes. "Tell me the secret to teenage boys, and you'll make my day."

"Drown 'em when they're young is the only fix, at least that's what my dad said fairly often."

She grinned. "Too late for that, and I'm pretty attached to Ben, it's just—"

Ben was fifteen and had taken his father's death hard, but he'd buried his grief and pitched in to help his mother—only now, nearly a year down the road, the toll was showing on him, too. But his way of dealing with his mourning was to act out. "My dad's solution was to work me until I was ready to drop. Kept me out of mischief."

"Nothing kept the Four Horsemen out of mischief."

He grinned back and shrugged. "Think how much worse it could have been."

She shuddered dramatically. "Doesn't bear thinking about. Want some coffee?"

"Wish I could, but I already had two cups at Ruby's, and Billy tells me my cattle are out on your land."

"Tank's land, not mine. I'm so sorry. Does he know?"

He nodded.

"And he was awful, right? Want me to talk to him?"

"You don't have enough on your plate? So what's on

today's menu?"

"Ian, you don't have to check in on me every day. I'll be fine."

Instead of arguing, he entered the greenhouse. "You ready for me to rebuild that set of plant benches yet?"

"I can swing a hammer, you know. I helped David build these."

He cast her a skeptical glance. "Yeah, I've always been wowed by those biceps, champ." Even if she didn't look as though a puff of air would blow her away, she was clearly too exhausted to be doing this by herself.

"I can do anything I have a mind to."

"Nobody's saying you're not gutsy, honey, but you have three children to care for in addition to this place, which was a difficult task even when you and David were doing it together. You look like you could sleep for a week."

"Ben can help me when he gets home from school. You have cattle to round up."

"It'll be dark an hour after he gets home on the bus. Let me get a hammer and a pry bar from my truck, and I'll tear these old ones out before I go."

She put her hands on her hips and shook her head. "I am doing fine, Ian. It's just hard this first year to figure out how to scale this to what I can manage—but I will manage."

"You do that, but in the meantime, I'm getting out my tools."

Veronica sighed. "David wouldn't want you burning the candle at both ends."

"David would want me watching over his family, same as I know he'd do for me." He paused. "God, I miss him."

Her eyes filled. "He was a good man."

"He loved you and those kids like crazy."

"He loved you, too, you and Jackson and Mackey."

They were both silent for a moment, thinking of long-absent friends.

"I heard from Mackey last week, did I tell you? He's doing stunts for Russell Crowe now. Some action movie where a lot of stuff gets blown up."

She followed him out to his truck while he retrieved his tools. "Right up his alley. I bet he loves it."

"Not as much as he loved being in the SEAL teams."

"I can see that. But being a stuntman should help satisfy his need for adrenaline. He always was in constant motion."

"He thought up every ill-fated prank we ever got involved in."

"Such as David's broken arm when you were about twelve?"

"Yep. Mackey decided jumping out of the hayloft would be fun." Ian began walking back to the greenhouse beside her.

"Those were good times."

"Easy for you to say—" He halted. "Sorry. I didn't mean—"

"It's okay, Ian. Really." But her eyes were dark with sorrow.

He felt it, too. Nothing was the same anymore, and innocent times held a particular sweetness in memory. Being an adult was a little short on the fun factor—lately, anyway.

Time for a change of mood. "You hear about the excitement at Ruby's this morning yet?"

"What? She told Arnie yet again that she won't marry him?"

"Actually, part of the news isn't that great—Ruby fell and was also burned by hot grease."

"Oh no! Is she okay?"

"I tried to get her to let me take her to the doctor, but you know Ruby."

"Just a wee bit hardheaded?"

"She swears she's fine and that the burns are no worse than others she's had."

"Tell me she's not back cooking already. I could go help

if—"

He rolled his eyes. "Yeah, because you have so much free time on your hands."

"We all pitch in where we need to in Sweetgrass."

He huffed a laugh. "Except for Veronica, who never wants to accept any help."

"Ian…"

"I know, I know. You have to figure this out yourself. I must just like the sound of my own voice, I guess." Seeing her frown, he shifted the conversation. "I'm going back this evening to check on her, using Dad as an excuse. How about if Ben joins us for supper? Let me spend a little time with him."

"You know he would love that, but—"

"But nothing." He rushed on before she could argue more. "Anyway, here's the real news: you don't need to go help cook because there's already someone else there doing it."

"Oh? Who?"

"A bona fide fancy-pants chef. Trained in Paris, no less."

Veronica blinked. "How on earth did someone like that get to Ruby's? Or Sweetgrass, for that matter?"

He rocked back on his heels. "Well, that's the thing—she says she's Ruby's granddaughter."

Her mouth dropped open. "Get out of town. Ruby has a granddaughter?"

He shrugged. "Maybe."

"You don't like her? Do you think she's taking advantage of Ruby somehow?"

"I didn't say that. I mean, sure she's bossy and kinda snotty, got that city girl thing going, but…what's in it for her? It's not like Ruby is rolling in the dough, and why would a fancy chef want anything to do with Sweetgrass Springs?" His own mother sure hadn't.

Veronica's brows snapped together. "Maybe I had better

pay a visit to Ruby's, too."

"You and the girls would be welcome to join us."

She waved him off. "No, that would ruin Ben's special time with you." Her head cocked. "I don't like to think of anyone hurting Ruby, and you know how she's grieved over Georgia. We need to watch out for her. I will be paying a visit very soon."

"Good," Ian said, and went to work tearing down benches. "But for now, you go inside and put your feet up. I'll leave when I'm done here and come back tomorrow afternoon to start the new ones. Ben can help me when he gets home."

"I am not putting my feet up."

He shook his head. "Suit yourself, hard case." But he softened his command with a grin. "Now get out of my hair. I'll be by to pick up Ben at six."

"Yes, sir." She snapped off a sharp salute and left.

Scarlett reached up to the order wheel to see what was next—

Only to realize the wheel was empty. She blinked and came up from that zone she inhabited when her mind and her hands were focused completely on the preparation of food.

"It's after two. The lunch rush is over," Ruby said.

They hadn't spoken much in the last hour or so while Scarlett's focus had narrowed to the dance of cooking, her visual field the grill and the prep area behind her. She zeroed in on her grandmother. "How are you holding up?"

"I'm fine."

But Scarlett could see the strain. "You should rest."

Ruby's back stiffened as she prepared to argue. Surprisingly, however, she didn't. "I generally sit and have a bite to eat, once I clean up and make sure everything's ready for supper."

"Do you do it all by yourself?"

Henry stepped up. "I help. I know how to, right?" he asked Ruby.

Her face softened. "You do."

"Then why don't you and I get things ready, Henry?" Scarlett said. "And you go home and rest. Unless you don't trust me," she said to Ruby.

"I can help, too." The timid waitress, Brenda, spoke from the doorway.

Scarlett smiled at her. "Thank you."

Jeanette walked up behind her, and Brenda scooted away to the side. "I'll keep an eye on everybody, Ruby." Her eyes were hard, her expression unflinching.

"I don't need supervision," Scarlett said.

"The three of them can get started on prep," Ruby decided. "You come with me—oh, shoot. I have to make Gordon's cobbler first."

"I can make a cobbler. Any idiot can."

"Not like Ruby's," Jeanette insisted.

Scarlett rolled her eyes. "Hello? What part of trained chef do you not get?"

"They don't make cobbler in Paris or wherever you've been."

"They make much more difficult and challenging dishes." She was right in Jeanette's face now.

"You're not helping Ruby by fighting," Henry said quietly.

Scarlett glanced over and realized Ruby's face was tight with strain. She exhaled and stepped back. "Okay. Brenda, you walk Ruby home. I'll get started on the cobbler. That way Ruby and everyone—" She glared at Jeanette "—can taste it and see while there's plenty of time to redo it." She arched an eyebrow at Ruby.

Ruby's lips curved slightly. "Fine. Except first you come with me."

"Why?"

"You got plenty of time to make a cobbler. Thought you might want to see where you're staying."

Protest burst from Jeanette's lips, but it might have come from her own. *Staying?* Truthfully, Scarlett hadn't thought past the plates she was filling. "I don't need—"

"There are no fancy hotels in Sweetgrass—no hotels or motels at all, actually. If you intend to help out tonight, you don't need to be driving another hour after closing. I wouldn't do that to my worst enemy, much less family."

Family. A pang struck Scarlett, a hunger for that sense of connection. "I don't want to impose..."

Ruby snorted. "I don't know how folks do things in the big city, but around here, family isn't just a word. You'll stay with me. I have plenty of room."

"Until the next stray comes along," Jeanette muttered.

Henry's face took on color, while Brenda blanched.

Scarlett wasn't sure why, but she was sure of one thing: Jeanette was a bully, and Scarlett knew how to deal with that.

But she also needed Jeanette's help in running the diner tonight. If Scarlett had her way, Ruby would be staying home and resting. She turned back to the other woman and spoke softly. "Look, you don't have to like me, but Ruby needs our help. If I can get her to stay home and rest, can we call a truce?"

The waitress appeared startled, but she quickly covered it. "Of course." She turned away, then back abruptly. "Good luck with getting her to chill, though." Her tone actually seemed slightly sympathetic.

Scarlett had to smile. "I suspect I'll need it."

Then she followed Ruby to the door. "Shall we take my car?"

"Not hardly," Ruby said, pointing to the big two-story red brick house out the back door. "There it is."

Wow. The structure was impressive, even though the white trim was peeling in spots. She matched her pace to

Ruby's, taking the older woman's elbow and noting that Ruby's gait was pained. "How much do you hurt?"

"I am perfectly fine, missy."

"You know you're not. I can't help you if you won't be honest with me."

Ruby halted at the back steps. Faced her. "Is that what you want, to help me?" Her eyes searched Scarlett's face. "Why are you just now showing up here?"

"I didn't know you existed until two weeks ago."

"Why not?" She frowned, then comprehension dawned. "You mean Georgia never…?"

The hurt she saw in the older woman's eyes made her wish she didn't have to answer, but the truth was the truth. "She told me we had no family." Scarlett pressed her lips together before continuing. "But I won't hear you criticize my mother. She was everything to me."

Ruby closed her eyes for a second, then opened them. "Well, of course she was. You're her child, aren't you? I just wish…" She shook her head. "I don't understand why she lied to you."

"You weren't in touch at all?"

Misery such as she'd seldom seen swam in Ruby's gaze. "Georgia ran away when she was seventeen. And don't ask me why because I don't know, except that she always wanted to be anywhere but where she was."

Scarlett blinked, seeing her mother in a different light but unwilling to expose her to anyone's criticism. But as she thought about how different her life might have been if she'd had a clue that there was anyone else in the world who cared about her, her heart ached. "Growing up, I would have sold my soul for a grandmother."

Ruby gripped her hand hard, just for a second. "Well, now you have one." She cleared her throat, then went silent for a moment, her gaze scanning the house. "The Gallaghers were part of Sweetgrass Springs from the beginning, and this was my aunt Margaret's home. I grew up out on the ranch, but she took me in when—"

Scarlett waited for Ruby to finish, but she didn't.

And she didn't feel like she could pry, so she switched topics. "You have a ranch?" Scarlett couldn't begin to absorb the notion of being related to anyone who owned one.

"Not really. I mean, it's part mine, but my nephew James lives there. It mostly belongs to him and his children." She glanced over. "Your cousins."

Cousins. "I never imagined…" She shook her head. "It was always just Mama and me. How many of them are there?"

"I had a brother William, but he's gone now. He had James and another son, Sam, who lived in Morning Star up near Abilene, but he's passed on, too. Sam's two sons, Boone and Mitch, are still there. James has three children. Jackson and Penelope are twins. Clarissa is the younger sister, and she still lives on the ranch."

Her head was spinning, trying to keep track. "But not the others?"

"Pen is a big-shot lawyer on the East Coast and Jackson, well…Jackson's been gone a long time. But that's another story." Ruby's eyes were dark with grief. "We have a lot to talk about. Come on inside, will you?"

Scarlett spared one more glance from the sidewalk up to the rooftop, trying to encompass the idea that she had a connection to this house. To a ranch.

To a family.

She'd had a lot of bold ideas in her life, but this one was nearly beyond her to assimilate. "Cousins? Really?"

Ruby smiled. "Jackson and Penelope are older than you, I expect. Boone and Mitch are the oldest cousins. There's also a half-sister Lacey. Rissa is the youngest, close to your age, I'm guessing—how old are you?"

"Thirty-two."

"Thirty-two…so Georgia would have had you not long

after she left. Who's your daddy?"

"I never met him." *You and I only need each other, baby girl,* her mother had said all the years Scarlett was growing up.

"Guess I shouldn't be surprised. Girl was as wild as a March hare."

Scarlett started to leap to her mother's defense, but in truth, Georgia had fit that description in some ways, especially when Scarlett was younger. Still, she would never have dreamed her mother could have been hiding so much.

She'd misjudged Andre badly, and if she knew so little about her mother, the closest person on earth to her, what else in her life was she wrong about?

And what did she do now? She couldn't, in good conscience, leave town without knowing Ruby was in shape to resume her cooking, but that would only be a matter of days.

She was desperate to know more.

But scared to death of the ugliness she might be bringing with her. "What should I call you?" Part of her knew it would be wiser to keep some distance until she understood more, but part of her was a greedy eight-year-old dying to call someone Grandma or Nana or... A memory of writing out various grandmother name choices—some the usual, some a little out there like Mimsey—had her grinning.

"What's tickling your funnybone?"

Scarlett stared. "Mama used to say that all the time."

Pleasure tangled with grief in Ruby's eyes. "My own mama said that to me, too."

In that moment, Scarlett's longing nearly overcame her good sense, but she was a stranger in a strange land, and she'd made serious errors in judgment only recently. "How about if I call you Ruby, just for now?"

"You didn't learn that caution from Georgia." But she nodded. "That comes straight from me. Ruby, it is...at least until I earn something better." She turned to mount the steps.

"Ruby, I didn't mean...you don't have to earn anything."

Her grandmother turned back. "I lost my daughter, and it had to be my doing somehow. I assure you I do."

Scarlett started to argue, but caution—learned or inherited—kept her silent and instead she focused on stepping up to assist the woman she found more fascinating every second.

Wide concrete steps led up to a screened-in back porch filled with plants, despite the time of year. Ruby wobbled a little. Scarlett hurried to put one hand on her elbow.

"I'm not feeble." Ruby pulled her arm away.

Scarlett hesitated, then took her elbow again gently but kept her tone crisp. She understood not wanting to be pitied. "You couldn't possibly be. Restaurant work is tough, and the weak don't survive. You've clearly built something amazing. How long have you been open?"

Ruby glanced at her, let her gaze linger. "Longer than you've been alive, little girl."

Scarlett drew herself up straight. "Not so little. Bet I have a good inch on you."

Ruby snorted. "You wish."

They smirked at each other, and Scarlett wondered if her grandmother felt easier, too, with the lighter topic. By the twinkle in Ruby's eye, Scarlett thought she might.

Meanwhile they'd reached the porch without Ruby yanking her arm away again.

"You raised Mama here?"

Raw grief rippled over Ruby's face, and Scarlett could have kicked herself. "She's really gone?"

Scarlett's own eyes stung. She nodded. "Two years ago in November."

"I always knew it was likely she was dead, however much I didn't want to believe that. It shouldn't hurt now, but knowing it's too late, that I'll never..." With rapid blinks, Ruby wrestled back her tears. "What happened? Was she...did she suffer?"

Scarlett tried not to think of the moment when her mother died, but a thousand times she'd pictured it and worried, wishing she'd been there to guard her mother as she left this world. The only way she'd found to go on was to shove her imaginings into a box and lock them away.

She fell back on what she'd been told. What she tried to cling to. "The doctors said no. It was an aneurysm. It came out of the blue. She just—" Scarlett swallowed hard. Shared the one thought that had comforted her. "She wasn't alone. I wish I'd—" She shook her head. "Mama was at the senior citizens center where she volunteered. She did that most everywhere we lived. They loved her, the old folks—sorry."

Ruby waved off her concern. "When you're old, you're old. No sense pretending otherwise. Go on."

"At this place, she had a group of old men she played cards with once a week, and she painted with a group of ladies another night."

"She was still painting? When she left here, she didn't take any of her supplies with her." Ruby's eyes were wide with wonder.

"When I was a kid, she made me picture books. Did them in watercolor. When I was older, I tried to get her to submit them to a publisher, but she said they weren't good enough."

Ruby snorted. "She was good enough when she was only a child herself."

The line of connection, the thread winding through two divided pasts, nearly stole Scarlett's breath. "Do you have anything from back then?"

"Oh, child, I have just about every drawing Georgia ever made. I couldn't bring myself to get rid of them. I always hoped…" Ruby looked both sad and inexpressibly weary, and Scarlett realized they'd been standing on the porch when Ruby needed to sit down.

"Here, let's get you inside."

Again Ruby bristled. "I am not an invalid. I can get my own self inside."

Cooking was clearly not the only thing she and this woman had in common. Fierce independence linked them, too—but how much longer had Ruby been alone?

She had so many questions. *Who was my grandfather? What was Mama like as a girl? Why wouldn't she tell me about you?* Anxiety built that she wouldn't get her chance if she didn't seize it now.

But she was afraid of answering questions Ruby might ask in return. She was more ashamed than ever of what a fool she'd been.

Anyhow, Ruby was exhausted and, truth to tell, Scarlett was tired herself, with more work on the horizon before she could rest. So she only grasped the handle of the door and held it open. "I have no doubt that you can."

Ruby cast her a skeptical glance.

Scarlett shrugged. "Hey, cut me some slack. I'm new at this granddaughter business. I don't know much about old ladies."

"Old ladies—hmmph!"

Scarlett grinned. "You said the truth was the truth."

Ruby's mouth curved. "You're my granddaughter, all right. Smart aleck. Now come on inside, and I'll show you your room before you get back to work."

"Slave driver."

They paused. Grinned again.

Abruptly Scarlett's eyes filled.

And she gave her brand-new grandmother a hug.

After a second's hesitation, Ruby grabbed her right back.

And held on.

Chapter Seven

Inside the kitchen, an old man rolled his walker toward the door. "What's wrong? What are you doing here?"

Scarlett halted, taken aback at the accusation in his tone.

Ruby never even blinked. "It's my house, Judge. I'll come home whenever I wish."

"But you never do." Tall and leonine, his full head of white hair and dignified mustache lending him a gravitas at odds with the walker upon which he leaned, the old man narrowed his eyes. "You're favoring your right hip."

Ruby bristled and opened her mouth, but before she could say a word, the man's sharp gaze focused on Scarlett. "Who are you?"

It wasn't said unkindly, which Scarlett appreciated after all the suspicion next door. "I'm Scarlett Ross. And you would be…?"

His head tilted, a grin teasing his lips. "You have to be related—even if you didn't favor Ruby, you certainly have her moxie." While Ruby spluttered, he extended his hand. "I'm Daniel Porter."

"I'm her granddaughter." Scarlett gave him her own. "You're a judge?" He looked like one, dignified and stately.

"Retired for many years." He nodded out the window. "My courtroom was right over there. Building was headed straight downhill once the county seat moved, but Ruby's going to change that."

Scarlett glanced at Ruby, catching sorrow fleeting over her face.

Ruby shook her head. "Going to show the girl her room."

His eyebrows lifted. "You're staying?"

"Oh, no, I—I'm only helping out while Ruby recovers."

Ruby's sharp gaze shifted to her, but before she could say anything, Judge Porter bored in. "I knew you were hurt. What happened?"

His interest seemed almost proprietary. Exactly how many men in this town were in love with her grandmother?

"I am perfectly fine. Just a little kitchen burn. Scarlett here is making a big fuss about it when I am completely okay." Ruby patted his arm. "Don't you worry one bit, Daniel."

Then an older woman entered the kitchen, in appearance younger than the judge, but no spring chicken herself. "What's going on back here? Judge, you should be taking your nap."

"I'll sleep when I'm dead," he muttered.

"You come on now," the woman urged. "Let me get you settled—oh! Didn't see you back there." She glanced between Ruby and Scarlett. "What's the matter? Who is this, Ruby?"

"It's her granddaughter, you meddling old woman," groused the judge.

The woman's forehead wrinkled. "Ruby doesn't have a granddaughter."

Scarlett opened her mouth to respond, but Ruby beat her to it. "Turns out I do. This is Scarlett Ross, Mrs. Oldham. She's all the way from Paris."

"I trained there," Scarlett explained. "But I've been back east most recently."

The other woman's eyes popped. "How on earth did you get way up there? You know, I once knew a gentleman who lived up there in New York City for a spell. He didn't like it one bit. Dirty and noisy, crowded as all get-out. Can't imagine why anyone would want to live in all that."

Scarlett felt a compulsion to defend Manhattan, but fortunately the judge leaped to respond.

"And that is why you will be a small town busybody all your life. Can't see the big picture. New York is a bustling place, full of interesting people and fine dining, all manner of cultural opportunities—"

"It's a heathen place, practically Sodom and Gomorrah—"

"Oh, what do you know? You've hardly read one book in your life—"

"I'll have you know I—"

Ruby tugged at Scarlett's arm. "They'll be at it for hours. A body could grow old and die, waiting for those two to finish."

"But—"

"You do not want to get in the middle of this, I promise you." Ruby headed down the hall toward a staircase in the front entry.

"Should you be climbing stairs?"

"And how will you find your room if I don't?"

"Directions?"

"That's no fit way to welcome strangers, much less family."

Scarlett touched Ruby's arm as they reached the bottom of a wide staircase that curved up and to the left. "Look, I'm not trying to make you into an invalid, but I'm pretty sure you want to be back at the café as soon as possible, right? Let me walk you to your room, then tell me where to find mine, but let me do the climbing, just for today. Please?"

She could tell the idea didn't sit well with Ruby, but it was a mark of how weary Ruby was that she stopped arguing. "All right." Instead of climbing, she moved around to the left of the staircase and down a hall, stopping at a door on the right. "This was once a library, and my uncle had his office in the next room, but I turned them both into my suite a number of years back. After a long day at the café, the stairs…"

"I hear you. Mama and I once lived in a fourth-floor walkup, and by the time I got home at night from the restaurant, my feet were screaming at me."

Ruby studied her. "In New York?"

She hesitated. Of course her grandmother would want to know her daughter's history, but Scarlett's own recent past was a minefield.

Ruby didn't wait for an answer. "I cannot picture Georgia confined in a city. She loved the outdoors as much as she loved painting and drawing."

"She did it for me. The noise just about drove her crazy." Scarlett had to swallow past a lump in her throat. Her mother had died in a foreign place, even more foreign than she'd ever realized, she saw now.

"Don't you fret. She wanted the bright lights badly when she was young." Ruby patted her arm. "I expect she found things to compensate."

"Maybe." Or maybe she just couldn't figure out where was home.

Ruby opened the door, breaking into Scarlett's bout with guilt.

There were bookshelves…everywhere. Untold numbers of books filled them, but more were stacked on tables or on the floor beside two overstuffed chairs that begged a person to climb in and retreat from the world.

Scarlett adored reading. In a life with little certainty, books had been the antidote to constant change. Even though she could seldom afford to own books because what she had should be ready to pack up at a moment's notice, she could find the dearest ones in most any library.

And these days she owned an e-reader, so that she could indeed take her most beloved books with her anywhere.

She glanced toward her grandmother, seeing her with new

eyes.

But her gaze was caught by a portrait that was surely her mother when she was young. Drawn to it like a magnet to true north, Scarlett drifted across the room, greedily taking in the sight of her mother's face as she'd never seen it. Carefully she traced her mother's cheek. "She was always so beautiful," she said softly.

"You should have seen her as a baby. Folks would stop me on the street to exclaim over her."

Oh, Mama... Scarlett wanted to sink to the floor and curl into a ball.

But she didn't. Couldn't. Instead she responded to the longing she heard, revolving to face Ruby. "I have pictures in my car. Want me to go get them?"

The yearning she'd heard in Ruby's voice was nothing compared to that on her face.

Then Scarlett noticed the white-knuckled grip of Ruby's hand on the chair back. The slight sway of her body.

"You need to lie down."

Ruby snapped back to the moment. "I'll decide that for myself. Let me get you some towels. I'll make your bed in a bit."

And the subject was apparently closed.

"I can make my own bed. Please...sit down. We don't have to stand on ceremony. If you'd just tell me where the linens are, I can help. Please, Ruby...Grandmother," she ventured.

Ruby's eyes flew up to hers, naked and vulnerable.

For a very long moment, emotion swirled in the air, too much of it, painful longing, grief, guilt...

Ruby looked away. Pointed toward the hall. "There's a linen closet out there. Pick out what you like. It's only a double bed. We don't run to king and queen-sized here. Furniture's old, just like everything else here."

Scarlett seized the escape, desperately grateful to get away from the tumult of both her grandmother's feelings…and her own.

Ian knew better than to open the pickup door for his dad, even though his dad only had limited use of his left arm and a slightly halting gait with his left foot.

Gordon McLaren might not be the man he once was physically, but his ferocious independence was not one iota diminished. The struggle was painful to watch, especially since getting into the truck involved hitching himself up to a seat high off the ground, not sinking down into an automobile.

But if Ian pointedly looked away, that would be an insult. He admired the hell out of his dad, he just… Wished things between them could be easier, he guessed. More harmonious.

"We picking up Ben, you say?"

"Yeah." Ian started the truck and pulled away.

"Boy doing all right?"

"Can't say. Veronica's sure not."

"Teenage boys are a lot to handle."

Ian glanced over at his dad, who'd had to handle him and his rowdy foursome without a partner. Knowing his father wouldn't like a blatant display of emotion, nonetheless an acknowledgment seemed only fair. "You sure didn't have it easy."

Gordon huffed a little laugh. "'Bout wore out a belt on your backside, not that it did much more than delay you a little."

"I should probably apologize."

His dad turned toward him. "Nope. Just being a boy, doing what boys do. Though—" His dad grinned "—you could have one of your own and give me the pleasure of watching you go through it."

Ian met his grin. "A little thirst for revenge, huh?"

"Might be." His dad hesitated. "You should marry Veronica."

Ian's hands nearly fell off the steering wheel. "You're kidding, right?" A glance disabused him of that notion. "Dad, it would be like marrying, I don't know, Rissa or something. Next thing to a sister, both of them."

"You're not getting any younger, son." His dad stared straight ahead, his voice lowering. "You think you've got all the time in the world, a lot of good years left, and then…"

His father never complained about the stroke that had so radically altered his life and removed so many of his options. What sort of plans had he had for his future that would now never come to fruition?

Sometimes life was so blasted unfair.

"I could drive you if you wanted to try physical therapy again," Ian offered. Maybe improvement could still be made, even if the doctors hadn't been encouraging.

His father shook his head. "That part's done now." He glanced over. "But you're spending the prime years of your life, breaking your back on this ranch, no woman beside you, no future McLarens to take your place."

Ian couldn't decide if his dad was praising him or complaining. Maybe a little of both. "Hard to meet a woman when you spend all day with animals and cowhands."

"Man needs a helpmeet. A good woman makes the rough patches smoother."

Ian's mind flashed to a petite frame, a full head of curly black hair and eyes that made him think of bluebonnets, that misty purple blue.

A city girl. A Paris-trained chef. Not even close to the kind of woman who could live in this area where the livestock outnumbered the people.

But she sure was pretty. Bossy bit of goods but a looker, heaven knows.

"That looks like a man with a woman on his mind."

Ian stirred. "What? Me? No way."

"So what's this I hear about a granddaughter showing up at Ruby's?"

"How'd you hear about her?"

"Got ears, don't I? She's the talk of the town. Not every day an old story resurfaces like that."

"Did you know Georgia, Dad?"

"Well, of course I did. Sweetgrass was small then, too. And she's from one of the original families. Everybody knew everybody."

"So why'd she leave? Why didn't she ever contact Ruby?"

"Georgia was a beauty—tall and a fine figure of a woman—but she had a restless heart. It was always just a matter of time before she took off. Ruby didn't want to hear it, that's all. Everybody knew she'd be gone at the first opportunity. What's her girl like?"

"Beautiful. Bossy. City girl all the way." Which was about the most damning thing he could say to his father, given his mother's desertion, and that wasn't fair to Scarlett. "She's small like Ruby, but she jumped right in to help when Ruby got hurt. And she's a good cook, breakfast at least. 'Course it's hard to mess up breakfast."

His dad snorted. "You manage."

"Hey—I'm not a bad cook now. A rough start, I will admit." When Ian had been about twelve and eating every ten seconds or so, plus bringing his buddies around all the time, Gordon had finally hired a housekeeper and cook because he couldn't keep up with the ranch and spend half the day in the kitchen trying to fill four sets of hollow legs.

But six months ago, Mrs. Hall's mother had broken her hip, and she'd had to return to Waxahachie to care for her. Ian had tried to learn to cook, but his heart wasn't in it and the results showed. His dad had gotten desperate enough that he'd taken over the cooking as he'd done when Ian was little.

"Good thing you're a better rancher than you are a cook. So this woman will be cooking tonight?"

"Ruby's supervising. Said she'd make you a cobbler."

"Ruby's a good woman. I sure like her cobbler." His dad glanced over. "I'd best get a look at this city girl if she's caught my boy's eye."

Ian shrugged. "Just 'cause a man looks, doesn't mean he's interested in buying."

"Lord have mercy, I have raised me a philosopher."

Ian chuckled and pulled into Veronica's drive.

Chapter Eight

"Hey, Ian. Mr. McLaren, Ben," greeted Jeanette as she led them to a table in the center of the room. "What brings you handsome fellows out tonight?"

"Heard tell there might be cobbler," his dad responded.

She was leaning over Ian's shoulder as she handed out menus and rearranged the condiments. "Might be is about right." She sniffed as though she'd smelled something unpleasant.

Ian leaned away from her and looked up. "Something wrong?" He glanced back toward the kitchen. "What's New York up to?"

Jeanette's eyes narrowed. "Trying to take over Ruby's kitchen and ruin everything is all."

Ian looked around, but people were behaving normally, chatting to others or simply concentrating on their food. "I don't see anyone upset by what they're eating."

"That's not the point." Jeanette slammed down his menu and flounced off.

"Wow. Jeanette's snippier than usual," observed Ben. "Who's New York?"

"You tell him, Dad. I'll just go check the kitchen." Ian rose and wove his way past the tables.

Or tried to. At every table, it seemed, someone wanted to talk. Only being neighborly, of course, but he was on a mission. If Scarlett fouled up Ruby's reputation…

He rounded the corner and approached the grill.

"Jeanette, if you look over my shoulder one more time, I swear—" Scarlett glanced up and her eyes widened. "What are you doing back here?"

"What's going on?"

"I'm trying to cook, in case you can't tell."

"Trying?"

She slapped the spatula on the grill and faced him, eyes sparking. "Do you see anyone not enjoying their food out there?"

"No."

"I know how to cook. I've been doing it most of my life. I am a professional, and if that skinny witch doesn't get out of my hair—"

"Whoa." He laid his hand on her arm. "You look tired. You probably didn't sleep very well last night, what with all the varmints outside, huh?" She was like a high-strung filly, a thoroughbred who'd been held back at the gate too long. "Then you show up and get put to work."

"I work all the time. I've never been afraid of hard work."

"Take a breath."

"I don't have time. I won't have anyone saying I'm slow. I am not slow!" She jerked from his grasp.

"Jeanette's just being territorial. Don't mind her."

She glanced sideways at him. "What kind of law enforcement presence do you have here?"

"County Sheriff's office responds to calls when we need them. Why?"

"Would I have time to get a running start if I drove my knife through her skinny ribs?"

He laughed. "I have a pretty good hideout on my place if you have to turn fugitive. Ignoring her is less trouble, though."

"Easy for you to say," Scarlett muttered.

"Want me to tell her to back off?"

Her spine went ramrod straight. "Absolutely not. I'll never get the upper hand if you run interference for me." Then she did take that deep breath. "Thanks. I just needed to blow off a little steam. I know how to handle cranky waitresses. She just—"

"She can be a handful, all right."

"You would know, I guess."

He frowned. "What do you mean?"

"She's got the hots for you. I assumed you two…"

He reared back. "Me? And *Jeanette*? No way. We were in grade school together, for Pete's sake."

"You're not in grade school now."

"There's nothing going on between us, New York." Then he grinned. "Would you be jealous?"

"Pfft—you're kidding, right? I'm not in the market for a man. Life's easier without them," she retorted. "And my name is Scarlett."

"That sounds like a challenge, *Scarlett*." He was surprised to feel one stir in his blood.

"Men are pigs."

He could swear he saw her lips curve, just a little. "Ooh, that is definitely a challenge." He rubbed his hands together.

"You wish. Now get out of my kitchen. I've got work to do."

"Speaking of that, my dad's all set for cobbler, but Jeanette's muttering about yours. Why is that?"

"Because she lives to complain? Here—" She turned, grabbed a spoon and scooped up a bite. She blew on it with lush lips that puckered in a way a red-blooded man could not possibly ignore, then brought it to his mouth.

"What are—"

She pushed the spoon gently between his lips.

The cobbler was very warm, so he had to suck air in and out over the bite a time or two before he dared eat. "You almost burned my tongue—oh, man." He swirled his tongue around in his mouth. "I can't tell enough from just one taste." He grinned. "Better give me another."

She smirked. "Great, right?"

"If you're through flirting with Ian and making a spectacle of yourself, the wheel's filling up," Jeanette snapped from the other side of the pass-through.

"Jeanette, cut her some slack," he said.

The waitress's eyes filled with hurt. "Not you, too. Men are such idiots." She whirled and flounced off.

"What did I say?"

Scarlett burst out laughing. "I told you. Giant crush."

He winced. "Aw, come on now. Not Jeanette."

"She's right, though. You're distracting the cook. Go away."

But he didn't want to. He stalled time. "Where's Ruby?"

"She went home, believe it or not."

"Before or after she tasted the cobbler?"

"After. Why?"

"She's probably packing to leave town. That's some fine cobbler, New—Scarlett."

Her cheeks flushed rosy. "Thanks. The secret is a little finely-chopped nuts plus a dash of allspice in the crust. But don't you dare tell a soul."

"Cross my heart and hope to die." Solemnly he performed the ritual over his heart. He knew he should leave, but he was liking the scenery.

"Ian...go away. People are staring."

He glanced out. She was right.

And no one was staring more than his father, who winked at him. Ben gave him a thumbs-up.

Oh for Pete's sake... "I'm going." At the corner he turned back. "So what would you recommend I order? Though I'm thinking a plateful of cobbler wouldn't be a bad start."

"Order anything. It's all good. Just try me."

Oh, I'd like to try you, all right. Starting with that delectable mouth and working my way down.

And he was certifiable for even thinking it.

"You're on, city girl." He saluted her with two fingers to his brow.

She merely tossed her head and went back to work.

But she was smiling, not frowning now.

Scarlett looked over the pass-through more than she wanted to as the evening wore on. She was watching to see how her food was received, yes.

But her eyes landed on the Hot Cowboy too often.

The name made her smile, as much as anything because she suspected he'd hate it. His discomfiture over Jeanette's interest in him was...cute.

Though he was far too physically imposing to be considered cute, plus she suspected he'd find the word offensive in its connotation of little, precious things.

He was neither little nor precious. He was one hundred per cent prime Grade A U.S. Male. Overbearing, to be sure, but not cruel about it. From the way people kept stopping by his table and seeking his opinion, clearly he was not only trusted but relied upon. He hadn't waited for someone else to take action when Ruby had been hurt, he'd simply stepped up and taken charge.

Was that his son with him? Was he...good grief, she'd never even considered that he might be married. She frowned and reconsidered what she'd taken as simple flirting. Maybe he liked to keep a number of women on his string. She was simply an oddity to be added to the number. Heaven knows every woman in the place watched. Found reasons to stop by the table and—

"Jeanette is getting all riled up," murmured the timid waitress Brenda. "She's snapping at customers."

"Why?" Scarlett glanced over and realized what it had taken from Brenda to speak up. "Isn't she always like this?" But then she recalled that last night Jeanette had actually been kind to her.

When she thought Scarlett was simply a customer.

Brenda shrank away. "I shouldn't—"

Henry stepped up to Brenda's side. "She's mad because Ian came back to talk to you."

Scarlett laughed, but at their solemn, worried expressions she sobered. "That's ridiculous." When Brenda hunched her shoulders, Scarlett touched her shoulder, which only made Brenda flinch.

"I'm sorry."

Brenda shook her head. "No, I'm the one who—"

She was so quick to apologize, so afraid all the time. What was her story? "You're fine. And you're right. Ian McLaren means nothing to me, and I should be more careful."

"Jeanette wants to marry him," Henry ventured.

How could she pass up this opportunity to be sure? "He's not married?"

Both heads shook in denial.

"Was he? Is that his son?"

Brenda opened her mouth but subsided. Henry spoke instead. "No, that's Ben Butler. His mom's a widow. His dad and Ian were good friends. Ben wishes his mom would marry Ian, though. She's having a hard time running their flower farm by herself."

So he was single…but maybe not for long. Just as well. "Flower farm?"

"It's the most beautiful place," Brenda gushed with an abandon Scarlett would never have imagined from her. "It's like heaven, all those flowers—" Abruptly she stopped.

"Having recess?" Jeanette asked sourly. "In case no one has noticed, we still have a full house."

Brenda and Henry scattered.

Scarlett knew better, but she couldn't hold back. "I have no interest in Ian, if that's what's got your knickers in a twist."

"Excuse me?" Jeanette towered over her, but Scarlett had long ago learned that nearly everyone but a child was taller. That didn't intimidate her at all. She leaned closer to keep the discussion private, however. "Ian is as protective of Ruby as you are, and that's why he came back here. He has no interest in me, and I feel the same. So will you please stop being such a bitch?"

"You think I'm a bitch? Look, Miss Fancy Pants, we all know you think you're too good for us, and we can't wait for you to leave. Ruby will be better real soon, and no one will be sorry to see you go, so just get off your high horse and cook, why don't you, and quit talking about what you don't know."

Scarlett watched her stalk off and turned her attention back to the meal she was plating. She was a little bit hurt, and a little bit chastened.

But Jeanette was also right. Scarlett had been constantly comparing this town and this café unfavorably to what she'd known, imagining the mockery of her competitors, should they see her working in this humble dot on the map. In this very pedestrian restaurant.

She wasn't in New York. Nor Paris. Sweetgrass Springs was a far cry from Atlanta or Denver or Boston. This food was a universe away from haute cuisine.

But she had a grandmother here. Someone who could put her life in context. Someone with whom she shared blood.

And that woman made her living feeding people, just as Scarlett had been doing for years.

That wasn't nothing.

She still didn't like Jeanette, but she understood her.

Jeanette saw her as a threat on more levels than simply the one on which Jeanette wanted to be more to Ian than a childhood friend.

Ruby is the heart and soul of this town.

Everyone here knew where they stood in relation to the others, and she'd upset the balance. They adored Ruby, and they would protect her from any perceived threat.

Scarlett had no idea where she stood in relation to anything, but that wasn't new. She'd been a fish out of water most of her life.

Except when she was cooking.

So she would cook. Period.

And as soon as she was no longer needed, she would be gone.

"You want to trade seats with me, son?"

"What?" Ian dragged his attention back to his father and noticed that both Gordon and Ben were grinning. "What are you looking at?"

"Nothing." Ben stared down at his plate. "She's pretty, I guess."

"She's a beauty, just like her ma," said Gordon. "Georgia could knock the breath right out of you."

"Why would you think—"

His dad snorted. "Son, I might be crippled, but it's not my eyes that got injured. You ought to have a crick in your neck from glancing back at that kitchen so often."

"I wasn't—"

"My mom's just as pretty," said Ben. "And she already lives here."

"What? Why— Look, I am not interested in Ruby's granddaughter. I was just making sure everything's going okay, since Ruby isn't here."

"Uh-huh," replied his dad.

"And why are you—" Belatedly Ian realized what Ben was aiming at. What was wrong with everyone? Jeanette could not seriously have a crush on him, and there was no way on this earth he could marry his lifelong buddy's wife.

But Ben was at that age when his feelings were sticking out all over him like antennae and he was so mixed up, the slightest thing could set him off. Ian was supposed to be making things easier on Veronica, not getting crosswise with her son.

"Your mom is a very pretty lady," he began, then decided this might be his opening. "She's also worried about you. Should she be?"

Ben flushed. "No."

"Look, you know you can talk to me anytime, right? We all miss your dad like crazy, and I know things are hard for your family. Your mom depends on you a lot, but you'd rather be hanging out with your friends, I bet."

Ben shrugged. "I'm okay."

"It won't always be like this. She's just trying to figure out how much she can handle on her own."

"She shouldn't have to." Ben kept his eyes locked on the table.

"Folks have to handle lots of things they might not want to, son," said Gordon. "Life's awful hard sometimes, but that's just a farmer's lot."

"I don't want to be a farmer," Ben muttered. "Rancher either. They're both stupid."

Ian and his father traded glances. He needed to proceed carefully. David's dream had been to pass his land along to his kids, and he'd especially wanted a future working side by side with Ben.

But David had died in a farming-related accident. "Well, you don't have to decide anything just yet. You might change your mind, but whether or not you do, right now your mother needs your help, and not only with the farm. How is school going?"

"Okay."

Which probably meant that his grades were suffering. "Your mom's not the only one who's got a lot on her shoulders. It has to be hard, helping her with the girls and the flowers and the stock, trying to play sports and still study enough to get the grades to give you options."

Ben looked up at last, his eyes anguished. "I have to be the man of the house. There's no one else."

Boy, did Ian understand that feeling. "Tell you what—there are a lot of people around here who would like to help. How about if we organize a work day at your place? You could make a list so we know what would be most helpful. I'd ask your mom, but—"

"But she'll say she doesn't need help."

"Exactly. I ask and ask, but finally I just have to jump in and do what seems to need work. I'd rather be taking care of whatever is critical, but I don't understand the flower business the way I understand ranching." He held Ben's gaze. "Can I count on you to be my spy? Help me keep your mother honest?"

"She won't like it."

Ian's dad spoke first. "But she'll be relieved as all get-out. And maybe even have a little time to ease up on herself."

"She could sure use it," Ben admitted.

And so could you, Ian thought. "I'm looking at it like an old-fashioned barn raising. Remember, Dad, years back, how everyone came together when old man Kinslow broke his leg right at harvest time? Everybody came over on a Saturday and got the crop in? Didn't even have church that Sunday, not at the various churches, but we had a nondenominational worship service in the pasture that Sunday morning, then everyone pitched in."

"Used to happen a lot," his father said. "Back in the beginning of Sweetgrass, that's how everybody got their houses built and barns raised. Same thing when it was time for roundup or harvest."

Ian was warming rapidly to the idea. Veronica always demurred, saying Ian was too busy, but she would remember the Kinslows, too, and know that there was precedent. Shoot, it went back all the way to their ancestors. He turned to Ben. "She'll go for this, don't you think?"

The boy's eyes lit. "She sure might." Then his shoulders sagged. "But why would people help us? We're Pattons, too, not just Butlers. And my uncle Tank would hate it."

Ian and his father traded glances. Dicey territory, given Tank's history as a bully and his father's as much worse. "People think a lot of your mom, and your dad and his family have always been favorites in this town."

"Yeah." Ben's voice was dispirited. "But people don't forget."

"Somebody giving you trouble at school?" Ian asked.

Ben shrugged. "Doesn't matter."

"What's the problem?"

Ben shot him a glance. "Do I have to call him Uncle Tank? I wish I could scrub that Patton blood right out of me."

Whoa. Ian had to tread carefully here and try to forget his own difficulties with Tank. He placed a hand on Ben's shoulder. "Has he done something to you, Ben?"

"Not really. He leaves me alone, but he's stopped some of my friends, and the kids at school talk about how he throws his weight around. He acts like that badge gives him rights that don't seem legal."

Ian's dad looked over Ben's head, eyebrows lifted. Ian shook his head. "Have any of them talked to their parents?"

"No. What good would it do? He's a jerk, and he's always been a jerk. I hate that kids know we're related."

"I could spout off some foolishness you'd tell a child, Ben, or I can treat you like a man."

Ben's eyes rose to Ian's. "I'm not a child."

"I know you're not. So here's the thing: your uncle is a troubled man, and I won't pretend to be his best buddy."

Ben snorted. "He doesn't have any friends. Except other jerks."

"Well, be that as it may, his old man set a very poor example for him."

"His dad was meaner than a feral hog," interjected Gordon.

Ian couldn't argue. "But Tank is not your dad, thank goodness, and you come from the best man I ever knew, except for my dad."

Gordon's eyes went wide, but Ian continued. "What both of them had in common is that they made the best of what life handed them. Your dad got married real young, and he didn't have a chance at an education, but he buckled down and worked hard, and he created a family anyone would be proud to call their own. My dad had to raise me on his own while trying to keep a ranch going, and he didn't shuffle me off to relatives like he could have, but instead he kept me with him. That's what a man does—he takes a look at the cards life deals out, and he doesn't give up and he doesn't whine about his sorry lot. He hunkers down and figures out what he can do with them."

"I'm not whining."

"I didn't say you were. What I'm trying to tell you, man to man, is that one of the cards you were dealt was to be related to Tank. But the way you got there was by being born to your mother, who is one very admirable woman. She couldn't control what family she was born into and neither could you. But she hasn't let it get in the way of being the best person she can be, and folks respect her for that, just the way they'll respect you if you focus on what you do have instead of what you wish you could change." He clapped Ben's shoulder. "That's a man's truth, Ben, not a child's pacifier. I believe you're man enough to step up like your dad did. Like mine did. Don't you?"

Ben met his gaze without the previous misery that had filled his eyes and nodded. "My dad was—" His voice broke.

"He was as good as they come," Ian agreed. "And he'd be real proud of you right now."

Ian looked away to give the boy a minute to compose himself and found his dad looking at him with new eyes. His own throat a little too tight for comfort, he settled on a simple nod.

His dad nodded back.

"So...your mom deserves a whole lot more than a simple work day, but it's a start. I'd sure like to help, and I know others would, too. How about you talk it up to your friends at school, and Dad and I will spread it around, too. We'll set it for, what, weekend after this? Is that good timing for the farm and what needs doing?"

"It would be real good, but—" Hectic color rose in Ben's cheeks, and he hesitated.

"Go on. But what?"

"Just...I think it would go down easier if we could point out someone else who needs help, some other place we'd go next." He shrugged. "So Mom doesn't feel so much like a charity case, you know."

Ian looked at his dad. "Boy's got a head on his shoulders." He grinned. "He might even lay claim to understanding women."

Ben rolled his eyes.

"No man should be so foolish as to think that. Speaking of women," Gordon said. "I want to meet Ruby's girl. That was some fine cobbler. Tastes different than Ruby's, but boy, is it good." He rose awkwardly, and Ian had to restrain himself from helping.

He cast a glance back at the kitchen and caught Scarlett looking. When she realized they were approaching, her eyes went wide, and she took a step back.

"Little girl, I never thought anybody's cobbler could hold a candle to Ruby's, but you did your grandma proud," said his father as he hobbled over.

The entire room's attention was focused on his dad and the woman behind the pass-through.

"You gonna come out here where I can take a look at you, or you gonna force an old man to walk all the way back there?"

Ian tried to catch Scarlett's attention to apologize. Asking her to come to him was a complete about-face to his father's usual fierce insistence on independence. He also had the sense that Scarlett wouldn't welcome the notoriety.

But he'd sold her short.

Scarlett came around and through the doorway, rounding the counter and making her way to them, wiping her hands on a dishtowel. "You don't look so old to me," she said, the faint huskiness in her voice competing with the humor. "You must be Ian's dad. He looks just like you. I'm Scarlett Ross." She held out a hand to shake.

"And you resemble both your mama and your grandma, don't you? I'm real sorry to hear about Georgia. She was something special, that girl."

"You knew her?" Naked longing filled her voice.

"Grew up together. Told her I was gonna marry her."

Scarlett's eyebrows flew upward. "I'm sorry that didn't happen."

"Well, considering I was about ten and she was all of seven or eight at the time and had just bloodied my nose, she can be forgiven for not taking the proposal seriously, I expect."

Scarlett burst into laughter, a sound as musical as fairy bells. "Why did she bloody your nose?"

"'Cause I had already asked Becky Tyler to go steady. Georgia didn't think much of that."

Scarlett's whole face lit. Then she glanced at Ian. "So is your son a chip off the old block, Romeo?"

Ian had never in his life seen his father blush before, but he was seeing it now.

"You're a pistol just like her, aren't you?" Gordon asked.

Her expression turned wistful. "I wish I could say so. I loved my mother very much. When I was little, I thought she was the most glamorous woman in the world."

"You weren't wrong." Then his dad stirred. "I'm being rude." He turned a little. "This is Ben Butler. His daddy and Ian got in a whole lot of trouble growing up."

Scarlett's gaze shifted quickly to Ian, then back, but not before he saw both mischief and interest. "I'm pleased to meet you, Ben."

Ben shook her hand, too. "That food was amazing, especially that cobbler."

"Boy's right," said his father. "Something makes it different—not better, of course, since nobody makes cobbler like Ruby, but still real good. No offense."

"None taken. I've had a taste of my grandmother's food. She's got the magic touch, doesn't she?"

All around him, Ian could see heads nodding and faces filling with approval that Scarlett would honor her grandmother.

"She sure does. Sweetgrass Springs would be nothing without her."

"Would you care to sit and have a cup of coffee?" Scarlett offered. "Decaf, since it's late?"

Then Ian realized what she had apparently already noticed, that his father was no longer standing so steadily. Standing up tired him greatly, but admitting it would pain him worse.

"Naw, I'm fine. We got to be going, anyway. Young Ben

here has school tomorrow."

Ben stirred in protest but thankfully said nothing.

"And Scarlett still has folks to feed," Ian interjected.

"I do," she agreed. "Will you come back, Mr. McLaren? Let me feed you again?"

"You gonna stay around for awhile?" His dad asked.

She looked startled for a second but quickly recovered. "I've told my grandmother I'll help out until she's well enough to take over."

Not exactly a long-term commitment, not that Ian was surprised. The last place she belonged was Sweetgrass.

"Now don't you get in a big hurry," his dad said. "I would indeed like to see what other surprises you might have to show us." He leaned closer. "And your grandmother could use the help. Woman's a force of nature, but she's not getting any younger."

"Well, I—" Her glance darted around at all the ears perked to attention. "I guess we'll just have to see how things work out, Mr. McLaren."

"That's pretty much a rancher's life, Ms. Ross. I'm real good at patience."

"Scarlett, please."

"Fine, but you call me Gordon, then."

She cast a quick glance at Ian as if checking out his reaction.

He shrugged.

"Thank you for stopping to talk to me, Gordon. Come back soon, will you?"

His dad jerked his head toward Ian. "Tell my chauffeur." He grinned and turned away.

"Bye, Ms. Ross." Ben followed.

"Bye, Ben. You come back, too."

Ian lingered. "Sorry he put you on the spot."

"He's great."

"The chauffeur can't really speak to that. I'm only the

hired help."

She glanced up, eyes sparkling. "Well, Jeeves, I guess you'd better get to it."

"Guess I will." But instead he lingered. "Good groceries. You do know your way around a kitchen, don't you?"

Pride swept over her features, followed by gratitude. "I absolutely do." Then her brows snapped together as she looked behind him. "But now I have a waitress on the warpath, so I'd better let her man go."

"Don't say that. I'm not—" He glared at her.

Once more Scarlett burst out laughing and patted his shoulder. "Night-night, Romeo."

Ian growled a little and shook his head.

But he was grinning as he left.

Chapter Nine

She hadn't had to clean her own grill in a long time. The world she'd come from was distinctly stratified, and a chef stood at the apex, even above the restaurant owner at times.

But the work wasn't so bad, she realized.

At least it wouldn't be if Jeanette would just go home and leave them in peace. Henry was a hard worker, Pete the dishwasher pitched in, too, and Brenda seemed to have taken a liking to Scarlett so even though she could have left already, she'd volunteered to mop.

Henry had insisted on picking up the chairs and upending them on the tables for Brenda first, though, like a gentleman spreading his cloak.

Brenda had an admirer, it seemed.

"All counted," said Jeanette from the cash register. "I'll take the bank bag with me."

"But Ruby always—" At a glare from her, Henry subsided.

"Ruby isn't here."

Scarlett stopped scraping. "Ruby what, Henry?"

He shrugged. "She takes the bank bag home each night then goes to the bank in the middle of the morning."

"Which I will do for her tomorrow," Jeanette said. "Because Ruby's not feeling well."

"Maybe—" Scarlett halted. Was this really her fight? Ruby

seemed to trust Jeanette to run things, so was Scarlett looking to step in simply because Jeanette was so unpleasant to her? Because Jeanette so clearly had set her cap for Ian?

Surely she was a bigger person than that. And she didn't want Ian, anyway.

Or not much. Not more than a passing fancy, at least—and only for that smokin' hot body of his.

Jeanette's posture screamed that she was waiting for Scarlett to argue.

This wasn't her café. She was the newcomer. She barely knew her grandmother at all. Making up her mind, she shrugged at Jeanette. "If you think that's what Ruby would want, far be it from me to interfere."

Jeanette did a double take. "More than you're already interfering?"

"Would you like to handle the cooking tomorrow?" Wow, the woman was annoying.

"Of course not," Jeanette snapped. Then she took a deep breath and released it. "Look, it was nice for you take over for Ruby today. She'll be up and around in another day, I'm sure, then you can be on your way."

Here's your hat, what's your hurry?

Wasn't that what she wanted, anyhow? She'd met her grandmother, but she didn't have to stay here to keep up the relationship. Anyway, Ruby might not want her around, once she heard that her granddaughter had been in jail.

But there was so much Scarlett didn't know yet. She wanted to see those drawings and paintings. Wanted to understand the seven-year-old girl who'd bloodied Gordon's nose.

Don't you get in a big hurry. Your grandmother could use the help. His words bothered her. She couldn't stay in this backwater forever, but what would happen to Henry and Brenda and the Judge? Ruby wasn't getting any younger, and the café was the saving grace of Sweetgrass Springs, best she could tell.

She's the heart and soul of this town.

Scarlett could do nothing about all of that, but maybe she could hang around for a few days and give Ruby a break. Santa Fe—or wherever she stirred up her courage to try—wasn't going anywhere.

Jeanette was still poised at the door with the bank bag on her hand, her purse over her shoulder.

Scarlett realized that Jeanette was waiting for her to leave first. She was the interloper, the stranger. Of course they wouldn't know they could trust her.

Still she offered. "I can lock up."

"There's no key," Henry pointed out. "Not much need to lock up in Sweetgrass Springs. Especially here. No one would mess with Ruby. She's special."

They didn't lock up. Seriously? Coming from a city where she'd had four locks just for her apartment door, the concept was astounding.

Wow.

"Well, then," she managed. "I'll turn off the lights. I'm guessing you're ready to get off your feet," she said to Jeanette. "Probably we all are."

Jeanette was curiously devoid of anger for a second, maybe still trying to take in that Scarlett wasn't going to battle her over the bank bag. She hitched up her purse higher on her shoulder and straightened. "You got that right. Five o'clock will be here plenty early." She glanced around her as if a little lost without the hard feelings swirling in the air. "Well…good night, I guess." She started out the door, then her head whipped around. "Wait. You don't have Ruby's biscuit recipe. She starts them at four sharp."

"I can wing it. I have my own recipes right here." She tapped at her temple.

"That won't be what people expect."

"My cobbler wasn't either. Different biscuits won't kill them for one day." Then Scarlett gave the waitress her back, too tired to start another argument. "I'll see you in the morning, Jeanette."

A long pause.

"I suppose they'll survive, just this once." The door slammed behind her.

Brenda exhaled a long sigh of relief.

Scarlett glanced up and grinned. "I hear that." She looked around. "Anything we still need to do, Henry?"

He seemed pleased that she'd consulted him. "Nope. I'm ready for bed—you?"

"I'd offer to race you, but I still have stairs to climb."

Henry laughed, and even Brenda grinned.

That all three of them were going home to the same place wasn't as weird as it probably should have been. It was a little like having siblings, except Scarlett's sibling of choice would have been an older brother, someone to depend on, someone who would—

She laughed at herself. She'd longed for a protector, but she needed no such thing—she'd made her way through growing up without one just fine.

"Something funny?" Henry asked as they climbed the porch steps.

"Nothing really," she responded just as he pulled open the door.

"Hey, Ruby," he greeted her grandmother, who was sitting in a kitchen chair. "How are you feeling?"

"Sore as the dickens, if you really want to know. A good night's sleep, though, and I'll be fit as a fiddle."

"That's good. We missed you tonight, but Scarlett—"

"—Did fine. Absolutely fine," the normally silent Brenda rushed to say.

Henry bristled. "Of course she did. I wasn't gonna say anything different."

"Good night, you two." Ruby's order was implied. "Dawn comes early."

"Don't you think you—" Brenda subsided.

"Don't I think I what?" Ruby's voice was kind, though her exhaustion was evident.

The young woman shook her head and turned away.

"Don't I think I should stay in bed? That it?"

The girl stopped midway down the hall. "It's not my business to say what you should do." Her voice was nearly too quiet to be heard.

"Honey, it is your business. You live here, and you make your living in my café. You are entitled to an opinion," Ruby said gently, then smiled. "I just don't have to do what you say."

The faint smile put the most fragile of curves on Brenda's lips, and Scarlett found herself wanting to cheer. "We did okay tonight, Ruby," Brenda said softly. "The cobbler was a big success and we worked together, so you could take it easy tomorrow. You work too hard." Then, as if she'd exceeded her quota of words for the day, she moved to the stairs and scampered up toward her room which was, Scarlett had learned this afternoon, right next to her own.

"Snuggle up," Scarlett and Ruby called out in unison, and Scarlett wheeled in shock once again.

Her grandmother's eyes twinkled even as they looked so very sad. "Who do you think your mama learned it from?"

Georgia had said that to Scarlett every night of her life. *Snuggle up.* And every night she'd respond back to her mother. *Sweet dreams.*

Her gaze met Ruby's, and warmth rose in her chest at the reminder that she wasn't alone anymore. Wherever she went, she would know that there was someone left who shared her blood.

"Sweet dreams," she finished with a catch in her throat.

Ruby's expression was surprisingly vulnerable. Then she straightened and cleared her throat. "Ground pecans, huh? You do know that pecans are expensive?"

Scarlett hadn't even considered that she would be costing Ruby money, and she knew better. Every chef had to guard the bottom line like a hawk. She'd been caught up in wanting to prove a point to all the doubters, or maybe to show her grandmother how good she was.

Or both.

"I'm really sorry. I should have asked you first. It's your kitchen. I'll replace what I used."

"You will do no such thing, missy," Ruby all but snapped. Then she smiled. "But you will show me how you did it. And you'll let me tell you how to make my biscuits for the morning."

"Probably a good idea. The citizens of Sweetgrass Springs might suffer a setback without them." She smiled back. "Though Gordon McLaren admitted that while your cobbler is best, mine is pretty good."

"He's not the only one."

Scarlett arched one brow. "You have spies observing me?" She glanced at Henry, who looked appalled.

"I don't—I wasn't—"

Her grandmother patted his arm. "With Jeanette there, I don't need anyone else."

"So you don't have any other spies?"

"I didn't say that. Shoot, every person in Sweetgrass is watching out for me. Can't be too careful with the slick stranger, come all the way from Paris, France." She laughed.

"They care about you. Ian is watching my every move, and Jeanette would gladly send me to the devil—and that's just for starters. You're a cross between Mother Teresa and Superwoman in their eyes."

"Pshaw. I'm just older than all of them, is all." She

winked. "I know where all the bodies are buried."

"They really do love you, though. It seems as though you and the café are all that's keeping Sweetgrass going."

Sorrow swept over Ruby's face. "And I'm not doing too well at it anymore."

"What does that mean?"

Ruby shook her head. "A story for another time. Right now, missy, you have put in one very long day, and I do believe I can hear your feet crying from over here."

"Yours hasn't been a cakewalk."

"Maybe not, but you well and truly saved my bacon. I don't know how to thank you." Without her customary fire and sass, Ruby seemed very small and fragile.

Scarlett desperately did not want to lose her anytime soon. She knew that, even if she knew little else right now. "You don't owe me a thing. We're family," she said simply. Her throat tightened unexpectedly.

She could swear she saw Ruby's eyes shimmer. "We sure are, and that is the best thing that's happened to me in forever." Then she cleared her throat. "You know how to make biscuits with yeast and baking powder both?"

"Both?"

"Yep. My grandmother's recipe. I'll write it down as best I can and leave it for you. I don't measure, I just do a dab of this and a handful of that."

Her breath caught. "I cook that way, too." And the likeness once again made something slow and sweet stir in her heart. "So you'll take it easy tomorrow and trust me with breakfast?"

Ruby looked up, held her gaze for a long moment. "You're family," she echoed.

Then her grandmother looked away. "You have the bank bag, Henry?"

"Um, no. Jeanette—"

Scarlett stepped up to take responsibility. "Jeanette took it with her. She'll deposit it in the morning, just as you normally do." She waited for her grandmother's response, oddly nervous.

Henry caught her gaze, and she could tell he was worried, too.

"All right, then," Ruby said.

Henry audibly exhaled.

"You go on to bed, too." But Ruby's order was gentle.

"I will." He glanced at Scarlett, his gaze tentative, his cheeks stained with color. "Good night, Scarlett. It was nice, working with you."

He was such a sweet boy. "I don't know what I'd have done without you. Snuggle up, Henry."

He nodded and made his way down the hall.

She was left with her grandmother, knowing she should hit the sack, too, but not ready to leave. She glanced around the kitchen, wanting to pore over it inch by inch for signs of her heritage. She had so many questions.

"So how much trouble was Jeanette?" The smile in Ruby's voice matched the one on her face.

Scarlett yanked herself back to the present. "She was all right, really." She hesitated. "Did I do the wrong thing, letting her take the bank bag?"

"No. She won't run off with it, if that's what you're worried about. Long as Ian's in the vicinity and available, she won't budge one inch from Sweetgrass, however much she needs to go."

"What do you mean by that?"

"Jeanette should have left after high school. She worked for me a little while she was in school, then went full-time after graduation to save up money for college. She wanted to see the world, but her folks needed her so she just kept working, and then Ian came home after college. There was no way she was going to go after that. Frankly, I don't know what I'd do without her. She knows how to run the diner as well as

I do. If she could cook, I'd have retired and given her the place long ago." Ruby's lips firmed. "But now you're here, and I'm glad I hung onto it."

"But I—" *Can't stay*, she started to say but halted. Ruby looked so tired. Sad, too, because she had no doubt completed Scarlett's sentence in her own mind. "You should go to bed. So should I," she admitted. "It's been a long day. I have no idea how you've kept this pace all these years."

Her grandmother shrugged. "You do what you have to." Her gaze rose to lock on Scarlett's. "I'm glad I stayed in place now. You might never have found me if I'd moved on."

Scarlett didn't have any answers, not for herself or for Ruby, but she knew one thing: she was profoundly glad Ruby had stayed long enough for Scarlett to learn of her existence.

"Me, too." And even though Ruby didn't seem to be a hugger, Scarlett wrapped her arms around the thin shoulders and embraced this woman who was such a miracle to her, such an unexpected blessing. *I love you*, she wanted to say, but she was so confused and so very afraid of hurting Ruby. Hurting herself. "I'm really glad."

Slowly Ruby's arms slipped around her waist and clasped her, too.

She felt so frail, and Scarlett realized that it was Ruby's spirit that was so powerful, not the fragile flesh that encased it. "You take it easy tomorrow, okay? I can handle the café just fine. Let me do this for you, would you?" *Even if it's all I can promise.*

Ruby's hug tightened, and Scarlett never wanted to leave her hold. Her head dropped to Ruby's shoulder, just for a second, while she soaked up the feeling of having someone in her life again whom she could love.

Ruby didn't move either, and one hand rose to stroke her hair.

"I'm so grateful you're here, Nana."

Ruby's arms tightened around her. Then she lifted her

head. "Nana? Peter Pan's dog?"

Scarlett tensed. "I hadn't thought about that. I just always liked that name for a grandmother, but I—" Now that she knew Ruby a bit better, Mimsey did not fit at all. "Should I call you something different?"

Her grandmother chuckled. "Nana was a good dog. I could sure do worse. You call me whatever you like." Her eyes shimmered as well.

"Snuggle up…Nana." If she didn't get up those stairs now, she'd fall apart.

"Sweet dreams, Scarlett girl." Ruby stroked her face, then released her.

Every step a battle, Scarlett climbed the stairs but stopped halfway up to see Ruby holding onto the newel post, watching her.

"Please sleep in, Nana. I promise I won't mess anything up."

Her grandmother's nod was solemn. "I know you won't. And yes, I'll sleep in—at least if I can, I will. A lot of years of habit, you know. Now you get on to bed."

Being ordered around warmed her. "Yes, ma'am." Scarlett blew her a kiss, then made her way to bed, her world a richer place already.

Chapter Ten

Her hair was still wet from the rain she'd awakened to this morning, but Scarlett couldn't care less. Standing in the café's kitchen, absently she blotted her hair with a kitchen towel as she stared at the piece of paper Ruby had pushed under her bedroom door while she slept. And boy, had she slept. She wasn't sure when she'd been more exhausted.

She dried her hands carefully and set the towel aside so she could pick up the recipe.

This was my grandmother's recipe.

Scarlett's great-great grandmother. It was ridiculous, but her hand was shaking. She traced over the letters. Her great-great-grandmother's recipe. Written in her grandmother's hand.

What was the woman's name? When was she born? Had she lived here in Sweetgrass Springs? What did she look like? Had she been the mother of Ruby's mother or father?

Her heart was pounding so hard it was almost audible. The recipe itself was interesting, and Scarlett could see how the biscuits turned out so flaky and delicious, but that wasn't what wowed her. It was knowing that a woman who shared her blood had mixed the same biscuits Scarlett was about to make, had served them to others who were also related to Scarlett. Had lived a life Scarlett could not begin to envision…but oh, how she wished she could.

"What's wrong?"

She jumped at least a foot at the sound of Ian's voice coming from the kitchen door. "Nothing. What on earth are you doing here at this ungodly hour?"

He grinned, and she saw that dimple again. Good grief, but he was gorgeous in a way unlike the men she was used to—not model-handsome but instead rugged and strong in a completely unstudied way.

"A whole lot gets done in the country before the sun comes up—hey, are you crying?"

"What? No—" She swiped at her cheeks and realized he was right—she had been. "I'm perfectly fine. I just—" She shook her head. "Never mind. I have biscuits to make. Were you worried I wouldn't be serving breakfast today, is that it?"

His eyes remained serious, but his tone was light. "Naw, I'm not worried."

She retrieved an apron and swiftly tied it around her waist, glancing back as she did so. "Uh-huh…you are so checking up on me. What, you didn't think I'd get up?"

"I said I wasn't worried." But his face said otherwise. "Hey, is that coffee I smell?"

Briskly she began to assemble the biscuit ingredients, mentally making notes about where she would move things if this were her kitchen. "So you made the trip to mooch coffee?"

"No, I just—" He busied himself pouring coffee into two mugs. "Sometimes I drop by and visit with Ruby while she's setting up. She seems to like the company. How is she?" He lifted one. "What do you take in it?"

"A little cream. Okay, and sugar. More than a little." She watched him. "One more spoon."

He recoiled. "Bet you make your dentist rich."

"No commentary on the cook's caffeine habits." She took the mug and sipped. "Ahh…I may live after all." Another sip. "Don't tell me—you're hardcore and drink it black."

He saluted her with his mug. "Of course. A rancher can't drink sissy coffee. At home I boil it over an open fire and drink from a tin cup."

She chuckled. "Because a real man only drinks coffee you can stand up a spoon in."

A second salute. "You got that right. So…Ruby."

"She was very sore last night and probably feels worse today."

"But she actually slept in and let you do this by yourself?"

"She actually did. Go figure." Another sip, then she set the mug aside and got to work. "She even asked for my cobbler recipe."

"Well, how about that?"

She ran warm water from the tap, then measured it into a bowl and sprinkled yeast on top. "She might have asked only to be nice to me."

"Ruby doesn't do nice. When she says something, she means it. Here—" He caught her glancing around for a large bowl for the dry ingredients and pulled one from below the counter to the left of where she was standing. "Ruby uses this to mix them in."

The enormous green pottery bowl showed its age, and Scarlett couldn't resist running her fingers around the edge.

If her mother hadn't stayed away, would she have learned how to make these when she was young? For a moment she was caught by the mental image of herself on a stool beside Ruby, learning. Waiting for her chance to sink her fingers into the dough.

"You okay?"

She dragged herself back to the present. "Of course." She consulted the paper again. "I was just…" She shrugged, then measured flour before she spoke again. "Did you know this was Ruby's grandmother's recipe?"

"I did. I remember her mama bringing them over to the house once."

Scarlett faltered while measuring out baking powder and had to force herself to count. "Ruby's mother? What was she like?"

"She was taller than Ruby and you. Not as tall as Georgia, though. Her hair was silver, of course. I don't know what color it was before. You might have gotten the black hair from Ruby's father. Jackson's hair is black, too, but it's not curly. His dad's used to be black."

"Jackson?" She cast back in memory. "He's my cousin, right?"

"Right."

"Jackson…Gallagher?"

He nodded.

"Where is he?"

Ian was silent a long time, and when she looked over, his expression was sad. She hastened to backtrack. "I'm sorry. Ruby didn't say he was dead—is he?"

"No. At least not that I know of, but then no one would."

"Why not?" She focused on cutting the shortening into the dry ingredients, reducing it to pea-sized pellets.

"It's a long story."

"I'm not going anywhere."

He seemed uncomfortable.

"Never mind. It's not my business, I guess."

"No, if you're going to be around, you should know."

She started to say she definitely wouldn't be around, but then she glanced at the recipe and thought of how much she didn't know. Maybe she could stay around a little while…

"Jackson's mother died when we were in high school. It was real hard on the whole family. On all of us, really. She was like a mother to me. I barely remember my own."

"I'm sorry. Did she…is your mother gone?"

"Not like you mean. She left us, me and Dad. She liked city life, and she didn't want anything tying her down. She hated the ranch."

"I'm so sorry."

"No big deal." But lingering bitterness in his tone said just the opposite. What child wouldn't be devastated by being left by his mother?

"How old were you?"

"Almost five."

"Oh, Ian."

He shrugged off any pity. "I did fine. It was real rough on Dad, not that I realized it then. Now that I've had to take over, I think of what it must have been like for him. He kept me with him all day until I got old enough for school. That couldn't have been easy. Anyway—Jackson's mom was the perfect mom, always baking cookies and such, and she never said she didn't have time to listen. I about lived over there half the time." He stared off into the distance. "Then she got cancer and died real slowly. It was awful. Jackson took it bad—he and his dad never got along anyway. He's pretty much a genius and the last thing he wanted was to be a rancher, but his dad wasn't going to let him do anything else. After his mom was gone, Jackson got wild, and one night..." His face filled with sorrow. "The boy with me last night, Ben? His dad had a sister who was riding with Jackson, and Jackson was drunk. He wrecked his car, and Beth died. He walked away with barely a scratch. No one in this town could forgive him, least of all his dad. He told Jackson to get out of town and never come back." Ian shook his head, his regrets clear. "He never has."

"Nobody knows where he is?"

"Not as far as I can tell. He was my best friend, and he sure never bothered to get in touch with me."

Scarlett tried to picture what it would feel like to have a best friend you'd known all your life, but she had no frame of reference. "That's tragic."

He shrugged. "That's life." He stirred and drained his mug, then walked over to rinse it in the sink. "Blue's waiting for me in the truck, and I got cows calling my name. Thanks for the coffee."

"You're welcome." She mixed the milk and bubbling yeast into the dry ingredients and began blending. "Are you coming back to see how I did?"

His eyes were serious. "Do you want me to?"

She had a sense of more being asked than simply about breakfast, and innate caution reared its head. "It's up to you. It's clear that you're a busy man." She sprinkled flour on the counter and turned out the dough.

"I'm sure you'll do fine. You strike me as a woman who lands on her feet."

If only you knew just how shaky my footing feels right now. "Absolutely." She glanced up once and saw him watching her. She brought her gaze back down. He was too close to becoming her touchstone in this unfamiliar place. "You do what you like."

"I generally do. See you." He headed for the door.

"Wait—does Blue get to eat people food?"

He blinked. "He'll eat anything he can find."

She turned to the refrigerator and retrieved some leftover beef she was going to put to use in a stew. She would reimburse Ruby for this, too, if need be. She crossed to Ian. He met her halfway. "Here—take this to him."

He didn't reach for it. "You should give it to him yourself. Make friends."

"I don't think so."

He grinned, and his eyes did that crinkle thing at the corners that was breathtakingly attractive. "Come on. I told you he won't bite. And after this, you'll be his new best friend."

Up this close, Ian was so big, so overwhelmingly masculine. She found it more than a little hard to breathe.

His eyes locked on hers, and his pupils darkened.

Oh my...

He bent to her, just the slightest inch, and she was caught in the spell of him. She was a tactile person, and her fingers itched to touch.

She heard a car door slam and remembered where she was. Who she was. She straightened. Retreated. "I have biscuits to make and customers to serve. Tell Blue hi."

His gaze was too serious. When he finally let the mischief in, she relaxed from the danger she'd just dodged. "Coward." He grinned.

"Think what you like." She tilted her nose in the air, then turned to resume her baking.

"It's a nice thing to do, New York," his rough velvet voice said behind her.

"Scarlett. And you're welcome. I guess I'll see you around." She placed a hand on her jumpy stomach and took a deep breath as she took her place in the kitchen.

But she couldn't resist watching him go, that broad back, the rangy gait of a man comfortable inside his skin. Just as he reached the front door and she thought she could settle down, he wheeled and came back.

"I forgot—how are you at hungry man food in large quantities?"

"What?" She shook her head to clear it. "Why?"

"Ben's mom needs help at the flower farm, and I try to pitch in wherever I can, but Veronica's a proud woman, and she won't ask for a thing. She's getting behind, though, without David, and Dad and Ben and I cooked up this work day for weekend after next. Like an old-fashioned barn-raising, you know? We even figured out how to keep her from feeling bad about it."

"So you need me to…?"

"Folks will bring food, I'm sure, but I want to provide the main part of it. Trouble is, I can't cook worth beans. Dad can, or he could once, but now with only one side working right, it would be too much for him. So I'm wondering if I could pay you to do it."

"I probably won't be here."

His brows snapped together. "You're leaving already?"

"Ruby thinks she'll be back here in a day or so. She won't need my help, and I have to finish my trip."

"I thought you came here to find her. So you zoom in, then take off, just like that? What about Ruby? Have you not noticed how old she is? You're going to desert her, just like Georgia did?"

Nothing got Scarlett's back up like someone criticizing her mother. "You don't know anything about my mother."

"You sure don't know much about family. You don't abandon family when they need you."

"Ruby says she'll be fine."

"And you believe that?" He was nearly shouting now.

Just then Jeanette walked in. "What's going on?"

Ian cast Scarlett a furious look. "Nothing. New York is itching to take off and leave Ruby to fend for herself."

"I'm not—"

"I have to go." Ian stalked out the door.

Jeanette cast a triumphant glance back at Scarlett.

Then followed Ian out the door.

Scarlett whirled and faced the dough. Picked up the recipe with shaking hands and tried to remember where she was in the process.

But looking at Ruby's handwriting only made her feel worse.

I can't stay. I can't. Even if trouble wouldn't follow me, this is not where I belong.

The bad part was not knowing where she did.

"I assure you that everyone takes a break in the afternoon,"

Jeanette insisted later that day.

"But what about the café?" Scarlett asked.

"It stays open, but we take turns. Ruby insists on everyone getting a break."

"For how long?"

"Two hours each, though she doesn't give herself the same privilege."

"What does she do?"

"She takes an hour, including halftime."

"Halftime?"

"That's what Ruby calls it. She climbs the courthouse tower."

"Seriously? Why?"

Jeanette glanced away.

"What?"

Jeanette shook her head.

"Please, Jeanette. Tell me." What on earth could make this woman who seemed bent on being her mortal enemy so uncomfortable?

Jeanette exhaled in a gust. "I think it has to do with your mother."

"What?"

"Folks say that she started it when Georgia first went missing." The waitress lifted one shoulder. "Sort of like she thought maybe she'd see her coming home or something."

A physical pain squeezed Scarlett's heart. "I don't understand what happened."

For once she and Jeanette were of one mind, apparently. "Nobody else does either. Ruby's the best person in the world, and she worked her head off to give Georgia the best life she could, but Georgia didn't care. She just took off." Jeanette snapped her fingers. "Like that, she left. And she broke Ruby's heart."

Everything in Scarlett rose in protest. "My mother was a good person."

"Couldn't prove it by me."

"You didn't know her. You have no idea how hard her life was."

"It didn't have to be. Ruby would have done anything for her. She couldn't help that she was a single mother at odds with her family."

"Why do you say that?"

"You never met Ruby's father. He was a hard man, and he was furious at her for getting pregnant."

"How do you know that? You weren't even born. You're younger than me, right?"

"I'm thirty-four. Am I?"

"No." Crap. "I'm thirty-two. But you don't know what you're talking about."

"Everyone in town knows. Her father would not forgive her because she wouldn't tell him who Georgia's daddy was so he could make him marry Ruby."

"No one knows who my grandfather was?"

A slow shake of the head. "Only Ruby. And whoever the father was."

"You think my grandfather knew about Georgia and didn't care?" That would mean her mother's situation had resembled her own.

"I can't speak to that. Lots of speculation, but nobody knows for sure. Maybe her aunt Margaret, but she's long dead now."

Would Ruby tell her?

Would she dare ask?

Why was her grandmother so closemouthed about it? A horrific thought struck her. "Had Ruby been...maybe something bad had happened." Scarlett snapped her mouth shut. She didn't want to be talking about this with a woman who loathed her.

But to her surprise, Jeanette touched her arm gently. "No one's ever said anything like that."

"But if that's not the problem, what—oh, no. Could he have been...married?" She felt sick.

"I can't imagine it. Not Ruby."

"For real?"

"Ruby has never been a foolish person, and though she's not judgmental of others, she holds herself to some pretty high standards. Whatever the reason she's kept her child's father secret, I have hard time believing it's because she did anything wrong."

Except not marry the father of her child. Not that Scarlett didn't understand losing her head over a man who didn't deserve it. Who was completely wrong for her. "I need to think."

She was astonished to see sympathy in Jeanette's eyes. "You might climb those courthouse stairs yourself. Ruby says it gives her some perspective. Swears it's the best place to ponder. And it's your turn for a break."

"What if someone comes in to eat?"

"Then they can either wait or I'll fix them a sandwich. Everybody in town knows about halftime. They wouldn't expect different."

Scarlett had thought to go back to the house and check on Ruby, but Henry had already done so and sworn that she looked better. "But wouldn't someone care that I'm in there?"

"Your grandmother owns it. I can't imagine her complaining. She seems pretty set on giving you whatever you want."

The bitterness sounded like the real Jeanette.

Then the full import of Jeanette's words sank in. "She...owns it? The *courthouse?*"

"She sure does. See, Sweetgrass used to be the county seat, but then it got moved. The courthouse sat there vacant for years, and the county wouldn't do anything to keep it up. Sweetgrass was dying by inches, so...Ruby went to the commissioners and managed to convince them to sell it to her."

Scarlett blinked. "Why would she want it?"

"I'm not exactly sure. She's had some idea to turn the town into a tourist attraction." Suddenly she grinned.

"What?"

"For a while, she and Henry would sneak over there and shine lights at odd times. Ruby was thinking we needed a ghost."

"A...ghost?" Scarlett couldn't help but laugh.

"Yeah. Like The Lady in the legend."

"What legend?"

"Of Sweetgrass Springs. Nobody told you?"

Scarlett shook her head.

"Folks tell about a dying soldier whose horse scented the water and brought him to the spring. The soldier couldn't manage to crawl far enough, and when he was dying, a beautiful woman rescued him. She gave him water from the spring, and she took care of him in a clearing right where the courthouse stands now. Though he expected to die, she healed him. When he woke up, he asked why she looked so sad. She was once mortal, she said, and she was loved, but she turned away from that love, so the Fates cursed her to linger there until she was freed. She asked him to stay with her, but he said he had to return to his men. He promised he'd come back for her as soon as the war was done, but she didn't believe him. He rose, healed and strong, and mounted his horse, but when he looked back, she had disappeared. She'd made herself invisible because she knew he would never be back. He rode off, and she's still there, waiting."

"Waiting for what?"

"Only true love can set her free." Jeanette's eyes went dreamy, and she looked like a different person. "Love strong enough to stay. That's what she's waiting for."

In Jeanette's expression Scarlett read the woman's longing for Ian and her reason, perhaps, for remaining here so long. The longing she saw there made her sad when she'd never imagined pitying Jeanette.

Scarlett had been burned badly by romanticizing a relationship that had turned out to be false, and she was determined never to do so again. Since Jeanette wouldn't appreciate her pity, she returned to the safer topic of the courthouse. "So my grandmother was hoping to use the legend to attract tourists." She had to give her grandmother credit. Places like Charleston or towns all over New England were chockfull of legends and ghost sightings to go along with them. "Not a bad idea." She glanced out the window at the town that was more than halfway to decay. "I guess it didn't work."

"Henry nearly got killed when a railing gave way, so Ruby called a halt to that, quick."

"The place is in bad shape?"

"It's sure not good. And Ruby doesn't have the money to fix it up."

Scarlett peered at the ramshackle building she'd barely spared time for up to now. "It looks as though it was once quite impressive."

"It was. Ruby has pictures. She's been assembling all kinds of historical information for a long time, so as to set up a museum someday."

Someday. For a woman in her seventies, would someday come too late? "I'd like to see it. How would I get in?"

"Best take a flashlight. Night falls so early this time of year, and you'll be coming back down those stairs in the dark. You don't need a key, though."

That no one locked doors still seemed amazing. "Nobody vandalizes a spooky old building?"

"Hon, this is not New York City. We're all neighbors here. Everyone knows who owns it, and not one soul in this town would ever want to hurt Ruby."

Scarlett wondered if she'd ever get used to the one-hundred-eighty-degree difference between where she'd been and this Brigadoon she'd come to.

A spirit in the spring, for heaven's sake.

"I think I will go." She removed her apron.

"Here's your jacket, Scarlett." Henry blushed as he handed it to her. "And here's a flashlight. You want me to come show you?"

"I'll be fine, Henry. I'd feel better, knowing you're here to help Jeanette. You have no idea how much I appreciate all you do."

His face flamed even more brightly, and he ducked his head. "I'm real glad to be helping you."

Over his head, she saw Jeanette's lifted eyebrows, but she refused to share in mocking someone with such a pure heart. She touched his arm. "Thank you, Henry. I'll be back in just a few minutes."

He stood a little straighter. "Take your time. Everything will be all right here."

With a smile, she left.

Heading back to the house after a long day of fixing fences and dealing with cattle in a cold and heavy drizzle that just would not let up, Ian reminded himself that they needed every drop. He dragged himself into the house, filthy and wet and longing to stand in a hot shower for about an hour. "Hey, Dad." He nodded to his father who was sitting in front of the computer he hated like he loathed drought and screwworms and mad cow disease.

His father only grunted and kept hitting keys. "Blast it," he muttered. "This can't be right." His head swiveled and he finally noticed Ian standing there in his sock feet after removing boots caked two inches thick with muck.

"What's wrong?" Ian asked.

His father shook his head sharply. "Nothing."

Definitely not nothing. "What's up?"

His father's expression was bleak. "When were you going to tell me we were bleeding money?"

Ian's jaw tightened. "We're not." *Yet.*

"How do you intend to pay this month's feed bill? To say nothing of the taxes, which are due at the end of the month?" His dad shook his head. "Dadgum rich folks, moving in and paying too much for land, driving property values through the roof."

Ian bit back what he badly wanted to say. *I have a solution, if only you'd listen.* "I'll manage, Dad. Haven't I been doing so all along?" Not that he knew how much longer he could keep juggling expenses. The ranch wasn't out of money, no. But another year of drought...

His dad raked one hand through his hair. "Blast this weak side of mine."

"Don't beat yourself up, Dad."

His father's face went thunderous. "I'm half a man! I am not good for one blasted thing around here because my arm and my leg—" He shoved to his feet and nearly toppled as he did.

Ian rushed to him and grabbed him.

"Don't!" His father shrugged him off, holding onto the adjacent counter for dear life. He braced his good arm on the edge while his head sagged in despair.

And Ian didn't know how to fix this.

At least, not as long as he hewed to his father's way of doing things. He did have answers, detailed ones he'd sweated over for hours—just nothing his father would want to hear because every one of them involved change. Big change.

Change that would forever say goodbye to a tradition nearly two hundred years in the making.

Ian blew out a breath and glanced over at the cold stove. He would have to have the discussion again, but tonight he was worn out, and it wouldn't be fair to hit his father with that conversation when he was already down.

His father would have to be brought into the modern era, but doing so wasn't easy. The ranch was still his dad's, and Ian wasn't trying to tear the reins from his father's hands, but that's how it would feel to his dad.

Never mind that a part of Ian longed to be free of all of it. He would do his duty to the land that had formed him. He'd never turn his back on his legacy. "I'll start supper in a little bit. Just give me a minute." He needed a shower and a brief respite from the never-ending list of problems. He turned to go, then halted and faced his father. None of this was what his dad had wanted, either.

"It's my turn to do the worrying, Dad," he said gently. "You've spent your entire life watching over this place. I promise you I won't lose it." He was still searching for a compromise his father could live with, but the old-school ways didn't work anymore.

"Let's go see Georgia's girl," his father said.

"What?"

The head more silver than dark now rose. "I said, let's go see Georgia's girl now. Find out what she's up to."

A bone-deep reluctance stirred inside Ian. He had absolutely no desire to be close to Scarlett Ross, and not because she didn't appeal to him.

She appealed to him way too much.

She had guts, he'd have to give her that. She'd walked into a strange place that was surely as foreign to her as New York City would be to him, yet she hadn't held back, hadn't quailed at stepping in when she was needed.

And she was saucy as all get-out. Tough, too, even if he hadn't given her much credit that first morning. She'd tried to fix her own flat, she simply didn't have the muscles to do it— but still, she'd wanted to pitch in.

And she didn't take guff off anyone. He grinned. For sure

not from him.

He'd gotten over being so mad this morning. He'd never liked holding a grudge. No, she wouldn't stay and she wasn't his type, not one bit, but he could enjoy her company while she was here, couldn't he? The thought of a little more sparring with Miss Scarlett had his mouth turning up at the corners. Let that saucy tongue and those lush lips of hers occupy a mind that spent most of its time full of worry.

They didn't have money to burn, not if the ranch was to survive, but Ruby's prices were so reasonable that it was hard to do better cooking at home, even if he were any good at more than the basics.

And his dad's eyes were sparkling at the notion.

Maybe as much as his own were.

"Yeah, we could," he answered his father. "I need to talk to her about the work day at Veronica's, anyway." He could try again. Not lose his temper this time.

His conscience rolled its eyes at him. *You could cover that with a phone call.*

Inwardly he shrugged. So what? They had to eat, didn't they? And after a day like today, someone else's cooking sounded damned appealing. "I'll just go get cleaned up."

His father smiled as though he saw right though him.

But Ian refused to let that bother him. New York was one fine cook. He hadn't gotten to taste her biscuits this morning, but he'd run across Harley Sykes, who swore up and down that Ruby couldn't have done better.

And their business would help Ruby out, after all.

Oh, you are pathetic.

Ian chuckled as he ascended the stairs to his room.

Chapter Eleven

S he hadn't been walking as much as usual, that was made clear as Scarlett climbed the three stories with more difficulty than normal.

She peered around her a bit as she climbed, but she still didn't feel all that comfortable leaving the café, however much the respite called to her. What she saw, though, made her itch to return in full daylight. The steps were marble, the railings beautifully carved, if grimy from wear and neglect. What might be oak panels lined the walls at chair rail height—again, dinged and stained by time and grime, but the craftsmanship, she thought, was excellent.

Ideas began to stir, and they helped distract her from the burning in her quads.

She really, really had to make time for a proper workout.

At last she reached the top level and opened a door to the belfry. She crossed the wooden floor and skirted around an enormous bell to reach the nearest opening. Cobwebs swung from up high, perfect horror story material.

But when she reached the opening, she gasped.

Even in the lavender light of approaching night, the hills spilled out before her in glorious row after row of curves dotted with trees, with the first few stars twinkling their frozen white light from above.

Scarlett drew her jacket closer. Shivered a little.

And drew in a deep breath for the first time since she'd

seen the sign for Sweetgrass Springs.

She'd always loved heights. Preferred the aerie to the earth, the whip of wind to the solidity of ground beneath her feet. When you were up high, everything else receded. Worry and doubt and confusion, all of them seemed to clear.

Her shoulders settled. She leaned against the framed opening and simply...breathed. Let her gaze range over the vista before her, the buildings around the square with the architectural details she'd missed from the ground. The smattering of houses beyond, in every direction, the river meandering its way to separate Sweetgrass Springs from the world beyond.

And past all that...the land. The ranches where men like Ian sweated and toiled.

You sure don't know much about family. You don't desert family when they need you.

She'd been too hard on him this morning.

Did she really have to go?

How can you possibly stay? said the voice whispering in her ear. *After what Mama did, abandoning Ruby, you think finding out that you're notorious will sit well with her?*

She couldn't be sure. Ruby was tough and demanding, but she understood hard knocks, Scarlett was beginning to realize. Maybe she'd understand.

But maybe she'd be disappointed. Having just found family and treading such shaky ground, Scarlett wasn't ready to risk Ruby's rejection. Even if she wasn't also courting potential danger if Kostov tracked her here.

You are meant for more than this, murmured the voice of her ambition. *You have talents. These people are stuck here, but you don't have to be.*

But Ruby was here. Her grandmother. Her only family—wait, no. She had cousins, too. Amazing. She'd never known anyone her age who was related to her. How could she leave until she met them?

And Ian was right. Ruby was not young.

Correction—*Nana* was not young. Scarlett smiled, recalling her grandmother's reaction to the name Nana. *You'd name me after a dog?* The memory of Ruby's feigned indignation, her shocked pleasure, made Scarlett laugh.

Yes, Nana. I love the name Nana. I love...you. She sucked in a breath. Could she say that? Seriously? She and Ruby had barely met. How could she love her, especially when she had not a clue why her mother had left. Whether Ruby had driven her away. *I lost my daughter, and it had to be my doing.*

Ruby was complicated, but she took in strays and helped so many. She cared for a whole town, so why would she have done less for her own child?

This place was full of mysteries, of unanswered questions.

Just then a pickup entered the square and caught her eye.

Ian. He was here, and they'd parted badly this morning.

She shook her head. She shouldn't care.

She left us, me and Dad. She liked city life, and she didn't want anything tying her down. She hated the ranch.

Another one who hadn't stayed.

Love strong enough to stay, wasn't that the legend? She swiveled her gaze below and off to her left, to the tree-shaded bend in the river where Sweetgrass Spring bubbled its bounty.

She thought of the woman still waiting... Something shivered up her spine.

Oh, good grief. It's a story, that's all.

But Ian...he'd been five. What did that do to a small boy, to lose his mother's love so young? To have the one person who should love you without reservation throw that love away?

She yanked herself back forcibly. There was no point in furthering this fascination for Ian McLaren. She would leave him, too—she would have to.

Not that he'd asked her to stay for him. In fact, he'd probably laugh at the very notion.

She could picture his dimple then. His teeth were white and even when he smiled. His eyes were beautiful.

And his body...

Best not to think about those acres of muscles, the impressive strength held in such tight check. What would it take to snap the reins on his formidable control?

Now she was the one smiling in anticipation...

Oh, just stop it. You have work to do. Get after it.

She stirred from her perch against the sill, then she threw her arms wide and breathed deeply, inhaling air so fresh she couldn't recall ever experiencing its like. With her head thrown back, her face open and willing, Scarlett felt her mind settling, dropping the day's worries, one by one by one.

One last deep breath, then a long sigh of satisfaction.

I see why you come here, Nana. Even if Mama's never coming back...this place is special.

Scarlett opened her palms to encompass the beauty like a canvas before her, the crisp wind, the starry, starry night. Had she ever seen so many stars?

A movement at the corner of her right eye.

A faint glimmer of white.

She glanced over, but no one was there. "Hello?"

The only answer was a faint rustle up high, maybe a bird or a bat... Again, a shiver crawled up her spine, and she couldn't help thinking about The Lady...

Oh, get real.

Scarlett straightened her spine. Time to return to the duties she'd assumed for the grandmother she still knew far too little about. On the way down, she cast away fanciful thoughts and instead she shone her flashlight over the spaces she passed, and her busy mind began to think about Ruby's idea. About what else could be done with this physical space and the town in which it existed.

The options her grandmother could realize in it.

Downstairs she quickly crossed to the back door to the

café, hastily trading her jacket for an apron, settling it over her neck and tying it swiftly around her waist. Then she turned to get back to work.

And nearly screamed at the shape that loomed in front of her.

"Hello, New York."

"You scared me," she accused.

"Been over to see the ghost?"

"You believe in that? Seriously?"

He shrugged, and she studied him more closely than before, aware of her undeniable attraction to him.

Ian wasn't pretty, no. He was far too masculine and rugged, too big and rangy and rough.

But wow...he sure made an impression.

"Can we start over?" he asked, his brown eyes serious. "I'm sorry about this morning."

Scarlett realized how much she would like the same. "Yes." She smiled. "I have to go cook now, but maybe later, you can tell me what you have in mind."

For a second, his expression went blank, then he stirred. "Oh. You mean the work day."

"What did you think I meant?"

His eyes twinkled. He glanced at her mouth, then dragged his gaze back to hers.

She couldn't help grinning. So they were both intrigued. She wondered how he would kiss. What it would feel like to be in his arms. "Yes, the work day."

His eyebrows rose. "For real? You're going to stay?"

"Probably not for long," she said honestly. "But I'll be here until your work day. Ruby needs my help." *And I need to understand Ruby.* Her life, her mother's choice to hide the truth, would never make sense until she did.

His smile lit him from the inside, and she began to see just how much worry this man carried around with him every waking second. "Good." He nodded. "That's real good."

They stared at one another for a long time.

"Anybody cooking back there?" came Jeanette's voice.

Ian stirred and Scarlett sighed. "No rest for the wicked. Are you staying for dinner?"

"I am. My dad really wanted to come back. You need some help?"

"You said you can't cook."

Color stained his cheeks, and delight rose inside her. "I guess I could wash dishes or something."

"Nope," she said, suddenly proud that she sounded a little like a native with that *Nope*. "I think you'd better—"

"—Get out of your kitchen," he finished for her.

She laughed. "You know me well."

His gaze grew serious, and his voice softened. "No, I don't." He stared at her again. "But damned if I don't want to." Then he turned on his heel and left.

While Scarlett stared after him.

"You think you might finish your supper anytime soon, son?"

Ian jolted. Swiveled his head to see his father grinning at him. "What?"

His dad shook his head. "Nothing. Can't blame you. She's a pretty little thing, isn't she?"

"I wasn't—"

His dad rolled his eyes. "Uh-huh. You haven't been looking back into the kitchen oh, more than every five seconds or so. No big deal."

"I was just—"

"Hi, Ian! Hey, Mr. McLaren." Ben approached their table, his twin sisters and mother right behind. Ben had already reached David's height and seemed to be sprouting by the day. His hair was black where David's had been a dark brown.

The little girls were blonde and delicate like Veronica.

"Well, hello there, young Ben. You all come to have supper?" Ian's dad asked.

"Yes, sir. My mom is treating us."

"We were a lot of help," chirped Abby.

At least Ian was almost certain it was Abby and not Beth. He wasn't around David's twins as much as he had been with Ben. "Really? What did you do?"

The girls launched into a recitation of the various chores they'd done after kindergarten let out for the day. Ian listened to them, but he spared a glance for Veronica.

She looked completely worn out.

As soon as the little girl slowed down, he nudged a chair from its spot. "How about you all join us? Bet we can grab another table."

"Oh no, we couldn't—" Veronica began.

"'Course you can," said his dad. "We insist on it, don't we, son?"

"We sure do. I have something I need to discuss with you, anyway," Ian said to Veronica.

"Oh?"

"Have a seat." He rose and made his way to the next table, which hadn't yet been bussed, and started dragging it to adjoin theirs.

Henry bustled over, as did Jeanette. "We can take care of this," she huffed. "All you had to do was ask."

Ian lifted his brows at her tone. "You're busy tonight. Henry can help me, can't you, Henry?"

"Yes, sir."

But Jeanette wouldn't go. "You really shouldn't—"

He looked at her. "Problem?"

He noted her sideways glance at Veronica and remembered Scarlett's scathing accusation that the waitress had a thing for him.

Seriously? *Jeanette?* He found himself studying the younger woman. He guessed she was attractive, but…

His gaze flicked involuntarily toward the kitchen.

Where Scarlett was watching him, too. With a slow, satisfied smile and raised eyebrows as if to say *See? What did I tell you?*

"Ian?"

He snapped back to attention and busied himself moving chairs around, settling the twins and helping Veronica into her seat. He listened to his dad josh with Ben and ask the little girls questions that made them laugh.

Then he resumed his seat, Veronica to his right.

Almost like a family, he thought. His buddy's family. For the first time, Ian let himself imagine being the head of a household, the dad who helped with homework and stole kisses from his wife. Who read bedtime stories and put out all the lights, the last one in bed, snuggling down with his wife as children giggled from their rooms and silence settled in.

Was that the life his father had hoped for?

Was it what he himself wanted? He was at a crossroads—if he could wrap his mind around selling the ranch, he could travel to all those places he'd read about and dreamed of.

He'd never felt so restless, not in several years. He'd never allowed himself to think about options besides the ranch—at least, not seriously.

Then Scarlett Ross had shown up and opened a window onto the bigger world.

Fish or cut bait.

Something had to be done, and soon, about the ranch. He could break his father's heart and sell out, securing a future for both of them, albeit nothing like the one his father had worked his whole life for.

But that life was over and done. The Double Bar M could not continue as it had for nearly two hundred years. It had to evolve…or die.

And if Ian let it die, it would probably kill his father.

Though he would be free.

Or he could push for the riskier plan he really believed was the best long-term option, raising solely organic beef for nearby city markets, then expanding into his own feedyard and certified organic processing plant. All those would create jobs beyond those Billy and his other two hands currently held.

But that, too, would be done only over his father's objections.

And he would be stuck here for the rest of his life.

In Sweetgrass Springs, the town he both loved and desperately longed to leave behind. Not forever, maybe, but how could he know for sure when this was all he'd ever known?

"Heavy thoughts," Veronica whispered. "You okay?"

He stirred. "What? Oh—no, I'm fine. Fine," he hastened to reassure her.

"I don't think so. Something's really bothering you," she murmured.

He arched one brow. "Something's bothering you—a lot of somethings, I'm pretty sure. Ladies first."

"I'm okay," she said automatically.

"Veronica, you're not." When she stiffened, he grasped her hand. "There's no shame in it. You're only one person. You're trying to do your job and David's too. Something has to give." He bored his gaze into hers. "David would never forgive me if that something turned out to be you."

Her eyes swam. He'd never seen her cry, not even at David's funeral, though many times in those days, her eyes had been red. "What else can I do?" she whispered, glancing to be sure her children didn't hear.

But Ben was listening, and he spoke up. "We have an idea, Mom. You should hear us out." He sat up straight, and Ian wished in that moment that his buddy could see the boy now. Even if he didn't much resemble David in looks, Ben would be every bit the fine, upstanding man his father had been.

You did well with this one, my friend, he said silently.

"What are you talking about?" Veronica asked.

Ben glanced at Ian, nerves in his gaze.

They both knew the footing would be dicey.

Ian nodded and took up the gauntlet. "You remember barn raisings? Like with Old Man Kinslow?"

She frowned and nodded. "My father wouldn't let us help, but yes, I remember hearing about it."

Of course that bastard wouldn't let them be part of anything good or neighborly, but Ian wasn't going there right now. "There are always people who could use help around here. I think we should renew the tradition. Neighbors all coming together on one day, maybe once every month or two, and helping other neighbors."

She cocked her head, and in her expression he could see both approval and the exhaustion of wondering where she would ever come up with the extra time. "It's a nice idea. Who are you thinking of? Where would you start?" Then she reared her head back as she understood where he was headed. "No. Oh, no, you don't, Ian McLaren. I don't need that."

Careful, he cautioned himself.

"So you're going to kill this great idea, along with your neighbors' chances to get assistance, because you won't serve as the pilot project?"

She narrowed her eyes. "Give me a list. Who else would you help?"

This was where it turned out to be helpful that much of Sweetgrass Springs seemed to turn to him when trouble arose. He rattled off a list. "Rissa could use help rebuilding fences, and Raymond's barn needs a new roof and a coat of paint."

"So let's help one of them first."

He bent closer. "No one is trying to embarrass you, Veronica. Everyone in this town loved David, and they would gladly pitch in to help his family. If we can make this work, then others will let us help them. You're going to let your pride stand in the way when there are folks who could really use this?"

She was clearly torn between embarrassment and the first faint stirrings of relief. Her jaw tightened. "Folks don't like the Pattons. I will not be a charity case."

"You've been a Butler for years now, and people have always liked you, regardless of your maiden name. It's not charity if you return the favor. Will you? You could help me think of others in need."

Her expression was so vulnerable. Across the table, Ben watched his mother like a hawk, clearly torn, too. The twins chattered on with his dad, for which Ian was grateful.

He kept his gaze firmly on Veronica. "Please. This could be a good thing for a lot of people. Sweetgrass is floundering, and with Ruby down injured..."

"You don't play fair, Ian."

But he could feel the capitulation. Still, he proceeded with caution. "Will you help?" he persisted.

"How is it helping if I'm the one who benefits most?" But her argument was losing steam.

"Because somebody needs to lead the way. You can't hide on that farm forever, Veronica."

Her eyes swam once more. "It hurts too much to hear people speak of him."

And he was pushing her too hard, perhaps. "I'm sorry."

She wiped her eyes with her napkin. "I'll survive." Then she touched his hand. "Thank you, Ian. You are such a good man."

He shrugged. "David was the good man. I'm just his lucky friend." He cleared a lump from his own throat and looked around the table. "Everybody ready to order?"

"Yeah!" cheered the twins.

Veronica bent to him. "One thing, that's all. One project. Something simple."

"Ben has already begun a list."

"Ben is not in charge. I mean it, Ian. One small project, then we move on to the next person."

Ian sighed. "We'll talk about it."

"I'm done talking," she muttered furiously.

Then she noted her children's anxious expressions and quickly sat up straight, pasting on a smile. "So what's good tonight, Mr. McLaren?"

"Anything that little girl back there cooks," his dad responded.

Ian looked up and saw Scarlett watching them, but immediately she turned away.

"I'd like to meet her," Veronica said.

"Well, Ian here can make that happen, I'm sure. He's gotten pretty well acquainted with her."

"Oh?" Veronica glanced back and forth between Ian and the kitchen.

Ian glared at his dad, who only looked innocent, then lifted his good arm. "Jeanette, we're ready to order."

"Something you want to tell me?" Veronica asked, bending close.

"Not a thing." Ian buried his face in the menu he could have recited by heart.

But the smile he saw curving Veronica's mouth was a welcome sight, even if it was at his expense.

Scarlett couldn't help glancing over the pass-through…again. The woman sitting next to Ian was likely Ben's mother, the woman she was supposed to help. Ian was right—she looked fragile and weary to her bones. She was a widow, her life was hard and Scarlett should feel sorry for her. She did, of course she did. She wanted to help, and she would.

Still…the woman had so much. She sat there, surrounded by family and friends, constantly sought out by other patrons who clearly admired her and were fond of her, and Ian hovered over her so protectively…

It was wrong to want to be in her place. It was.

But a terrible piece of Scarlett would have traded with her in a heartbeat. However much that woman had lost, she knew where she belonged. Knew she wasn't alone—

Scarlett ripped her attention away and focused on the meal she was plating.

With shaking hands.

She set the plate down for a second while she struggled to breathe past the ache that choked her. *How can you envy her? You are horrible. Mean and unkind.*

"You okay?" came a familiar voice from far too close.

She jolted. Opened her eyes and realized Ian was right beside her. She glanced up at him, then quickly away, focusing for dear life on her plate before her.

He took it from her hand and set it on the pass-through. "What's wrong?"

"Nothing." She cleared her throat. "I'm busy and you're in my—"

"—kitchen. I know. Can you spare a minute?"

"I'm really jammed, Ian."

One long finger touched her chin, turned her face toward him. "Can I help?"

His warm brown eyes made her want to fall, to lean into his strength.

So she stepped away. "Not unless you've learned how to cook since I saw you this morning," she said briskly.

"I'd like you to meet someone. Jeanette says things are slowing down. Just for a second?"

She glanced over at the table where one girl had crawled into her mother's lap and Ian's father was leaning close as they spoke and—

She didn't want to. She was always on the outside looking in. Going over there wouldn't change that. "She's important to you."

"She is," he agreed. "Her husband was my best friend except for Jackson. We all grew up together."

"You're good with her kids."

He shrugged. "I try to be. He would have wanted me to take care of them."

She risked a quick glance. He'd make an amazing father, a devoted husband. "She's very pretty." Veronica Butler looked the way Scarlett had grown up wanting to, all doll-pretty blond hair and china blue eyes.

"She's too damn skinny. She needs about a week in bed and someone to feed her up."

"So you're elected? Or self-appointed? Or is that all you want?"

His brows snapped together. "What does that mean?"

She was way over the line. She didn't know this place or these people. She wouldn't be around long enough to change that. Didn't want to be.

"Give me five minutes," she said and reached for the last ticket on the wheel.

He hesitated, and she could feel his gaze on her. She didn't like anyone looking too close. "I don't need an audience," she snapped. "I'll get there when I can." She risked a quick glance, and she could almost see that brain calculating. "Shoo." She motioned the same with her hands.

Still he hesitated. "You're not obligated to do anything. You're a free agent."

Yes. She was. And she liked it that way.

Mostly.

She exhaled in a gust. "I'm sorry. It's been a long day, that's all." Or all she would confide. "I do want to help, and I'd like to meet her. Just…five minutes, okay?"

He reached toward her as though he wanted to touch her.

In comfort? In apology?

She didn't know. And he wasn't hers—he was clearly attached to that woman in the other room. If that didn't work out, there was always Jeanette. There was nothing between herself and him, couldn't be even if he wanted it.

But she missed touching. Missed human contact. Her mother had been free with affectionate gestures like a stroke of her hair or a cradling of her cheek, the quick hug for no reason. Here she was the outsider, and that's how it had to be, but...

His hand was back at his side, but his eyes were still asking questions.

"Beat it, okay? Or I'll never get done."

His reluctance to leave her was obvious, but she also understood its cause. The picture of him that was beginning to form was a man who accepted responsibility without being asked, who took charge in a crisis, the man everyone knew would be there for them.

She didn't want to be another of his burdens.

Chapter Twelve

She lingered as long as she could, hoping they would leave. Knowing it was foolish. That she was no coward. Hadn't she met strangers all her life? Wasn't she good at it?

So why was this different? What was she waiting for?

Do it. She started to take off her apron, but hesitated. Keeping it on made her situation clear, gave her an excuse to escape. "Brenda, come get me in a couple of minutes, okay?"

"Me?"

"You."

"Why?" The girl's forehead wrinkled, but immediately she began apologizing. "It's none of my business."

"It is." She sighed. "I'm being a coward."

"You?"

Scarlett shook her head. "It's ridiculous." She started forward, then hesitated. "No more than five minutes, are we clear?" She didn't wait for Brenda's answer but forced herself to move.

Ian's dad spotted her first. "Well, there she is—good groceries again this evening, little girl."

She really liked Ian's dad. "Hi, Mr. McLaren. Glad you enjoyed it. Hello, Ben."

Ben's cheeks reddened. "Hi, Ms. Ross."

"Scarlett, please." She glanced at the girl next to Ben. "Hello, there. Are you Ben's sister?" She cast her gaze toward the other girl. "Wow. You really are twins, aren't you?"

The little girls giggled. "I'm Abby and that's Beth," said the one on the other side of their mother.

Scarlett glanced back and forth, looking for anything to tell them apart. "Ah, now I see it." She pointed to the quiet one, Beth. "Your left ear is a quarter inch lower, right?"

The girls giggled.

Their mother spoke. "Hello, Scarlett. I'm Veronica. You are a blessing to Ruby, taking over like this. I know she must be grateful."

Well, crap. She was nice. But of course Hot Cowboy would insist on falling for someone perfect. "I still can't get over finding out that I have a grandmother," she admitted.

"She has to be over the moon herself. All these years, she's prayed for Georgia to come home, and now…"

"I loved my mom." She knew there was warning in her voice.

"Of course you did. I'm sorry for your loss."

Scarlett settled her ruffled feathers. "I'm sorry for yours."

Veronica's eyes went soft and painfully sad. "Thank you." She took Scarlett's hand and squeezed.

Great. Now she couldn't hate the woman for being a perfect angel. Scarlett squeezed back before pulling her hand away. "I'd better…" She nodded her head toward the kitchen.

"I know you must not get much time to yourself, but would you come see my flowers one day?" Veronica smiled ruefully. "I can't leave often myself."

The Hot Cowboy didn't matter, Scarlett discovered. She could like this woman. Could see that she'd make a good friend, but—

"If I can, I'd like that. I won't be here long."

Veronica frowned. "But Ruby—"

Just then the door burst open. A man entered, and the people at the table visibly tensed. Scarlett glanced at Ian, whose jaw hardened.

Who was this guy? He wasn't as tall as Ian, but he was big and beefy. He wore a cowboy hat, like so many others and—

He had a gun on his hip. A badge pinned to his shirt.

She took an involuntary step back. Had he been sent after her? How had anyone found her?

His gaze scanned the room until he spotted Ian and began stalking toward them. The twins leaned into their mother, and Ben shrank in his chair. Ian stepped forward as if to protect them all.

Veronica squeezed the girls' shoulders, then rose. "Tank, how are you?"

He took in the inhabitants of the table, his gaze stopping at Scarlett with a frown. "Who are you?"

Ian started forward, but Veronica put herself between them. "She's Ruby's granddaughter, Tank. Isn't that wonderful?"

His startled gaze shifted back to Scarlett. "Ruby doesn't have a granddaughter."

He was a bully, that much was easy to figure. Scarlett had faced down bullies all her life. You couldn't let them see you were scared. She moved around the table. "I didn't know I had a grandmother, either, until recently. I'm Scarlett Ross...Sheriff?" She held out a hand.

"Deputy Sheriff Patton," he said, and his gaze raked her.

She didn't like the expression in his eyes one bit, but she didn't want to give him any reason to take an interest in her, so she shook his hand. "Pleased to meet you. Are you here for dinner? The special tonight is pork chops with mashed potatoes and gravy." Ruby had a rotating list of specials Jeanette swore the townspeople expected.

"It's not Thursday." He frowned.

"She's from New York, Tank," Jeanette sneered from behind her. "By way of Paris, France."

Yeah, Jeanette was not going to be her friend. Not that it was any surprise.

"What's the Friday special?" she asked Jeanette.

"Catfish."

"I see. Fried, I suppose?"

"No other way to fix it."

Scarlett glanced around her. "It's not Ruby's fault that you were disappointed," she said to the room in general.

"Nobody here is disappointed." Ian's voice was iron.

"Not one bit," echoed his dad.

"I liked the mashed potatoes," piped up one of the twins.

"Me, too," Ben said with belligerence in his voice.

The deputy flushed. Glared at Ian. "You get that damn pasture fence fixed yet?"

"Don't swear around my children," Veronica said.

"Don't you—" Tank's hand fisted.

Ian's muscles coiled, and Scarlett could see the punch coming. The air was thick with suppressed violence.

She stepped forward. "Deputy, I would be happy to make you some catfish if that's what you'd prefer. Or would you like to try the pork chops?" With one hand on his elbow, she urged him toward the counter.

He resisted, and he was twice her size, but he wasn't the first hothead she'd dealt with. She kept up her patter. "I've done a good job with Ruby's biscuits, if I do say so myself, and there's peach cobbler for dessert. Would you care for iced tea or…?"

He narrowed his eyes as though she were a gnat he'd like to squash, but she also noted curiosity there.

She smiled brightly as she went around the counter and handed him a rolled-up napkin with silverware inside. "Or I've made a fairly decadent chocolate cake you might want to try." She'd learned long ago that her will could overcome the limitations of her size. "Pork chops or catfish? Or would you like to look at the menu?"

He exhaled and finally settled on the stool. "Pork chops is fine. And iced tea."

"Excellent. I'll get your order started and—" She glanced at Brenda, but the girl was almost literally shrinking into the woodwork. "Jeanette, would you please get Deputy Patton some iced tea?"

As she made her way to the kitchen, she glanced at Ian and willed him to take his party and leave, but clearly he was spoiling for a fight himself.

In the end, however, his concern for Veronica and her brood overrode the rest.

She nodded at him as they rose to go, then gave Veronica and her bunch a smile.

And went back to cook.

Crisis averted.

It was late by the time Ian had escorted Veronica and her brood home, then gotten his dad settled. He had to be up early, as always. He should be in bed himself.

Instead he paced. Stared out across the front porch at the winter moonlight.

She wasn't staying. They were light years apart in virtually everything. She was bossy and had a temper, to boot. She had traveled that world he would never see.

But she was a burn in his belly. He liked her spirit. He liked her looks.

He wanted his hands on her in the worst way.

He glanced at the clock. She would likely still be there, closing down.

Morning would come early. There was a front coming in later in the day, with a freeze expected. He had preparations to make, a to-do list a mile long...

Screw it.

He yanked the keys from his pocket, thought a second

about telling his dad he was leaving—

He was thirty-five years old. He didn't have a curfew.

Blue wanted to follow. "No, buddy. Only one fool per mission." He held his palm out. "Stay."

Blue settled but his ears were still perked up, watching Ian as he left.

Scarlett had sent everyone home, Jeanette grumbling as if Scarlett would abscond with the silver if left unsupervised.

Like the thin, worn flatware possessed even the faintest trace of precious metal inside.

She had needed to be alone. Too many strangers, too much emotion…she needed some space from everything. She was about ten seconds from throwing down the towel, literally, and racing out the door.

She could do it. She had a spare tire again, courtesy of Ian.

When did the man ever get his own work done, after taking care of half the known universe?

She didn't care. It didn't matter. In a day or two Ruby would be better, and she would go—

A sound outside.

She was all alone. In a strange town.

Anyone could—

Abruptly Scarlett was catapulted back into that night when her apartment was invaded, a meaty hand slapped over her mouth as she lay in her bed—

She grabbed for the nearest knife, her heart thudding.

The back door opened.

She edged into the shadows.

"I have a knife," Ian heard. The voice was nearly feral.

What the hell?

She was a city girl, he reminded himself. Probably geared for muggers. "Scarlett? It's only me." He stepped into the light, swiveled to see her but couldn't.

"Ian?"

"Yes. Where are you?" There. At last he spotted her outline, tucked in behind the prep area. "Are you okay?" As he neared, he could see that she wasn't. She was nearly panting, and her face had lost all color. "What happened? Did somebody—" His jaw went rigid. "Did Tank—" *I will kill that bastard.*

"Tank?" She seemed not to know the name. Her pupils were huge, and she was trembling.

"Here." Gingerly he plucked the wicked big knife from her hand and set it aside, then drew her closer. "You're okay," he soothed as he wrapped her up in his arms. "You're all right."

Still she trembled, so stiff she could break.

He bent his head and laid his cheek on her hair, rocking her gently. "You're safe," he murmured. "No one's going to hurt you."

She shuddered.

Then she grabbed onto him like a drowning victim. Slid her arms around his waist and fisted the back of his shirt in her small hands, plastering her body against his. "Ian?"

He'd never imagined hearing this spitfire sound so frightened. So lost. He tucked her into him yet tighter still, caught in the grip of fierce protectiveness, a violent urge to fight off anyone or anything that threatened her. "Hush, now," he soothed. "You're safe. I've got you."

Explanations would have to wait. Whoever had scared her like this, though…a low growl rose in his throat.

Then she lifted her face to him, that face that had somehow crept under his skin when he wasn't looking—

Her eyes were huge and dark and lonely.

And he was lost.

"Scarlett…" He cradled her cheek in one hand and low-ered his mouth to hers, at first brushing his lips gently over hers, only a benediction, a comfort.

Then she rose to her toes and opened her mouth under his. Let her tongue graze the inner edges of his lips.

With a growl he lifted her off the floor and melted into her the way she was yielding herself to him. Her kiss tasted of desperate need, of crackling flames that set fire to the tinder of the desire he'd been banking ever since his first sight of her.

He pulled her more tightly into him, and she climbed his body, her legs parting to wrap his waist, bringing the heat of her against his aching, raging erection.

He went blind with the hunger he'd ruthlessly stifled since he'd first encountered a tiny virago, a smart-mouthed city girl who would—

Leave. As his mother had.

For a second he faltered, but she slid her fingers up his chest and over his shoulders to plunge them into his hair while her mouth did unspeakably amazing things to his.

He shoved one hand under her shirttail—

Only to encounter the tight cinch of her apron.

Apron. They were in Ruby's kitchen, for God's sake. The cafe was closed, but the doors were never locked.

Anyone could walk in.

Was he planning to take her on the prep table, then? Or maybe splay her over one of Ruby's dining tables? The image clawed at him, Scarlett, her riot of black hair around her like a nimbus, the body he was desperate to see, to touch…

Abruptly she scrambled down. Backed away, out of reach. "What was that?" she demanded.

"Darlin', you know exactly what that was." He took a step toward her.

"Stop right there." But her chest was heaving, and her lips were wet from his tongue.

"I don't think so."

"I'll—I'll—"

"What? Pull a knife on me?"

Her expression morphed into fear again.

He was appalled. He had never harmed a woman in his life. Never would. "Who made you afraid?" he asked gently.

Her face went vulnerable for a moment, then she shook her head. "No one. I'm fine."

"Scarlett," he warned. "Now is not the time to lie to me. Who are you so scared of? I won't let them hurt you, you know."

Her head cocked as she considered him. "You can't—" She broke off. "I'm fine."

"You are not fine. You were scared to death when I got here."

"Doesn't anyone in this town ever knock? And how stupid is it to leave doors unlocked? Don't you people know—"

"That there are bad people in the world? Yes. But we have a code around here."

She laughed but it was derisive. "You don't even have proper police or an emergency room or—"

"We take care of our own, Scarlett. We'll take care of you, too."

Her expression was astonishment. "Me? You don't know me. I don't know you."

"You had your tongue in my mouth a couple of minutes ago."

"That's just sex."

"Pretty damn good sex, I'd say." He found a smile so he wouldn't howl with unquenched need. "But I'd need another taste to be sure."

Her eyes met his. Temptation flirted with her, too, he

could see. "I don't think my grandmother would appreciate it much." She grinned. "I know Jeanette wouldn't."

"Oh, give it a rest. I don't want Jeanette."

"She hasn't gotten the message. Think that's fair to her?"

"I've never given her one reason to believe there was anything between her and me."

"Again—she missed the memo. I think you're gonna have to spell it out, cowboy."

He prowled toward her. "Later."

She grabbed a dish towel. Flicked it at him. "Back off, bud." But her eyes were sparkling. She flicked it again.

Thank God. She wasn't afraid anymore. He could handle the spitfire just fine.

He caught the end and yanked her close, grinning. Oh, he knew they weren't going to finish what they'd started, not here, not right now.

But he was having fun playing. When was the last time he'd felt playful?

He started reeling her in.

She dropped her end and ran.

He caught her within three steps.

She squealed.

He swung her up in his arms and planted a kiss on her laughing mouth.

Again it turned scorching hot in a heartbeat. Scarlett gave as good as she got, and soon her legs were around his waist again and he'd backed her against a wall, ready to yank open those apron strings—

Instead he clenched the front of her apron in one fist and tore his mouth from hers.

Then banged his head against the wall. "We can't."

Her chuckle was shaky with unspent passion. "I know. Damn it."

That she hungered for him, too, cheered him immensely.

He straightened. Looked her in the eyes. "I want you."

So typical that her gaze never faltered. "I want you, too."

"The cafe is closed on Sunday. You'll want to spend time with Ruby, but you'll give me part of your day."

She nodded. For once she didn't say she wouldn't be here. He had no idea what that meant, but he wasn't complaining.

He knew he should let her down, but he didn't want to back away yet. Even though he was rock-hard and aching, having her against him was the best thing he'd felt in a long time.

But she'd had a long day. So had he. They would both work hard tomorrow. He loosened his grip. "What else needs doing so you can get home to bed?"

"I'm done."

He nodded. "I'll walk you over." But he didn't let go.

And she didn't either.

At last she sighed. "I wish you weren't so sexy." Before he could recover from his astonishment, she tightened her fingers in his hair and laid another devastating kiss on him.

He was halfway to tearing off her clothes when she shoved at his shoulder. "Now let me down, Hot Cowboy."

Astonished laughter burst from him. Then he frowned. "Don't call me that."

"Why not?" Her eyes were bright with mischief.

"I'm not—aw, man. That's—" He could feel his cheeks heat. "Just...stop it."

She rose to her toes and pressed a smacking kiss on his lips, then danced away, drawing her apron off and tossing it into the laundry bin. "But you are hot. And you are a cowboy. Deal with it."

She was so damn beautiful, her hair a mess from his hands, her eyes full of laughter, the body he'd so wrongly called that of a boy feeling just right in his hands...

"Don't you ever say that in public, you hear me?"

"Or what, Hot Cowboy?" She opened the back door, laughing.

He charged her, swung her up in his arms and muffled her squeal with his lips.

They lost another few minutes making out.

But at last she sighed. "Ruby waits up for me."

"She's got Arnie."

"What do you mean?"

"You never saw him there? It's the worst-kept secret in town that she and Arnie sleep together every night."

She blinked. "Seriously?"

"The man's been proposing to her for close to twenty years. She insists it's only sex."

Scarlett burst out laughing. "Wow. That's…crazy. And…sweet."

"I go with crazy. No idea why he puts up with her stubbornness."

"She's not—" Scarlett halted. "Okay, she's a little hardheaded."

"Sorta like her granddaughter." He stroked her cheek.

Their eyes locked. He lowered his head and kissed her again.

She kissed him right back. Then sighed. "I still have to go."

"I know. I've got a list a mile long in the morning myself," he commiserated.

Their eyes met. "Sunday is at least a year away," she said.

"Yeah." But he was cheered that she thought so, too.

Cheered enough that it didn't occur to him until he was driving back home after seeing her to her door—

That he'd never found out what she was so afraid of.

Scarlett crept up the back steps, abruptly sobered by what she'd done.

She'd promised Ian Sunday. Had let him kiss the socks off her. Had given back in full measure, been ready to tear off his clothes. She wanted her hands all over that lean, powerful body. Oh, my word, but the man was built—

Her lips were tender, her whole body buzzing with unrelieved need. She wanted to jump in her car, chase him down and have her way with him.

Or let him have his way with her. Either would do. Both. He was freaking gorgeous. And...fun. That was a surprise. Mr. Responsibility, the unofficial mayor of Sweetgrass Springs.

"Scarlett?"

And she was in her grandmother's house. Lusting after a cowboy, for heaven's sake. Of course, according to Ian, her grandmother had a man in *her* bed.

Go, Nana.

"Coming," she called out while brushing back her hair and drawing a deep breath to steady nerves that were still on fire. She stepped inside the kitchen, resisting the urge to glance around for Arnie. "You should be in bed," she said.

"I've slept enough for ten people," her grandmother grumbled from the kitchen table.

"How are you feeling?"

"I'm—" Her grandmother paused. "Still a little sore."

"Maybe we should take you to a doctor, after all. How's the burn?"

"It's...tender," Ruby admitted.

"I'll get my spray."

"Mrs. Oldham treated it for me before she went to bed."

"You aren't thinking of coming back to work."

Ruby hesitated. "I miss it, but..." Her shoulders sank. "Not yet."

I have more time, Scarlett thought. Then wondered why she wasn't upset instead of feeling relieved. Or what the reasons for her relief were.

She wanted that Sunday, she realized. One day with a seriously sexy man. Just sex, that's all, but she already knew it would be sensational.

"Are you coming down with something? Your cheeks are red. Do you have a fever?" Ruby rose and put a hand to her forehead as Scarlett's mother had always done.

"I'm not sick." No way she was explaining that the heat in her cheeks had nothing to do with illness.

"You're working too hard."

Scarlett grinned. "Pot, meet kettle."

"I'm used to it."

"So am I. And I'm younger."

Ruby frowned. "I do all right for my age."

"You are amazing for your age, but you deserve some rest." When she could see protest rising to her grandmother's lips, she jumped in with a distraction. "I was supposed to serve catfish because it's Friday."

"I heard you made pork chops." Ruby grinned. "Folks could use some shaking up around here. They'll live."

"Jeanette squealed on me, right?"

"Jeanette's a good girl."

She could see the conflict on her grandmother's face. Jeanette had been with her a long time. Scarlett was a new wrinkle.

"She doesn't like me."

"She's given up her life to help me out."

"And to hang around for Ian?"

Ruby nodded. "She doesn't want to see the truth."

"Ian was dumbfounded to realize she had a thing for him. How can he be so dense?"

"When you live around the same folks, day in and day out, it's easy to see them only as you first knew them."

"Does he take responsibility for every single soul in this town?"

"Pretty much. I don't know what Sweetgrass would be

without him."

"He says the same of you."

Ruby shrugged.

"Tell me about the courthouse. It's an amazing space. How on earth did you ever decide to buy it?"

Her grandmother looked wistful. "An idiotic notion, that. I had some idea I would save the town, bring it back to life." The sadness and resignation in her voice were painful to hear.

Scarlett didn't like seeing her look defeated. "I hear you and Henry played ghost." She grinned.

Ruby chuckled. "It was fun, even if it didn't work out so well." Then her expression saddened again. "Anyway, it will be a moot issue soon."

"Why?"

"The note's coming due. The bank isn't inclined to extend it without a substantial reduction in principal, which I can't afford."

"Oh, Nana…" Scarlett thought about mentioning the ideas that were coalescing, but she was pretty sure they'd be expensive to implement. "I have some savings…"

Ruby's brows snapped together. "Absolutely not. It was my wild idea. I'm not taking your money."

"I wouldn't mind." She upped the ante. "We could be partners." Now why on earth had she said that?

"No." Her grandmother's tone brooked no opposition. "Not that I wouldn't love being partners with you, honey, but that's throwing good money after bad. This town can't be rescued, and I should just accept that."

Scarlett started to argue, but to offer hope she couldn't back up because her own life was such a muddle would be inexcusable. "I am so sorry."

"That's life." Ruby looked away.

Scarlett seized upon a distraction. "I met Veronica tonight."

"That girl's had a rough life. Coming from the family she

did, there was never any reason for her to turn out to be such a sweet person, but somehow the meaner her dad got, the more she went in the other direction."

"Apparently her brother isn't much like her."

"Tank? You met him, too? He doesn't come in often."

"He's the only one who pointed out to my face that I cooked the wrong thing."

"Be careful of that one. He shouldn't be wearing a badge. Too much of his daddy in him."

"He and Ian don't seem to like each other much."

"That's an understatement. Tank always envied Ian and Jackson and their bunch. The Four Horsemen, everyone called them."

"Of the Apocalypse? Why?" To think of Ian in a sinister context was a stretch.

"They were tight as brothers, the four of them. It was three, originally, the sons of the town's four founding families."

"The fourth didn't have a son that age?"

"Tank was the fourth. His daddy kept them all away from the townfolks much as he could."

"Why?"

"He was...there was just something wrong with him. And his wife never said boo to him. Nobody liked him, and Tank is too much like his daddy."

"So where did the fourth Horseman come in?"

"Mackey." Ruby shook her head. "That boy was trouble from the second he set foot in Sweetgrass. He and Ian and Jackson and David became a unit after Mackey fought Tank when he was picking on a younger boy. Tank was big even then, but Mackey had lived all over the world because his dad worked in oil fields, and he'd learned to be handy with his fists."

Ruby smiled. "He was a sweet boy, though, under all his posturing. And those four...lordy, they could get into some mischief. Mackey was always the one who thought up the schemes, but the rest of them were no angels. Not bad boys, not really, just a lot of excess energy that needed better channeling. It was a good day for Sweetgrass when they all turned their attention to athletics. They were unbeatable on the football field or the basketball court. Ian was the quarterback, and Jackson was his favorite receiver, but all four of them had a real gift." Ruby's face filled with sorrow. "Then Jackson's mama died, and…well," she said briskly. "It's late, and you need to be in your bed."

"Let me ask something first. Have you heard about Ian's work day idea?"

"No."

Scarlett proceeded to explain.

"That boy is good as gold. Veronica needs the help so badly, and he's working himself to the bone trying to take care of his place and hers, too. Good for him."

"Could we close after the breakfast rush on Saturday? He asked me to cater the work day, but I thought maybe we could all pitch in, too—but it's your income I'm volunteering. Jeanette and the others might not be able to afford to skip their pay, anyway, but I've got some money and I could make up the lost receipts so they would still earn something."

Ruby put a hand on her arm. "You will not use your savings on my cafe in any way, shape or form. That said, I'm all in favor of your idea, and none of them will balk at giving up a day's wages. Around here, we pitch in. Good for you for suggesting it."

Scarlett wasn't sure when she'd ever felt the glow of pride quite like this. "Thank you."

"Thank you, sweetheart." Ruby hugged her, and Scarlett lingered in her grandmother's embrace, warmth filling her.

When Ruby released her, she pointed to the stairs. "Four o'clock comes early. You get on to bed, hear?"

It was nice, having someone fuss over her. "Snuggle up,

Nana." She kissed her grandmother's cheek.

Ruby cradled her face in her weathered hands. "You are a blessing to me, child. Even if you never cooked a dish. I'll be back at work soon, though, so you don't have to put in such long days."

"Like the ones you've put in for how many years?"

"But I chose this life." Ruby sobered. "You didn't. I know you won't want to stay, but I'm grateful for every second you're here. That has nothing to do with the fact that you're keeping the cafe open, in case you were wondering."

In that moment, Scarlett wondered if she would ever be able to think of settling in a place like Sweetgrass. Right now, her life was too much a mess, and no one here would thank her for dragging them into her troubles. For the sake of this woman and this town, she would have to go soon.

But not yet.

"I love you, Nana. And I'm happy I can help. Snuggle up," she repeated.

"Sweet dreams," Ruby responded.

Scarlett took one more hug for herself. Her grandmother held on as though she needed it, too.

Oh, Nana…I will miss you so.

Ruby watched her granddaughter climb the stairs and marveled. She'd long ago given up on surprises, yet the biggest one ever had arrived just when she needed it most.

"Quite a girl, that one," said Arnie from behind her.

"What are you doing out here? Someone could see you."

He wrapped one arm around her. "I thought you might need me. You weren't sleeping."

"I never had trouble sleeping until I started taking afternoon naps."

"Because you were so weary you couldn't help yourself once you finally made it to bed, but now you have help. Good help, too—hate to say this, Ruby, but her cobbler might be better than yours."

"Old coot." But Ruby smiled because she agreed. "The girl has a deft hand in the kitchen, that's for sure."

"You ever think about going to Paris?"

She laughed. "Never even imagined such a thing."

"What do you suppose they taught her in that fancy cooking school?"

"Not biscuits or chicken fried steak, that's for sure." Ruby grew solemn. Scarlett was meant for much more than this little town or her simple cafe, anyone could see that. She'd leave, of course, but in the meantime, Ruby thought she just might take her time recovering. She wanted every last minute she could claim.

"What are you smiling at?"

"Nothing." Except wondering what Scarlett would think if she saw Ruby climbing the stairs twice every day to build up her strength. Now that she wasn't on her feet all day and into the night, she'd discovered both an exhaustion she'd never let herself consider…and a restlessness. She wasn't used to so much leisure time.

She'd spent more time on the phone in the last two days than the last two years. She'd exhausted her friends in town, even called her great-nephew Boone to tell him about his surprise cousin. Boone, of course, had taken it all in stride, but Maddie had gotten on the phone and practically shrieked with joy.

That girl did love family. She, like Scarlett, had been all alone in the world when she'd come to Texas. She was the reason Boone had found Mitch again—and the driving force behind locating the sister they'd never known about.

Now she and Boone had two boys and an infant girl, Mitch and his Perrie had two boys, and their sister Lacey and her Dev had an adopted daughter and a baby girl, with a boy on the way.

But Maddie was already planning a trip to Sweetgrass to gather Scarlett into the fold. She'd once been a chef herself and now owned a diner in Morning Star. She and Scarlett would have cooking in common.

Besides, there wasn't a soul on earth who didn't love Maddie at first sight.

Well, maybe Boone at first, when his dad had willed his home to Maddie right out from under him…but he got over that in time.

She hoped they would be able to come, but they'd better do it quickly, she'd made sure Maddie knew. Scarlett was already eyeing the door.

Which Ruby could not help mourning, however much Scarlett was destined for broader horizons. She loved the girl, and was positive the affection was returned.

She missed her customers and the feeling of being in the thick of the action.

But she'd stay right here and go bug-crazy if that's what it took to keep her granddaughter around a bit longer. And selfishly hope to give Ian McLaren a little more time to sweep that girl off her feet.

She'd seen his truck outside the cafe, all right. Watched the two of them walk over here.

Body language said more than people realized. Those two might have kept distance between themselves on the walk over, but their bodies still leaned toward each other, and the air around them practically sizzled.

Scarlett could not do better than that boy.

And Ian needed some shaking up. He was too serious. Gave up too much of himself to others.

"You are plotting, Ruby Gallagher, don't you try to tell me you're not." Arnie glanced up the staircase, then murmured. "Best watch yourself, little girl. Your grandma has plans for you."

"I do not." Somehow she managed to keep her lips from twitching. "I would never force her to do anything she didn't want to do. Like as not she'll hightail it out of here, just like her mama."

"But you hope not."

She leaned into Arnie's side, her heart aching. "I do."

"She's awfully fond of you. Maybe she'll stay."

Ruby wanted to believe that. Scarlett needed family worse than anyone she had ever met.

Well, except maybe herself. "I love her so much my chest gets tight," she whispered.

He wrapped her up in his embrace. "Everything will work out, you'll see."

She leaned into him, this sweet, steady man who put up with so much from her. After waiting for Georgia in vain for so many years, she was trying her best not to get her hopes up.

But it didn't seem to matter to her old, stubborn heart.

Chapter Thirteen

S aturday, Scarlett kept expecting to see Ian all day, and she found herself making mistakes as she glanced up, again and again, whenever the front door opened.

"What's got you so jumpy?" Jeanette slapped down a plate. "You screwed up this order."

Scarlett didn't even try to argue. She was a professional, and she had to leave everything else behind. "I'm sorry. What was it supposed to be?"

"Hamburger, no onions, no cheese. Get it right this time, will you? Ruby deserves better." She walked off, nose in the air.

"She shouldn't talk to you that way," Brenda ventured. "You're saving Ruby's bacon, and you work as hard as anyone here. More so than her." The young woman jerked her head in Jeanette's direction.

For her to be speaking up at all was revolutionary. "But she's right. I made the mistake, and I know better." What had she been thinking, agreeing to meet Ian tomorrow? Making an appointment for sex, for heaven's sake? Nothing good could come of it.

"Brenda's right," Henry chimed in. "Jeanette should be thanking you. We'd all be out of a job if you hadn't stepped up. You're a really good cook," he said, cheeks flaring bright with color.

Scarlett cast aside thoughts of Ian and focused on them.

"Thank you. You know, Ruby needs backup. Do either of you want to learn to cook?" She tried not to think how concerned she was that her grandmother didn't seem to be improving very rapidly.

"I would," volunteered Brenda.

"Me, too," said Henry.

"Do you have any experience cooking at home?" Wherever that might have been.

"Not me," said Henry.

"I've cooked a little," Brenda responded.

"How about if we get together tomor—" Tomorrow would be simplest, and she could make her excuses to Ian, but both of them worked as many hours as she did and would no doubt like some time off. "—this afternoon," she corrected. "We'll do a trial run of the special tonight, then during halftime we can do more. We'll use whoever is in the cafe as our guinea pigs." She smiled. "Are you game?"

Both enthusiastically nodded.

"You don't want to take a break at halftime?" Henry asked.

In truth she would, so she could get a better look at the interior of the courthouse for an idea that had been percolating, but this need had to take precedence. "Ruby should have backup. This is more important."

"But you'll be here," Henry said.

She didn't try to argue. "This will give you more career options later on when you leave here."

Henry looked alarmed. "I'm not leaving. I like it here."

Brenda looked terrified.

"I don't mean you have to go, just…you never know what will happen in the future. It's always good to have contingency plans." *The way you do? What, exactly, are you planning to do next?*

"Look, you may not care about this place, but I do. What's the hold-up?" Jeanette complained.

Scarlett had been working while she was talking, so she took great enjoyment from shoving the new plate under Jeanette's nose. "I cooked new fries, as well. Take this off their check, and I'll make up the difference on the check and your tip, too." She stared right back at Jeanette, daring her to bitch again.

Brenda stood on one side of Scarlett, and Henry flanked her on the other.

Jeanette glanced between them as if about to order them back to work, but in the end, she only shook her head and turned away.

Scarlett almost felt sorry for her.

Instead she nodded at first Brenda, then Henry. "Thanks." She reached for the next ticket.

Scarlett didn't send anyone home at closing time this night. Even if Ian showed up, she'd decided she wasn't going to risk being alone with him. Yes, their date would be for just sex, just fun—but she felt it wise to reconsider. Ian was far too attractive in more ways than the physical, and the last thing she needed was one more reason to regret having to go.

She had to, it was that simple. None of these people deserved the trouble that could come their way if Kostov came looking for her.

And the DA might clap her in chains, anyway. She would have to call him next week to check in and find out if there was any progress toward scheduling the trial.

"Okay, that's everything," she said. "Great job, everyone. Enjoy your day off."

Brenda and Henry ranged beside her again as Jeanette gathered her things and left. When she was gone, Henry spoke. "I want to come in tomorrow and practice dicing the way you showed me. That was amazing."

To Scarlett's surprise, it was actually he who was the better cook, even with no experience. She vowed right then and there to buy him his own chef's knife. She'd caved to temptation and brought out her own, performing a little culinary wizardry with carrots and onions and celery.

But she didn't want Henry hurting himself with no one around, and she planned to spend her morning with Ruby.

The afternoon was supposed to be Ian's, but she'd heard not one word from him. "I can't be here with you. Could you wait and practice on Monday when things are slow?"

Henry's voice grew quiet. "I don't really have anything to do tomorrow."

Scarlett's shoulders sank. She wouldn't give up her time with her grandmother, but the excuse to cancel on Ian would be welcome.

"I'll come with him. We'll both practice," Brenda volunteered.

"I thought you wanted to go to the flower farm." He frowned.

"I can go there some other time." From the shy glances she was giving Henry, being with him had trumped flowers.

Scarlett hid her smile. "It's your free day to do whatever you wish with it."

"How about we fix our own breakfast over here?" he suggested to Brenda. "That's one more thing to practice. We won't have the biscuit recipe, but—"

"I'll give it to you. You'll need to cut it down drastically, though."

"I'm not so great at math," he admitted.

"I am," Brenda said shyly.

"Good," Scarlett responded. "Just come get me if you need help."

But the two of them were too busy smiling at each other.

Scarlett kept her own smile to herself. She gestured them

out the door and followed, making a quick detour to retrieve a photo album from her car's trunk.

Henry and Brenda had already gone inside when she started up the porch steps.

Ian rose from one of the chairs. "Sorry I couldn't make it earlier. Some problems came up with the livestock and one of the hands."

"Is everyone okay?"

"Yeah." But when he took a step toward her, his movements weren't as fluid as usual. "You sure?"

"Just had a bull shove me against the fence. You looking for an excuse to ditch me tomorrow?"

"It's not— I just—" She faced him. "You know I won't be here long."

"You could be."

"No, I can't."

"Because you hate this place the way your mama did?"

"You didn't know my mother. I don't know that she hated it."

"But you don't know that she didn't, either."

She shook her head. She didn't understand at all. "I know I don't hate it."

He stepped into her space. Tipped up her chin. "You might be happy here, even if it's not New York or Paris. You fit in better than I thought you would."

"I can fit in anywhere. I've had to all my life."

"I'm sorry for that. Everyone should belong somewhere, even if—"

"If what?"

"Sometimes you don't have a choice in where you belong."

The porch light didn't cast enough illumination to be sure, but she thought she saw wistfulness on his face. "Did you ever want to belong somewhere else, Ian?"

"Doesn't matter. I'm here." He straightened. "I'll be by to

163

pick you up at one o'clock."

This was her chance to back out. It was the wise choice.

But she so very much didn't want to.

Still, she'd better exercise some caution. "Just sex, right?" She tried to ignore how impersonal it felt to be making an appointment for sex.

"Anything wrong with having some fun, too?"

"Fun?" she echoed.

"Fun." Then he stepped closer and proceeded to give her a sample of his idea of fun.

Man, he could make her head spin.

"See you, New York," he said, brushing a last soft kiss over her tingling lips.

She barely resisted sighing out loud. She did stand there and watch until his lights were out of sight.

When she finally gathered herself to go inside, she was disappointed not to find her grandmother waiting.

But Nana's absence was equally a relief. Scarlett greatly feared she was wearing her confusion all over her face.

Chapter Fourteen

I an was up early, as always. On Sundays they kept the chores to a minimum, but farm animals couldn't read a calendar. He gave the hands the day off, though, and performed what needed to be done himself before he and his dad went to church.

But today would be different, he thought as he gathered eggs, milked the cow and checked the hay rings for the herd. After he and his dad took the easy way out and had sandwiches for lunch, he would head into town to pick up Scarlett. The day was cool but sunny, a perfect day to show her his refuge.

He'd packed a blanket, along with some wine and cheese and fruit. Maybe he couldn't cook worth beans, but he'd scrounged the time to drive to Fredericksburg yesterday and throw himself on the mercy of a friend with a vineyard and gift shop. Scarlett was probably used to fancier—no doubt was—but he wouldn't try to compete with all the men who'd wined and dined her in big cities.

Not that he could.

He frowned. Feeling nervous wasn't his style. He didn't like it one bit. Anyway, this was only sex, right? He did know how to make a woman happy in bed.

Though maybe not like those playboys she'd no doubt known.

Damn it. He was getting cold feet.

I wish you weren't so sexy. Abruptly he recalled her words.

Hey, he was the Hot Cowboy, after all. He snorted, then whistled to call Blue back from his dog chores. Somebody had to pee on every fence post and weed, didn't they? Blue pulled his weight even when he wasn't herding.

Ian glanced at his watch and discovered it was only twenty minutes past the last time he'd looked.

Blue bounded up, tail wagging.

"Women," Ian complained. "Be glad you're neutered, bud."

Blue's tongue was hanging out in adoration.

Ian crouched and gave him a good rub. "You have to stay with Dad this afternoon, pal. I'll make it up to you, promise."

Blue licked his jaw.

"Yeah. I'll miss you, too. Okay, not really." Ian grinned and ruffled his fur, then climbed back in the truck.

Scarlett woke up at four and grumbled at her body clock.

Then she turned over and fell back asleep.

At six the increasing light in her room did the trick, not truly daylight yet, but not night either.

She'd dreamed of Ian—torrid, aching dreams that had her restlessly imagining how their two bodies would be together.

He couldn't possibly look as great naked as she'd imagined him.

But she would be so much less, with her barely-there curves. Why couldn't she have been blessed with bountiful cleavage like her mother? Georgia Ross had been centerfold material. Men had salivated over her everywhere they went.

Scarlett looked like her kid brother.

Well, tough, Ian McLaren. If your eyes don't already tell you there's nothing there, then shame on you.

But he hadn't seemed disappointed when he'd had his

hands all over her.

And she did have nice legs. Long for her height, however pathetic a measuring stick that was. She shoved the covers back, disgusted with herself. If they hadn't so clinically made an appointment for sex...

But she didn't want romance, not even the illusion of it. There was no point. She grumped her way to the bathroom and showered, being careful to be as quiet as possible so Henry and Brenda could sleep in. Then she grabbed the photo album she'd retrieved from her trunk and headed downstairs.

At the bottom step, she halted in surprise.

Arnie turned. "Good morning, Scarlett. May I make you some breakfast?"

She glanced around.

"Your grandmother's still sleeping. The Judge and Mrs. Oldham, too." He smiled. "She won't be happy I'm still here."

He had the sweetest eyes, and his smile was infectious. "You don't like being her dirty little secret?"

"Maybe now that you're here to take over, she'll give in. I've tried to get her to ease up for years and let me take care of her. I'm not rich, but I've been careful with my money. We could travel, or she could just relax for a change." His face was filled with longing. "We can't know how much time we have left. She carries too heavy a burden. However, I'd be glad you were here even if you weren't such a wonderful cook. You've made her so happy, simply being here." He took one hand in his. "I know I'm not your blood grandfather, Scarlett, but I'd be proud to be an honorary one."

She felt like the lowest kind of scum. Why hadn't she thought harder before stopping here? She'd never even considered that other people besides her grandmother and herself would be affected by her decision to come. The mere notion of having a grandmother had been so surreal.

But others were indeed involved. How could she refuse this kind man's plea to help a woman she already adored?

Yet there was Kostov. He seemed less menacing now that she was here in Texas, but her nightmares reminded her that he was scary real.

"I'm sorry. You just woke up. Of course you wouldn't want—I understand why I can't be—"

"Oh, no!" She couldn't let him believe he was the one who came up short. "I can't think of anyone I'd rather have as a grandfather, Arnie." That, at least, was the truth. She'd grown fond of fixing his oatmeal and one egg every morning while chatting with him a little.

Even if she'd never suspected that he was her grandmother's lover. Her smile came naturally. *Go, Nana, indeed.*

Then the woman herself walked in. "What on earth are you doing still here?"

Arnie winked at Scarlett, unfazed. "Fixing breakfast for two beautiful ladies."

"Oh, you old goat. Now get on out of here. Scarlett, I don't know what he's told you—"

"Give it up, Nana." she chuckled. "I like Arnie. And the only shame here is that you're hiding him."

"Oh, see here—" Her grandmother blustered.

Scarlett deftly derailed her rant. "I have a photo album I thought you might like to see."

That did the trick. Soon they were ensconced at the table next to each other, poring over photos of Scarlett's life with her mother.

"She's not in many of these," Ruby pointed out.

"I'm sorry for that. She took most of them, and it was just the two of us."

Ruby traced Georgia's features in one photo, then turned to Scarlett, eyes suspiciously bright. "I hate that you two were alone. Your father really never…?"

"Mama said he was a six-week mistake, but she wasn't sorry because she got me out of the deal." Scarlett shrugged. "We had each other. It was enough." But she wondered all over again why her mother had chosen to leave everything familiar.

"Would you like to look through her drawings?"

"I would love that."

"Do we have time, Arnie?" Ruby asked.

"Take all the time you want, sweetheart."

Ruby's forehead creased as though she wanted to chide him for the term of endearment, and Scarlett couldn't stifle a grin.

But her grandmother didn't say anything as she led Scarlett out of the room.

"Should you be climbing stairs?"

"Now don't you start in on me. I have more than enough nursemaids around here." Ruby gestured for quiet since everyone upstairs was still sleeping, and she made her way to the door at the end of the hall that was always closed.

Inside was a wonderland that stole Scarlett's breath. "It looks like you kept everything."

"I did," Ruby said sadly.

Scarlett couldn't look around fast enough. Bookshelves filled with dolls and books she wanted to take down and read. A cork bulletin board loaded with notes and pictures torn from magazines. And the walls...

"She really had talent, didn't she?" On one wall was a sketch that was surely Ruby, only a much younger one. "You're beautiful, Nana."

"Not hardly. Maybe once, a little, but not now, for sure."

Scarlett tore her gaze away. "I think you are." Her eyes filled. "I wish I understood why she never told me about you. I'm so sorry, Nana," she whispered. "But I can't love her less. She only had me."

Stricken, she looked more closely at her grandmother. "But you didn't have anyone, did you?" The knowledge broke something inside her.

"Don't you worry about me, child. I was fine. I was

home." Suddenly, Ruby's composure cracked. She grabbed Scarlett and held her close, her frail body shaking. "I lost my child," she whispered. "And I will never stop missing her, but oh—" She hugged Scarlett hard. "If I couldn't be with her, I am so eternally happy she had you." She pulled back and framed Scarlett's face in her hands. "I would have waited longer than this for the joy of knowing you at last—but thank heaven I didn't have to." Tears spilled over her weathered cheeks. "I am so grateful you're here."

Scarlett already felt horribly guilty and conflicted, but now...

She desperately wanted to explain, but how could she? She thought she knew this woman well enough now to understand that Nana would insist that they tackle Scarlett's past head-on.

And trouble would follow her to Texas.

To these people she already cared about too much.

So she kept quiet.

And hugged her grandmother harder.

Ian had showed up promptly at one, and loaded her into his pickup.

"So...Arnie stayed around," he noted.

Her nerves steadied a little. "He cooked me breakfast."

Ian's eyebrows rose. "And what did Ruby do to him?"

"Chewed him out until I told her it was foolish to hide him. She blustered a little, but she didn't make him go."

"Well, well, well, Miz Scarlett. You have effected a sea change in this town. First we don't have catfish on Friday, and now Arnie's out of the closet."

Fresh on the heels of the clear evidence that her grandmother would be crushed if she left, his remark stung. "It would have been better if I'd never come."

His head whipped around. "Why?"

"Because—"

"You can't stay," he completed the sentence for her. "Explain why not."

"Because I have a life," she snapped. "Places to go. People to see."

He stared out the windshield. "Like Paris."

"Exactly." She braced for him to argue.

"What was it like?"

Was that wistfulness in his voice? A rancher wanted to go to France? "It was…amazing. So much to see that I'd only read about in books—of course, I mostly was working, but every chance I got, I explored."

"The Louvre? Did you make it there?"

Now she really was astonished. A cowboy longed to see the Louvre. "I did. It takes days to cover even a fraction of what's there."

"I don't know a lot about art, but I always wondered what something like the Mona Lisa looks like in the flesh." He shrugged. "Not that a country boy would fit in over there."

She studied him now. "The French aren't as unfriendly as is rumored." she grinned. "And they would be all over you, cowboy. Texas possesses a powerful charisma in so many places."

He snorted. "No idea why." He glanced into the distance. "I always wanted to see where my ancestors came from."

McLaren. "Scottish?"

He nodded. "To the bone. A lot of Scots came to America after Culloden. The British left nothing for them. It was emigrate or starve." Another shrug. "It was lucky for my family that my great-great-great-granddad made his way here in time to fight in the Texas Revolution. That's how we got our land—a land grant for veterans."

"Revolution against what?"

He turned a shocked gaze on her. "And you with roots as deep as mine here. Don't know your Texas history?"

"Never in my life did I once consider coming to Texas. I didn't even know my mother was born here."

"Wow. When Georgia left, she left all the way."

"Do you understand why?"

"Sorry. I really don't. Nobody talked about her much when I was growing up, out of respect for Ruby, I guess. Oh, I grew up knowing she'd had a child who'd left, but…" A lift of the shoulder. "Kids don't pay much attention to that stuff. You really had no idea about Ruby or Sweetgrass?"

"Not until two weeks ago. When my mother died, it was such a shock and I felt so lost, I just boxed up her things without looking through anything." She glanced over. "There were four founding families, right?"

"Right. McLarens, Gallaghers, Butlers and Pattons. Four veterans with adjoining parcels. Each family donated land at the intersection to create the town."

"Where is the Gallagher land?"

He pointed off to the left. "Starts just up the road and goes west."

She stared in the direction he'd indicated, wondering if she could get a tour.

Just then he started to turn. "Here's our place, the Double Bar M." They began winding down a caliche road.

Scarlett observed eagerly. Live oak trees dotted the pastures, but most of what she saw was open. On the left side of the truck, she spotted more cattle than she'd ever seen in her life. And horses.

She'd always wished for a horse. "Are all these yours?"

He nodded. "This isn't the best part of the state for cattle because much of the terrain is hilly and the soil is thin, but we have an advantage in this valley. We have our own spring plus a section of river cutting through our land. We also have deeper soil that's been improved by every generation."

"You can improve soil? What, with dirt lessons?"

He burst out laughing, and his already handsome face was transformed by the broad smile.

Oh, she so did not need to be noticing that. "No dirt lessons, huh?"

"I could explain how it works, but I'm not sure that's the most stimulating conversation we could be having." He placed his hand on hers.

The heat of his skin made her fingers curl. Sex. They had an appointment for sex.

When had sex last made her nervous?

He laced their fingers together. "Relax, New York. I don't bite, and I gave up sacrificing virgins a long time ago. Your virtue is safe, if that's what you want. We're just having a picnic."

She squeezed his hand. "I'm not scared."

One eyebrow arched. He drew her hand up to his mouth and pressed a kiss to the back of it.

Then he turned their hands over and swirled his tongue in her palm.

Sensual lightning arced through her body. "That is so not fair," she said more breathlessly than she'd intended.

His single dimple flashed. "It wasn't meant to be." He held her hand to the front of his jeans. "You're killing me, honey. I'm holding on by my fingernails." His eyes were warm and teasing.

Her hands itched to roam that big, hard body.

He exhaled. "You keep looking at me like that, and we'll never make it."

She raked her gaze over him. "I don't care."

"Now who's unfair?" He laid her hand back in her lap and gripped the steering wheel with both hands. "I have someplace special I want to show you, but I promised my dad we'd stop by the house first so he could say hi."

Right. She was supposed to be a cordial visitor when she

desperately wanted to get this man naked. She inhaled. Straightened in her seat. "Okay."

"I don't want to stop either, but my dad really likes you. I promise we won't take long."

"I like your dad, too."

He turned off into a grove of trees, and the road climbed a little. She spotted barns and pens and various pieces of equipment she had no idea how to use. "You have a lot of…stuff."

He chuckled. "Next time I'll show you around the place and name everything."

"Next time?"

He looked at her very seriously. "I know you won't be around long, but while you are, I'd like to see more of you."

"You're such a gentleman." So different from the edgy, competitive men she was accustomed to, so brittle and concerned about trends, always grasping for an advantage. "But this is—"

"Just sex. So you say. But we can be friends, too, right? Any reason not to?"

Because you're too attractive in more ways than the physical? Because knowing you better will only make leaving harder?

She shrugged. "I guess not."

He'd stopped the car in front of the house but didn't move to get out. "What the hell kind of men have you been around? Somebody needs to be better to you."

Absurdly touched, she pulled the door handle and made her escape.

Then she finally focused on his place. "This is…amazing."

"In a good way?"

A very good way. The house looked so…solid. So much like…home. A real home. It was two stories and built of rock weathered by time. The wood trim was faded to silver, a foil for the mixture of aged gray and brown stone. "I've never seen anyplace like it. It...fits." She glanced around her. "As though it's a piece of the hillside." Behind the house, a short distance away, the hill rose. When she revolved to put her back to the house, the vista stunned her. "Oh." Her mouth wouldn't quite close. "Oh, Ian..."

He came to stand beside her. "The view is better on top of the hill, but there's a spring over there. The house was put here because of it."

"You use water from a spring?"

"Not as much anymore. My grandfather dug a well, and my dad improved on it. The spring helps water the stock, though, as does the river."

"River?"

He pointed off to the east, and she caught the glitter of light on water. "This place is gorgeous, Ian."

She couldn't quite read his look. "It's home. Everything is old, but there's history here."

History. Something she could barely imagine possessing.

And you with roots as deep as mine here.

But they weren't. She had been transplanted, again and again. She felt like she'd been merely surviving for a long time, nothing more. She envied him this place. He'd never doubted where home was.

But before she could respond, his father came out on the porch. "Son, I raised you with better manners. You ever gonna invite that girl inside?"

Ian's face revealed his conflict.

She felt the same way. She did like his dad a lot, but... The afternoon was young, she reminded herself. "Hi, Mr. McLaren."

His face creased in a broad smile. "Nice to see you out in the fresh air, young lady. Come on inside, but I won't keep you two long. Ian planned a picnic—don't worry, though. I promise you he didn't cook."

She grinned, but she noticed that he looked lonely. Eager

175

for the company. "We're in no rush, are we, Ian?"

His eyes were hot on her. "Speak for yourself," he muttered.

She locked gazes with him and smiled her understanding.

He sighed. "On our way, Dad."

She looked good in this house, surprisingly so. None of the furniture was new, and the wood floors were scarred by time and many pairs of boots. The rugs were worn. There wasn't one shiny thing in this whole house.

Except her. She shone bright as a beacon, laughing and chatting with his dad as he showed her around.

"Wow," she said, "A lot of books. Yours?" she asked his father as she studied the shelves.

"Nope. Mostly Ian's. Boy has a fascination for learning."

She gave him a quick glance, but Ian couldn't read it. He had the crazy urge to shuffle his feet.

"A lot of reference books. History…geography," she noted. "Don't you have internet access out here?"

"I like books," Ian muttered.

"Yes, we have internet access," his dad replied. "Off and on. Not that I'm much good at using it, but Ian researches stocks and keeps up on all the latest trends in ranching."

"Stocks?" Her eyebrows rose.

"Boy's got a head for figures, so he started trying his hand at investing. Done good so far."

Not good enough to do more than buy time, though, Dad. Especially not if you won't change your tune. "Anyone can get lucky."

"I've had a lot of Wall Street traders eat at my last restaurant. I'm not sure they'd agree."

He shrugged and turned away. "Want some water or something?"

"I'd love to see the kitchen. Let me come with you."

"It's just a kitchen."

"I'll be the judge of—oh! Oh, will you look at that? A wood cook stove!"

He and his dad exchanged puzzled glances.

"Can't you just see her here, the woman who cooked in this kitchen a century or so ago?"

For the first time since his mother abandoned them, Ian looked at the room without seeing only the disuse, the emptiness of a family fractured. "My grandmother rolled out pie crusts there—" He pointed to a section of countertop with an inset of marble.

Scarlett's mouth literally dropped open. She crossed to the counter, her hand hovering over the slab. She glanced back. "May I?"

"May you what?"

"Touch it?" Her tone was filled with reverence.

"Of course," his dad said. "It hasn't been used since my mother passed."

Her hand stroked the slab, her fingers trailing over the top. "I would love to bake a pie here," she said so low Ian wondered if they were meant to hear. Her head rose. "You wouldn't happen to have her rolling pin, I guess."

"Probably. Somewhere. We don't get rid of much." A lot of what was in this kitchen had long lain unused, but memories were returning as he opened the drawers beneath the section of counter where she was standing. In one of them, he found what he was looking for, his grandmother's old rolling pin with its painted red handles, the wood darkened with time and countless uses.

He held it out, and you would have thought he was handing Scarlett the crown jewels.

"Oh." She bit her lower lip. "Oh, this is amazing. I wonder how old it is?"

"Older than me," his dad said.

Ian had never thought to woo a woman with ancient cooking utensils, but the rapture on her features told him to go for it. "Here." He opened one of the cabinets above and pulled out a big white pottery bowl, then fished in another drawer for a set of old, dented measuring cups with small rounded handles.

"Ian, this is amazing." Scarlett ran her hands over every last piece.

"She had a drawer especially for flour." He reached around her and opened the handle to the right of her, showing her a bin lined with metal.

Her smile was bright as the sun and her eyes were glittering when she looked at him. She clutched the pottery bowl to her like a baby. "Ian, I know you have a picnic ready, but afterward would you let me cook here? Please?"

He goggled. "You want to cook here? In this old place?"

"I do. I want to make bread. Do you have any flour?"

"Some. I think."

"But not yeast, I bet."

"Um…"

"Never mind." He could see her brain firing. "I'll get ingredients from the cafe and pay Nana back. Is that okay, Mr. McLaren?"

"Do I look stupid? And call me Gordon." His dad's face was alight. "We'd be honored, wouldn't we, son?" Then he frowned. "But it's your only day off."

"I love to cook, and this kitchen…may I look around to see what supplies there are?"

"Knock yourself out," Ian said, trying not to mind that his plans for the afternoon were evaporating before his eyes.

But she looked so damn happy.

And his dad's face bore more hope than he'd seen there in a long time.

This kitchen had been used with love by four generations of women until his mother had snapped the links of the chain.

Now another woman would treat the space with affection. Use it as it was meant to be.

Things were not going to be simple with Scarlett Ross.

And she was going to break his heart. He might as well get used to that.

Still, he wondered if she would enjoy this kitchen enough that, along with her growing bond with Ruby, she might find reason to stay.

"Okay," she said after poring through cabinets and drawers. "I know what I need." She approached and held out her hand to him. "Let's go have a picnic."

Hallelujah.

He didn't fool around and give her time to change her mind.

They drove across his land in silence. With every yard they traveled, she began to see a different man than the sexy cowboy she'd first met, different even than the man others looked to for solving problems. Ian McLaren was those things, but he was more. When they stopped the pickup and emerged, Ian carried the picnic basket and two blankets tossed over his shoulder, every step proclaiming his connection to this land. He belonged here, was solidly grounded in this earth and sky and hills.

But there were all those books, all those windows into other places. He'd wanted to see the Louvre. The Mona Lisa.

Who was this man? The more she learned of him, the more she was confused.

And fascinated.

And fearful.

He, like her grandmother, would not be easy to leave.

But how could she possibly stay and not—at a minimum—expose them to embarrassment, if not outright danger?

She desperately wished the DA could make the case without her testimony and leave her to go on with her life. Still, though, she would have to be honest with these people, and she wasn't proud of how she'd been so ambitious and blind and foolish, so focused on gaining acclaim as a chef that she missed all the signs.

She sure wasn't proud of the pictures in the paper of her in handcuffs.

But it could get so much worse. If she went back and testified, would Kostov's men haunt her forever? The DA had once mentioned the witness protection program, and at the time, it had seemed like a good idea.

But when you went into witness protection, you had to cut all ties. Forever.

She had ties now.

She should cut them. Leave immediately and spare these people—

"Regretting your impulse?" Ian asked. "You don't really have to cook for us tonight." His brows snapped together. "You work too hard already. You should rest."

Incomprehensibly, his pique made her cheerful. "If you think you can retract your permission for me to cook in that wonderful old kitchen, you better think again."

He looked back at her and shook his head. "You are insane."

"Will you ever be able to travel?" She couldn't get those books off her mind.

"What?"

She drew up beside him. "No one has that many books about other places and doesn't want to see some of them in the flesh."

"Not gonna happen." He shook his head brusquely and reached for her, pulling her up the last incline. "We're here."

She halted beside him and looked around. "Oh, Ian…it's beautiful." A small clearing, with one side open to the view, a well-used fire pit at the center of it, nestled in the midst of live oaks. "Did you come here as a kid?"

"As often as I could. There wasn't a lot of time, between chores and school."

"I heard you were the quarterback. The Four Horsemen. You were good, Ruby says."

He shrugged. "That was a long time ago."

"Did you ever want to play at a professional level?"

"That wasn't in the game plan. I played for awhile at Tech. Football paid for my education."

"You were the college quarterback? Did you date a cheerleader? Or the homecoming queen?"

Color rose on his cheeks.

"You did!" She grinned. "I want to see pictures of you in your pads and those tight football pants. I bet you were hot then, too."

He waved off her compliments and concentrated on spreading one of the blankets. "How about some wine?" He opened the basket and drew out a bottle. "Red okay? I'm not much of a wine guy, but at the winery they said this was a good one."

She was incredibly touched that he had gone to the trouble she could see as he brought out bread and cheeses and fruit. "Where did you get all of this?"

"Fredricksburg." He squirmed. "A buddy of mine from school owns a winery there. I threw myself on his mercy."

"You did all this for me?"

"You'd prefer a baloney sandwich?"

She laughed. "Not really."

"Then just drink. And eat."

His discomfort was absolutely charming. "You did all this yesterday, on top of getting smacked against a fence by a bull."

"So?"

Oh, she was in so much trouble… She accepted the glass of wine from him abut remained on her knees, brushing her lips over his cheek. "Thank you. I feel terrible that you went to so much effort, but I'm also impressed."

"Yeah?" Then he caught her mouth with his.

The kiss quickly turned so carnal that she nearly dropped her glass.

He took it from her hand and set it aside, safely nestled in a corner of the basket. "Taste the wine from me instead." He took a sip of his own, then put his glass aside.

Then he kissed her again. Dragged her body over his and began to ply his hands over her body.

Oh. She'd been so worried that things would feel stilted, but—

"Stop thinking," he growled. "Kiss me back."

Gladly. Suddenly it was all too easy to get back to that place where she thought she would die if she didn't get her hands on him.

And he was right there in front of her, within easy reach. She yanked his shirttails out of his jeans, thanking her lucky stars that it was January in Central Texas, not New York. The air was crisp, but they'd just have to get closer, wouldn't they?

And then she was done with thinking.

Those big, strong hands cruised over her body with a skill that left her breathless, she who'd thought herself the sophisticate and him the rube.

"If you stop, I'll kill you," she managed, and rose to straddle his lap.

"Not on your life." He backed up his words with action, skimming his hands up her side and pulling off her shirt and jacket together.

She worked at the buttons of his flannel shirt, muttering as she fumbled.

"Here—" He skinned the whole thing off over his head.

Beneath he wore a plain white t-shirt.

And about an acre of muscles. "Gimme," she said, and pulled at that garment, too, until his chest was bared. "Oh, my…" It was all she could do not to rake her nails over his chest. It was broad and lean and muscled, but not the gym muscles she was accustomed to.

This was a working man. A real man, the way God intended. She closed her eyes and bit her bottom lip.

Then she spotted his bruised side. "Oh!"

"It's nothing–" He gasped when she pressed her lips to the bruise

She could swear that strong body trembled, just a little. She smiled. "My mother used to say kisses make anything better."

"I'm healed already." He grinned, but his eyes scorched her.

She could swear her heart fluttered. Her insides melted like butter.

Before she could get too fanciful, she bent again. Swiped her tongue over his chest and up the strong column of his neck.

"Sweet mother of—"

Abruptly she was on her back on the blanket, endless blue sky overhead. He fastened his teeth to one of her nipples, and she yelped.

"Sorry—I didn't—" He halted. "You're so delicate. I don't want to hurt you."

She reared up and took his mouth with hers. "You didn't. Don't you dare stop. I could eat you alive."

He laughed. "Not if I devour you first." He unzipped her jeans and drew them down her legs, nibbling his way as he went. He seemed to catch every sensitive spot she possessed as he cruised his way back up.

Then he drew her panties off with his teeth.

She nearly swooned.

Then his eyes widened. "You have a tattoo." He grinned at her.

A youthful indiscretion. "It's a tasteful one," she protested. Well, sort of.

"Betty Boop." He winked. "I always thought she was kinda hot."

"Of course you did. Don't laugh at me."

"Oh, darlin', I'm definitely not laughing." He bent and swirled his tongue over the image, ending with a kiss that felt like a benediction.

She couldn't seem to get her footing with him.

Then his tongue traveled to more intimate places.

She gasped. Dug her fingers into his hair.

After that, it was all heat and need and speed, as they took one another to the brink and beyond.

She'd made love outside before, but it had never been remotely like this.

Nothing had ever been like this.

He nipped and suckled, licked soft, slow stripes over her skin. Pressed intimate kisses to her core, then used his tongue and teeth to devastating effect over tender tissues crying out for him to let her fly over the edge.

But he was taking his time, heat and need notwithstanding.

Then he switched the pace. Made her scream.

And she flew. Collapsed, melting in the aftermath. Wanted him inside her in the worst way.

Instead he started all over again, building a fire that was quickly consuming her.

She shoved at his shoulder, caught him off guard and tumbled him to his back. "My turn," she said, and began working her way over his body, nipping at his hip, licking his navel, dancing her tongue down his happy trail to—

"No. Scarlett, don't. I'm too close—"

She took him into her mouth, and he groaned from deep

in his belly. She tormented them both for precious seconds—

Abruptly she was picked up by her waist.

Lifted clean off the ground.

God, he was so strong. So freaking gorgeous.

He slid her down over him with agonizing slowness...

She couldn't help moaning aloud as she took him in.

His laugh was shaky. "Yeah. Me, too."

She opened her eyes and looked into his beautiful brown ones.

For a moment they were both suspended on the edge of something she couldn't name.

"You are so beautiful," he said.

And then he lifted her and settled her again, until she took over the rhythm. She rode him until need was screaming through her—

Then found herself on her back once more with his powerful frame over her as he sent them both soaring.

They napped in the sunshine beneath the second blanket he commended himself on thinking to bring. When he awoke, she was cuddled in his arms.

And she felt exactly right there. Ian stared around him at this place that had always been special to him, but never this special before.

Could he figure out a way to keep her?

Did he want to?

Hell, yeah, he did. But that wasn't the problem.

He had to find out why she was so intent on leaving.

Then she stirred in his arms and opened her eyes. Smiled up at him. "Wow." She pressed a kiss to his chest and opened her mouth on his nipple.

The whys and the hows would just have to wait.

They made love again, more slowly this time, but more playfully as well. She drizzled wine over his chest and sipped it from his navel.

He painted her body with wine and suckled every drop.

You know this is special, he thought. *You have to.*

Her eyes said she did.

He wouldn't risk screwing this up with words.

Instead he took her mouth with his and told her with his body everything he didn't think she would want to hear.

Afterward, they devoured every bite he'd brought.

She was surprised that the kitchen was clean, and she smiled ruefully at herself. Just because two guys lived here didn't mean she should assume they couldn't clean up after themselves.

Hadn't she learned that Ian McLaren was a man of purpose who managed to accomplish whatever he intended? Hadn't she just gone on a picnic with him even though she'd meant as recently as this morning to find a way out of it?

And oh, what a picnic it had been. A delicious shiver trembled through her body. He was an extraordinary lover. Built, yes, mouthwateringly so, but even if he hadn't been such eye candy, he took care of her…in so many ways. Satisfied her, yes. Made her scream. She bit her lip to stifle the grin that kept wanting to pop out.

"What can I do to help?" said that very voice, the one that seemed to resonate inside her as no other had.

"I've got it under control. Why don't you go relax with your dad?"

"I can hang with my dad anytime." His voice was a deep burr that abraded her nerves like velvet on tender flesh.

She couldn't resist glancing up, only to see his gaze hot on hers.

"Why would I want to be anywhere else but here? For once I don't have to share you with the whole blasted town." He grinned, but his eyes were dark and serious.

"Don't look at me that way."

"What way? Like I could devour you in one bite?" His dimple popped. "If I weren't so hungry I'd drag you off and do exactly that."

"What about your dad? And how can you be hungry again? You ate every crumb of your picnic share and half of mine."

"I just did chores. I worked up an appetite again." His gaze locked on hers, then dropped to her mouth. "Or maybe I'm just hungry for this." He lowered his head and took her mouth in a sweet, spicy-hot kiss.

"You're getting in the way of my cooking," she murmured, but couldn't resist grabbing a kiss of her own.

He drew her into his arms and slid one hand into her hair, cradling her head close while he brought their bodies together.

Clearly he was hungry for more than food.

She was, too.

"Okay for me to—" His dad halted at the door. "Sorry."

Scarlett broke away. Was she blushing? "Please don't be. Your son is distracting me."

"Maybe you should put both of us to work," his dad said. "What can we do to help?"

Scarlett was torn between a wish to commune with this kitchen in private and the desire to know them better. *You shouldn't. It's not wise.* No, it wasn't. But this was their kitchen, wasn't it? "You said you had more red wine."

"I do. Want a glass?" Ian answered

"I would because it was wonderful, but no—I want to make this beef dish from a little bistro on the Left Bank."

Ian's eyes lit. "Glad I bought a couple of extra bottles while I was there."

She smiled. "Me, too."

"I'll just go get it."

"You using beef from the cafe?" his dad asked.

"Ian said you have plenty here."

"Sure do. What cut do you need? You won't find better than Double Bar M beef. Ian's got some he raised organic." His brows drew together. "Had to set aside a whole blasted pasture to meet the requirements."

"You wouldn't have to go slaughter the cow right now if I said yes?"

Gordon chuckled. "No, ma'am. Got a freezer full right there. You'd have to thaw it, but we have a microwave."

"I would love that. Is it marked? Should—would you rather get it out?"

"You make yourself right at home, little girl. *Mi casa es su casa.*"

"Thank you." She went to the freezer and picked out what she wanted. On her return, she first stopped at the wood cook stove that she'd spotted earlier. "You never use this?"

"Naw. Many a meal has been prepared there, and my mom used it all the time, but my wife—" He shook his head. "She only wanted the new."

Ian had still not returned, and Scarlett itched to know more about this mysterious woman. "Where was she from, if you don't mind my asking?"

"I don't. I met her when I was in the service. She was from San Francisco. Should have left her where I found her. She'd have been happier." He grimaced. "But I wouldn't have Ian. Boy's the light of my life."

"It must have been hard, raising him alone." She smiled. "I hear he was a handful."

Gordon laughed. "There were days when I swear I coulda worn a belt out on his behind and never made a dent in his determination. Boy always did know what he wanted, and those other three…" He chuckled. "I took him out on the range with me every day until he started school. Life was busy, but I wouldn't trade for a second of it."

"He seems to have turned out very well, Mr. McLaren. You did a good job of raising him."

"Told you to call me Gordon, and yes, he's a very good man. I worry about him, though. Boy's got too much on his shoulders, and I'm not worth a damn to help anymore." He looked off into the distance, his expression sorrowful.

"I bet he'd say that you already did a lifetime's worth of shouldering the load."

Gordon lifted a shoulder. "Weight gets heavier on him all the time." He glanced over, eyes eagle-sharp. "Don't make it harder on him, Scarlett. You're not interested, I'm gonna ask you to back away. You might be eager to leave this place like your mama was, and that's your privilege—but I don't want my boy being left with a hollow chest the way I was."

She wanted to feel indignant, but the clear love for his son trumped that. "He's a wonderful man, Mr—Gordon. I just...things are complicated."

"Life is complicated, but I've always found that some plain talking fixes most anything." In his eyes was a warning.

Hadn't she tried to keep herself apart from Ian until today? Didn't she know getting involved was wrong?

But there was something about him that she just could not resist. "I don't want to hurt anyone, Gordon. I never expected to find so much to care about here."

They both heard Ian's footsteps on the wood floors.

With one last exchange of glances, they dropped the subject.

"I brought you a present," Ian said. "Fresh cream and butter from our Jersey."

She pressed a hand to her chest. "I swear my heart just skipped a beat."

They both laughed.

"I'm serious. I have never had a chance to cook right at

the source of the ingredients. I tried in my restaurant to have everything as fresh as possible, but still it had been trucked in. I would dearly love to have a place where I could cook with solely local ingredients."

Ian was watching her with a look she could only classify as fond. "So you can do something with these?"

"Are you kidding? Just you watch me." She opened the package of meat. "This beef is beautifully marbled."

"It's Brangus, a cross-breed of Brahma and our Angus bull. Brahmas can tolerate the heat, and Angus marbles well. I'd like to take the whole operation organic."

"Too damn expensive," his dad said.

"There's a market for it, Mr.—uh, Gordon. Maybe not here in Sweetgrass, but I bet you money there are high-end restaurants in Austin or San Antonio that would jump all over it. Grocery stores, too. People care a lot about what goes into their food these days, and cities provide customers who can afford it."

She didn't miss the look Ian cast his father.

"Nothing wrong with the old ways," his dad grumbled.

"There's room for both," she said. "But Ian is onto something." It wasn't her business.

Two hours later, the place smelled like pure heaven. Bread was baking, and whatever that French dish was had an aroma that made Ian's mouth water. At Scarlett's request, he'd invited Ruby and Arnie, Brenda and Henry out to share in the bounty. The Judge and Mrs. Oldham had already been settled in for the night, but he'd promised them leftovers—if there were any, given how amazing this stuff smelled.

Scarlett had asked him to make a salad while she whipped up a fresh dressing out of thin air, it seemed. "You have a recipe in your head for that?"

She glanced up. "No, I've never made this particular dressing before. I'm used to having an array of fresh herbs to work with, so I'm inventing with what I could find."

He shook his head in amazement. "You really know your way around a kitchen, don't you?"

She performed a little curtsey. "I do indeed, sir." She looked over toward the wood stove. "I bet the bread would be even better if I knew how to use that."

"Dad might remember some. Ruby would probably know, too. You're welcome to try it anytime, though it doesn't feel fair to have you over and make you work."

"I asked, remember?" Her eyes sparkled. "This is a wonderful kitchen. I know you'll think I'm crazy, but I swear I can feel the women who used it. I've never been in a space with so much soul to it."

She surprised a laugh from him. "A kitchen with soul."

"Don't scoff, unbeliever. You don't understand kitchens the way I do. You don't like being in here, so it doesn't do its magic for you."

"You think those pioneer women felt magic here?" He shook his head. "New York, their lives were about as hard as it gets. They weren't in here having fun."

"I know that. Or I guess I would if I'd ever given a second's thought to what a woman's life was like on the frontier. But still, when you cook with love, there's a kind of magic to it that seeps into the walls. If these walls could talk…"

His face closed down. "Not all the stories would be good."

She touched his arm. "You don't know that she didn't love you, Ian."

His jaw flexed. "She left me, that's what I know. Never looked back." He shook his head. "But she's nothing to me. I never spare her a thought."

He was wrong, she thought. The loss of his mother had

marked him for good.

Just then laughter erupted in the living room.

He glanced back, and his frame relaxed. "You've brought this house back to life. Dad and I just rattle around here."

"I like feeding people."

"You couldn't be more like Ruby if she'd raised you."

"Thank you. That's a real compliment."

"You don't have to go, you know." Damn it, why had he said that? She was tensing before his eyes.

She turned away. "It's just about ready. Want to help me put out the food?"

"Scarlett…" He stopped her. Turned her toward him. "Some day you're going to explain to me what's troubling you. How can I fix it if I don't know what's wrong?"

"Oh, Ian…" She traced her fingertips over his jaw. "You don't have to fix everything." Her gaze slid away. "And sometimes things are beyond repair."

"You can still talk to me. Tell me what's bothering you."

"How about you start by telling me how losing your mom really makes you feel?"

"I already told you. I don't feel anything."

"Yeah. Sure thing." Her disappointment was clear. Damn it, he didn't want to talk about his mother. Ever.

Then she drew a deep breath and turned to her work. "I still can't believe you brought me fresh churned butter. I'm more excited by that than anything else, I do believe—though the organic beef is a close second."

All he'd done was go to the woman down the road who churned butter in exchange for milk from his Jersey. "You'd think I'd given you diamonds."

"Oh, no. I don't care a whit about diamonds, but fresh cream and butter…" She rose to her toes and gave him a quick kiss. "Now that's a present." She danced away to stir her fancy French dish.

His hands itched to draw her back.

"Little girl," Gordon said, patting his belly, "I am stuffed tighter than a tick. I do believe that was the best meal this ole boy has ever eaten."

"Here's to Paris, France," said Henry, raising his glass of fresh milk.

Fresh milk, straight from the cow. She still couldn't get over the bounty they took for granted.

"Hear, hear," chimed in Arnie.

"Sweetheart, you have left me in the dust," Ruby declared. "But you have got to show me how you did that. I would have been glad to help."

"No way," Scarlett said. "How many times has anyone cooked for you in your life? Not enough, I would imagine. I was happy to do so."

Ian said nothing, but his gaze was fixed on her, his expression one she couldn't read.

"What was that dessert?" Brenda asked.

Scarlett was grateful for the rescue from the dark gaze that drew her again and again. "It's a cousin of what's called a trifle, a very old dish, eighteenth century British. When I learned I could have fresh cream to work with, I just made a quick sponge cake for the base. Nana had peaches in the freezer and Gordon generously donated some brandy. I whipped up what's called a syllabub with the cream, some sugar and a few spices…simple."

"Not simple to produce heaven on a spoon in an unfamiliar kitchen," her grandmother argued. "You have the touch, Scarlett."

"Magic in the kitchen," Ian murmured from beside her.

She cast him a quick glance steeped in memory and smiled. "Thank you." Then she looked at Gordon and her grandmother. "Speaking of unfamiliar kitchens, do either of you know how to use a wood cook stove?"

"That old thing is probably rusted inside," Gordon said.

"I remember some," Ruby offered. "My grandmother cooked on one. Your mom did, too, right, Gordon? Why do you ask?"

"I am dying to try it. Ian said I could, but neither of us has ever used one. I'm thinking it might be comparable to a brick oven for bread, but I'm curious to see what I could do with it."

Abruptly she subsided. She couldn't be here long enough to make use of it. What was she thinking? "Never mind." She rose. "Time to clean up and head for bed."

"You are not cleaning that kitchen. You've already worked far too hard on your only day off. Sit." Ian picked up her plate and his. "I've got this."

"But—"

"We can all pitch in," said her grandmother. "You go put your feet up."

"Nana…"

But none of them would hear a word otherwise. "Go with her, Dad," Ian suggested. "Keep her out of the kitchen."

She was summarily shuffled off to the living room with Gordon, but soon Ruby and Arnie followed.

"We've been ejected," Arnie said. "Anyway, your grandma should get home to bed. We can take you with us."

She cast a glance toward the kitchen, where Ian and Henry and Brenda were working and talking, laughing now and again.

She wanted to linger, to ride home with Ian.

Which was exactly why she shouldn't.

Don't break his heart.

What about her own?

"How will Brenda and Henry get back?"

"Ian can take them." His dad studied her. "But you are welcome to wait here and go with him, too."

If Henry and Brenda were with them, they would provide a barrier to any meaningful conversation. Or any other activities.

Which was probably just as well.

"I'd appreciate the ride," she told Arnie. She turned to Ian's dad. "Will you tell Ian goodbye for me?"

His dad looked at her knowingly. "If you're sure that's what you want."

She had no idea what she wanted, except too much she couldn't have. "Thank you."

As they made their way to the door, she saw Ian glance her way. She tried for a jaunty wave even as her heart squeezed.

No. She couldn't do this. If nothing else, it was rude. "Excuse me." She made her way to the kitchen, seeing nothing but his dark eyes. "My grandmother needs to go home. I'd still be glad to stay and help clean up."

He didn't say a word as Henry and Brenda faithfully repeated their insistence that she take it easy. He remained across the room, and she felt an aching sense of loss. One more embrace, even a slight hug...

"Thank you, Ian. Thank you for...everything." She bit the inside of her cheek to stem the ache of unshed tears. "I'll...see you at the cafe, I guess."

He only stared impassively. "Sure." He turned away.

They needed distance, she reminded herself. He wasn't sharing his feelings with her, either. This was how it had to be.

How can I fix it if you won't tell me? He already took on too many burdens, and hers seemed unfixable.

She turned to go before she broke down. At the door, she gave his dad a wordless hug.

"You take care now, little girl," Gordon said.

She held onto him for a little longer, his frame an older version of his son's powerful one.

She would never see Ian as an old man, she realized. Grief pierced her to the bone.

"I'm sorry," she whispered.

And she fled.

Chapter Fifteen

Monday started out busier than ever. Scarlett knew she'd have to stay late that night to begin preparing foods to take to the workday, since the activity was nonstop during the hours the cafe was open.

But that was okay. She would have time alone, which she desperately needed. She had a lot to think about after she'd taken a quick break and called the DA when his office opened.

He'd been icy at first, then he'd threatened and blustered about how she needed to get back in her car and return immediately.

She'd told him about Kostov's men but refused to say where she was.

"I can have you tracked down, you know. You need to be in protective custody."

"I'm needed where I am. I'll—" She'd swallowed hard. "I'll come back when you need me."

"You have to agree to call me once a week," he'd insisted. "Miss one time, and I'll have the US Marshals after you. No one can hide for long."

So she'd gone back to work, more unsettled than ever. She was grateful for the work that consumed her attention, but she equally felt the need to get away, to plan her next destination. There seemed no question she would have to go—and soon.

She wouldn't wait for Ian, hoping he'd make a late night stop. He likely wouldn't come, not after she'd fled with such clear cowardice. That was best, really. Soon she'd be all alone again, and she'd better get used to it, stop having ridiculous fantasies about being part of a big family, of belonging here.

Don't hurt him.

"Excuse me? Hello?"

Abruptly she looked up to see two strangers and a baby standing in her kitchen. "Can I help you? We're really busy right now, but if you'll just go back into the dining room, I'm sure Jeanette—"

But the dark-haired, curvy woman only smiled and handed the baby to the tall, rugged cowboy beside her. "I can see that. Here, Boone, take Lilah Rose. I'll get an apron."

"What? No— You can't—"

Then Ruby spoke from behind Scarlett. "You know where the aprons are, Maddie."

The woman named Maddie laughed. "I don't mean the elf-sized ones. Where's a normal one?"

Scarlett's brows snapped together. The nerve— "What's going on, Nana? Who are these people? I don't have time for pranks."

"It won't take you two seconds to meet your cousin Boone and his wife Maddie."

Cousin? She blinked.

The man grinned. "I'm Boone Gallagher, and I'll apologize in advance that my hard-headed wife got too antsy to wait to meet you." He moved closer and stuck out a hand.

"Oh, good grief. No handshakes—we're family." Maddie bustled up and grabbed Scarlett in a hard hug. "When Ruby told us about you, there was no way we were going to wait. Family is too important. Only thing more important than food."

"She should know," Ruby said. "She used to work up in New York, too. Now she owns a diner in Morning Star, and she stole half my menu."

Maddie only laughed gaily. "Ruby stole half of mine, so we're even." Then she took the baby from Boone. "This is our daughter, Lilah Rose. Our sons Dalton and Sam are back home, staying with Boone's brother Mitch and his family. We didn't want to overwhelm you with the wild bunch, but she's too young to leave just yet. I'm still nursing her."

Scarlett couldn't seem to form a response. Maddie was like a big, friendly tornado sweeping right over everything in sight.

"You're scaring her, babe. Take a breath." Boone grinned. Rugged and rangy, he was the perfect image of a cowboy, his Stetson over tawny hair, his blue eyes friendly. "A force of nature is my Maddie. Aunt Ruby, let's take Lilah Rose into the dining room and get out of Scarlett's way. I know those hungry folks out there would thank us." Swiftly and easily he cleared everyone out, but only after a kiss and a long, loving look at Maddie. "Behave. Don't try to take over."

"As if I would." Maddie shook her head. "Well, I wouldn't mean to, at least. Okay—" Maddie turned to her, tying on her apron with swift professionalism. "Tell me where you need me. I know this menu like the back of my hand."

"Then why don't I just go sit in the dining room, too?" Scarlett worked to keep her temper in check.

Maddie grinned at her. "I know. Sharing your kitchen sucks, doesn't it? I should have waited, but today is the only day my place is closed, so if we were going to visit, it had to be now." She burst into laughter. "If you could see your face…"

When Scarlett didn't join in her laughter, Maddie stepped back. "I'll take the apron off right now if you want me to. I honestly only want to help. It's a great way to get to know each other, cooking together."

Scarlett stared. "Does anyone ever say no to you?"

"Not often. I'll grow on you." She held out her open

palms. "So what will it be? You can give me the grunt work." Her eyes twinkled. "And while we're working, I'm going to shamelessly beg for every scrap of information on the state of New York restaurants today."

"How could you leave there for a diner in—where's Morning Glory?"

"Morning Star, which is even smaller than Sweetgrass. It's two and a half hours north of here." Her smile went wide. "And I did it for love, of course. Best move I ever made, but boy, did I agonize over it." She glanced out toward her family. "To think I nearly missed out on them…"

She turned back. "But that doesn't mean I don't want to hear the skinny on what's hot that I'm not learning on the food blogs. Like explain to me how anyone up there thinks they can possibly turn fried okra into an avant garde appetizer. Excuse me? Some things are sacred."

Scarlett couldn't help grinning. "Where did you grow up?"

"North Carolina. You?"

"All over. But we lived in Durham for a bit. And Boone for six months."

"Boone. One of my favorite spots in the world. Wouldn't you know I'd fall in love with a guy by that name?"

She really was impossible not to like. And the orders were stacking up. "The breakfast rush will be over soon—or I hope it will. Half the world has shown up here today, it seems."

"Ruby says your cooking puts hers in the shade, and that's no small compliment. Of course they're coming here in droves."

Scarlett mentally surrendered. "Where did you work in New York?"

Maddie rattled off several names. "I was offered owner-ship in Sancerre once my thirty days were over."

"Thirty days?"

Maddie grinned. "Long story. Boone's dad willed me his ranch, and—"

"Willed *you* Boone's ranch?"

"Yeah. Boone was away in the service at the time. He was a SEAL. Turns out it used to be my family's ranch, only I knew my father under a different name."

Scarlett blinked.

"It's complicated. You kinda need a scorecard, and I've barely scratched the surface." Maddie laughed. "Anyway, Boone and I had to stay on the ranch together for thirty days before he could buy me out. He wasn't happy. Not a fan of city girls."

Like someone else Scarlett knew.

"But somewhere along the way, we fell crazy in love, only I couldn't imagine staying in Nowhere, Texas when I could have New York at my feet. You know?"

Scarlett had to look away. "Yes." She also knew what it was like to fall from such a lofty height.

"You okay?" Maddie asked. "Sorry—just blabbing on about me when you're the one who's interesting. So where did you work?"

Scarlett froze, her conversation with the DA on her mind. She didn't know what to do about him. Didn't want anyone here knowing how spectacularly she'd failed.

But she could be exposed so easily. And this friendly woman posed a danger she wasn't ready for. She seized upon the first distraction. "Your daughter is darling. Did you say you have two boys?"

Maddie hesitated and looked at her curiously.

At last, though, thank heavens, she let Scarlett off the hook. "I do. They're five and three and they—"

Gratefully Scarlett listened and continued to work.

After Boone and Maddie left that night, Scarlett's head was

whirling. She'd managed to dodge more conversations about her past, if just barely. Her cousin Boone—

Wow. A *cousin*. And there were more in that branch—his brother Mitch was married and had two boys, plus Boone and Mitch and Maddie shared a half-sister named Lacey. She frowned. Lacey was the product of Maddie's...dad? Yes, her dad and Boone and Mitch's mother. So Lacey was a half-sibling to them all, only they hadn't known about her until five years ago.

And here Scarlett had thought her past was convoluted.

Lacey was married to...Dominic? No—Devlin. And they had two daughters, one adopted and a biological daughter named, um...Jenny. After the mother Lacey shared with Boone and Mitch. And she and Dev had a boy on the way.

Whew. She thought that was all of them. She was dying to meet them. Boone raised quarterhorses, and Mitch was an adventure guide who'd built a house on the same ranch. Lacey and Dev lived in Houston where her adoptive parents lived, but they all saw each other all the time, according to Boone.

When Boone could get a word in edgewise, that is, but he never seemed to mind how Maddie chattered. Who could? A friendlier person had never been born. Scarlett felt like a curmudgeon in comparison, and she had great social skills.

Scarlett had a standing invitation to Morning Star, along with an implied threat that if she didn't use it soon, Maddie would be on her doorstep.

Scarlett grinned. A force of nature, indeed.

She adored them all. That precious Lilah Rose had taken to her and cuddled up in her lap so trustingly... Scarlett hadn't been around children much and hadn't given a lot of thought to having any, but that little girl could make a believer out of anyone. She had her daddy's blue eyes—which were remarkably like Scarlett's own, she'd realized with a shock—and her mother's chestnut hair.

What would her own child look like?

Suddenly her brain was blasted with an image of a baby with sun-streaked dark hair and brown eyes like—

No. Ian and she would never have babies. The hollow that opened inside her was something she just had to will away. It was beyond unrealistic.

Besides, for all she knew, she would never see Ian again. He hadn't come to the cafe all day, nor had he shown up that night after closing.

Just as well. She would, of course, see him at the work day Saturday, she realized, but after that—

Don't think about after that. It was impossible not to, though, now that Ruby had come back to the cafe. She hadn't cooked, but she'd sat out in front and visited with her customers, who treated her like royalty. She wasn't strong yet, but she would be.

She wouldn't need Scarlett here forever. The thought was surprisingly distressing.

Go to sleep. Tomorrow will be a long day.

She lay awake, staring at the ceiling, for a long time after.

On Thursday night Ian couldn't stand it anymore. He climbed back in his truck and headed into town.

She was in there, working alone, as independent as ever. Determined not to lean on anyone.

Tell me what's wrong.

How about you start by telling me how losing your mom really makes you feel?

He had never wanted to talk to anyone about his mom, at least not since he was a little boy. His dad felt bad enough— why make things harder? So he'd learned to lock it away. Forget her.

Damn it, Scarlett…

He stepped inside. Exhaled hard. "I cried every night for weeks after my mother left."

She whirled, knife in her hand again.

"Now you tell me what you're so scared of." He stalked toward her.

"I…can't. I'm not— I have my reasons. I'm not simply holding back."

"The hell you're not."

They stood like opponents in the ring in that moment before battle is joined.

She set down the knife, her huge blue eyes so deep a man could drown in them. "What are you doing here?"

"Living up to my half of the bargain. Your turn."

She looked so small. So sad. "Ian…I would if I could. I just—it's complicated."

"Life is complicated."

Suddenly she threw herself into his arms. "I missed you. I didn't want to."

He gathered her in. "I was only going to come tonight to remind you about the work day." He pressed her closer. Lifted her chin. "Not."

Then he kissed her.

She answered him fully, wriggling closer as if she could crawl inside his skin.

He wished she would. Maybe then he'd know what the hell was standing between them.

He was so lonely. Never once in his life had he acknowledged that feeling. Never knew he could feel so damn sad and empty. He lifted his mouth from hers, prepared to try again to convince her—

"Don't," she murmured, fingers over his lips. "Just kiss me."

There should be a way to fix this. Damn it, he was good at solving problems.

I missed you so. But she wouldn't tell him one detail. How could he make it right for her, for them? Was he kidding himself to think there could be a *them*? She'd walked away from him, run from him, truth be told. Whatever her reason was…

It wasn't that she didn't like it here. She did, he was positive. What could be holding her back?

But he couldn't fix what he didn't understand.

She was so close, so sweet. He was so hungry for her. Later…they would hash this out, he vowed.

But for now he let go of everything but this moment. This sense of coming home. He gathered her closer, but nothing was close enough. He deepened the kiss and let his hands roam over her, wishing he could take her inside his skin.

She responded fervently, locking her arms around his neck and standing on tiptoe until he was tempted to just scoop her up and carry her off, except he couldn't seem to stop touching her.

Every kiss was a torture, a blessing.

"We can't—Ian, we can't make love here."

He didn't release her, but he stared down into that beautiful face. And sighed. "I know."

He didn't want to share this with anyone. Sure, he could take her home, but…he didn't want to share her with his dad. Ruby's place wasn't any better. Ruby had half the town living there.

He still had blankets from the picnic in his truck, but it was too cold outside.

"The courthouse," she said suddenly, eyes twinkling. "Is that crazy?"

"It's genius. Come on."

He retrieved the blankets, and they crept across the courthouse lawn like two truant kids. The door was never locked, so getting inside was a piece of cake.

"I feel like I'm fifteen," she said with a giggle.

"Twelve. The four of us snuck in here one night when we were twelve. It was still a working courthouse."

"What did you do?"

"Nothing, really. Just…" He shrugged. "We were boys. It was there." He paused. "Well, okay, we were looking for The Lady. We were hoping she'd help us scare the crap out of Tank."

"Why would she be scary? I think her story is just…sad. It breaks my heart."

"Twelve-year-old boys don't think about mushy stuff. Give 'em the gross, every time."

They'd reached the top, the cupola where Ruby held her halftime vigil.

"I—" She hesitated.

"What?"

"I… I think I saw something the other night when I was up here."

"You saw her?"

"I'm sure it wasn't—"

"It was her."

"How would you know? Did you ever see her?"

"I did once, actually. Never told anybody, though. The guys would never have let me hear the end of it."

"Did she say anything?"

He shook his head. "She only looked at me. She…" He shrugged.

"What?"

"She —I could swear I felt her stroke my hair and—"

"And what?"

"It's crazy, but for a second, I thought she kissed my forehead."

"Were you scared?"

"No, that was the weird part. I felt…safe. She almost felt like a mother or something. The only thing she said to me was *Wait*." He felt foolish and busied himself spreading out the blanket, but he was too restless to lie down. He made his way to the parapet and looked out.

"You love this town, don't you?" she asked.

"Love it and hate it."

"Because you're trapped here?"

"I'm not trapped." But he felt that way sometimes, like he was a bird in a cage, beating his wings against the edges of the bars, sometimes so full of rage and longing he didn't know what to do with. "I'm needed here."

"Ian." Her small hand came to rest on his forearm. "Maybe you're meant to go. You've given up your dreams for this town, but you don't have to. If it's not working, you just move on."

The ache of it, the grinding pain of his lifelong wish to see what was out there, to choose his own path, nearly leveled him. "That's your answer?" he accused. "Times get tough and you run? Is that what your mother taught you?"

She looked stricken.

"Running is no answer. Life gets hard, but you don't run away. You don't leave everyone who needs you behind."

A tear fell from her lashes, and she turned her back on him. Put distance between them. "You don't understand."

"I understand plenty. Your grandmother needs you here. This town will die without her cafe. Hell, *I* need you here." He cursed and wheeled away. Why had he said that? He felt like the little boy who wanted to beg his mother not to go.

Who *had* begged her.

His mother had looked at him for a long time. For those moments, he'd thought he'd succeeded, that she wouldn't go, that she wouldn't abandon him.

Then she'd said those few fatal words. *I have to. I'm dying here.*

And she'd walked out, leaving him behind. He'd wanted to go with her, desperately, but even a boy had known instinctively that doing so would kill his dad.

So he'd stayed.

Scarlett turned ravaged eyes to his. "I'm sorry. Sorrier than you can possibly know. If I could stay, I would. There's nothing I'd like better. And Nana's note is coming due, I found out. I wish I had the money to help her, but she won't take what I have."

She gestured to the building in which they stood. "This place could be an amazing space. You could turn the ground floor into a restaurant serving locally-grown foods. You could make it a destination restaurant people would drive to from miles away, and it could serve your organic beef and your fresh butter and cream. The rest of it could be an events center where people held weddings and corporate gatherings. There's so much—"

"Then do it." The surge of hope was painful. "Do it for your grandmother and yourself and the town where your ancestors lived and died so that you could have roots."

Torment rode hard over her delicate features. "I wish I could," she whispered. "But I...can't. Ian, I *can't.*"

"Why not?" He tore the plea from his gut. "You can do anything you really want to."

"If that's true, then why don't you go? Why don't you see the world you're dying to travel?"

I...can't. He looked at her, seeing his own confusion and misery mirrored in her blue eyes.

"I'll do your work day," she whispered. "Then I have to go. Please—let me tell Nana myself."

He watched her and felt the shimmer of dreams dying. The agony of what would never be. "I don't understand."

"Yes, you do." She rose to her toes to plant a kiss to his cheek.

As she turned away, he hauled her back hard against him. *Fight for me*, he wanted to shout. *Fight for us.*

But he could feel her trembling, and he knew that whatever it was that held her back, she truly believed the obstacle to be insurmountable.

He could bark at her, lecture her, he could plead.

Or he could feed his soul one last time.

Even though he would pay later with agony.

"I am so sorry." She started to draw out of his arms.

"Not yet," he said. "Don't leave me yet."

He sensed her hovering on the edge of indecision, but he could feel her longing as deep as his own.

So he seized the moment and kissed her.

She hesitated.

Then melted into his arms.

This was going to hurt ten times worse, but he wanted the memories, however painful. So he took her down to the blanket, and proceeded to love her the way he wished he could do for a lifetime.

Scarlett felt worshiped. And ravaged. Raked by a pain so intense she wondered if she'd survive it. Yet at the same time, her body responded to the glories of Ian's lovemaking, the steady strength he possessed in such abundance. He teased all her senses, willed her flesh to fly with his, her spirit to match his, her body to revel in touch and taste, teeth and tongue, hard against soft. He drew out the lovemaking until she thought she could not bear one more second, yet she never wanted it to end.

She wept through most of it, the passion and the glory of him too much for her heart to bear. They soared together into the chilled moonlight, but he warmed her with kisses, with caresses of hands so strong yet so gentle. Never in her life had she experienced lovemaking of such splendor, of such power.

She crested again and again until she finally begged for him. "Ian, I need you—"

His powerful thrust made her gasp. His deep groan, his teeth nipping at her throat, their rushed breathing—

"I wish..." he murmured.

I wish.

She did, too. Wished for more than she could put into words.

"Don't think," he demanded, and sealed his mouth to hers, setting up a rhythm that hurled her into the starry night, into the realm of dreams, into the bliss of union she knew she would never feel again with anyone else.

The thought of this intimacy with any other man was unbearable. She spread her fingers over the back of his head, yearning to shield them both from the future she could not bear to anticipate.

Then he changed the rhythm, and shot them both out past the edge of thought, where it was only possible to feel, to fly—

And when at last they fell to earth, he held her as though never to let her go. As if she were special.

Scarlett's tears slid into her hair as she held him close, this man she had to protect from the ugliness she would bring into his life if she faltered.

At last he relaxed into slumber.

It was like tearing her own heart out to slip away and dress quietly. To cover him as best she could.

To kneel beside him and study a face that had become beloved.

She wanted to kiss him again, but one of them had to be the last, and every last one would be painful.

Better to let him sleep.

And let him go.

Tomorrow was the work day.

The next day she would have to depart.

She moved quietly toward the stairs—

A wisp of white flitted past her vision.

Stay.

Scarlett halted. Blinked. She stared, but there was no one there.

Then Ian stirred.

Quickly she escaped.

Chapter Sixteen

I wish.

Stay.

Damn, had he really said those things?

What part of *I can't stay* don't you understand, numb nuts?

And why had he bared himself to her the way he had, talking about the Louvre, telling her about his mother, for Pete's sake? Opening his heart to her as they loved—

So she could leave him to wake up alone and cold. Feeling a worse fool than he already had.

"What's wrong, Boss?" Billy asked.

Ian whipped his head around, read to bite off Billy's head—

But Billy was innocent. All these people were. He'd organized this workday, and he was being a jerk.

Veronica cast yet another worried glance at him, and he could see guilt written all over her features. Didn't she have a hard enough time accepting help? Now here he was, behaving like a jackass, ready to snap at anyone just because—

Because he'd been left. Again. How did he even know Scarlett hadn't skipped town last night?

Just then Henry came around the corner of Veronica's house. "We got the cafe closed. What can I do to help?"

Who's we? he wanted to ask. But then he saw her.

Scarlett was walking over with trays of food in her hands. Brenda and Jeanette also bore trays. "Go help Scarlett," he told Henry.

"That's the last. I already unloaded everything else. It's in your kitchen, Mrs. Butler," he said. "That's okay, right?"

"It's perfect. Thank you, Henry." Like everyone else here, Veronica was dressed for hard work. Already they'd gotten a lot done. None of this would solve her day-to-day problems, much less long term, but the work being done would buy her some time. The greenhouses were being repaired, and the gate for one of the pens sported new hinges. The stalls had all been mucked out and replaced with fresh hay. Jonas was tuning up the tractor, while Harley Sykes changed the oil in David's old pickup.

And Ian was watching Scarlett walk away. Not once had she met his eyes.

Coward. That's all she was, a coward, like her mother. Like his. *Run away, then. We don't need you.*

"Ian?" Veronica's touch on his arm jolted him.

"What?"

"What's wrong? Can I help? You should take it easy. You've been working ten times harder than anyone else."

"There's a lot to get done," he snapped, then immediately felt like slime. "I'm sorry. It's not…" He exhaled. Made himself get a grip. "This isn't about you. I apologize."

She glanced at Scarlett, then back. "What has she done? I'll go give her a piece of my mind."

Hell. He was letting his bad mood contaminate the entire crew. "It won't help. There's nothing to talk to Scarlett about, anyway."

"She's been sad all morning," Henry volunteered. "She nearly didn't come out here."

"She shouldn't have to," Veronica said. "It's not mandatory. She's already done so much. I'll go tell her she doesn't need to stay."

"Leave her—" Ian barked. Then yanked off his ball cap. "Look, I apologize. I just got up on the wrong side of the bed,

I guess. Ignore me." He turned to Henry. "I think Dad could use some help over at the chicken coop. With that cold front coming late next week, he's creating a second wind break. Would you mind?"

"Not a bit!" Henry brightened and left.

"Ian...has she hurt you?" Veronica asked.

Great—just what he needed, to become an object of pity. Scarlett hadn't invited him to fall for her. Had done everything possible to warn him off, in fact.

But damn it, what was she so scared of? What on earth could be dogging her? "She's hurting herself worse. And she's going to break Ruby's heart when she goes."

"Are you so sure she's leaving?"

"Yeah. But I don't know why. Guess she's just like my mom. Sweetgrass isn't exciting enough for her."

"She's seemed so...engaged. She's making a place for herself here."

"She doesn't want to. And we can't force her." He sighed. "But I don't know what to do to help Ruby. Her note's coming due, and I don't think she has the money to pay it off."

"Oh, dear. I—maybe we could take up a collection."

"You know anyone in this town who's got an extra dime?" he asked with more bitterness than he intended to betray.

"No. And Ruby's too proud to accept it, anyway."

"Scarlett had this great idea, but it would take money to fund it plus a star-quality chef." He laughed without humor. "Which is about as likely as calling the moon down to earth."

"Isn't she an actual chef?"

"Yeah. A damn good one. She cooked a meal last Sunday that was out of this world. Conjured it up from nothing. She's got a touch, that's for sure." His mouth turned down. "But she's not staying."

Veronica was staring in the direction Scarlett had gone.

"I'm going to have a word with her."

"No." He stopped her before she could. "Please. She—I don't think she's happy about leaving, despite what I just said. I have this sense that there's something else going on, but she refuses to talk about it."

"Well, then," Veronica put her hands on her hips. "You just have to make her tell you."

He snorted. "I've tried. I'm done with trying. Let her go. We don't need her."

She was quiet for a long moment.

He turned away. "I've got work to do on the well pump."

"Ian...don't lie to yourself. Don't give up on her, not yet."

"I know when I'm whipped." He tugged down the bill of his cap as he left.

"So you're my cousin," said a voice from behind Scarlett.

She whirled, a tray of sandwiches in her hand. "I am?" Another cousin?

The woman who'd entered the kitchen was half a foot taller than her, with a long, glossy red ponytail and challenging brown eyes. She wore beat-up jeans like they were second nature, with a western shirt rolled up to her elbows and a thermal undershirt beneath it.

She was lean and lithe, a tomboy as a girl, Scarlett would bet.

"I'm Rissa Gallagher. And you're the woman who's got Ian chewing nails. You leave him alone, you hear? He doesn't need some snotty city girl bothering him."

"Excuse me?"

"Exactly. Snotty. Prissy." The woman glared at her. "Ian was like a big brother to me growing up. He's had plenty of heartache, and his life is hard enough. My own brother abandoned us, his twin took off to be important like you, and Ian stayed behind to clean up the damage. He doesn't need your bullshit. And Aunt Ruby deserves better."

Wow. "What do you know about anything? I've never even seen you before. If you care so much about my grandmother, how come you've never come around?"

The woman Nana had called Clarissa—whose sweetly feminine name didn't suit her one bit—tugged her ball cap down further on her brow and frowned from beneath the bill. "I don't get to town much. Running a ranch doesn't leave a lot of free time, even in the slow season. Ian's lost a lot of sleep to be with you."

"What do you know about it?"

"I hear plenty. It's a small town."

"You're telling me," she muttered. "I don't see what business this is of yours."

Rissa stalked over and glared down her nose. "Because I will kick your prissy little behind from here to Mexico if you hurt the closest thing I have to a brother one bit more than you already have."

Scarlett stood her ground. "Then you'll be delighted to know that I'm leaving tomorrow, first thing."

"Figures. Another Gallagher running away. Our great-great-granddaddy is turning over in his grave at the cowards who lay claim to his name. And Grandma Gallagher would hate that you've been making her biscuits."

Longing, sharp and bittersweet, pierced her. "Did you know her?"

Rissa shrugged. "A little. She used to save me peppermints and sneak them to me when Mama wasn't looking. She was really old then, but I can still see her and those bright blue eyes that were just like Aunt Ruby's."

Like mine, Scarlett realized. "What was she like?"

"What do you care? You're running away, remember?"

"I wish I didn't have to." Why was she admitting anything to this woman who clearly loathed her?

"Then don't."

"It's not that simple. Trouble will come if I don't."

"What kind of trouble?"

It was an odd thing that this woman who didn't like her seemed to be someone she could tell the truth to, someone who wouldn't be destroyed by it. "Nothing I can discuss, but maybe I can come back someday."

"Yeah, right. So you can upset everyone all over again."

The tiny flicker of hope sputtered out. She was right. "I have work to do." Scarlett turned away. "Nice to meet you."

"Sure thing, *cousin*." Scarlett didn't need to see the sneer on her cousin's face to hear it in her voice.

The door slammed behind her.

Scarlett stared into the distance, despair turning the sunny day dark.

Then she shook herself and went back to work.

Ian gave her wide berth, pointedly working as far from where she was as possible.

But even he had to eat. She dished him up a mug of thick, beefy stew and proffered the plate of thick-sliced ham and cheese or roast beef sandwiches she'd compiled with two kinds of her own homemade bread. A heaping bowl of potato salad sat beside the platter, and fruit filled another bowl. All sorts of side dishes had been added by various townspeople.

Though Ian didn't look at her as he filled his plate, she was gratified to have the chance to nourish him.

"You do good man food," said Harley Sykes.

"You sure do, Miz Ross," chimed in Ben Butler. "Thanks for your help."

"I'm very happy to be a part of this," she answered honestly.

Ian's dark gaze flicked to hers. *Liar*, she could practically see on his lips.

She met his gaze steadily. It wasn't a lie. If she cared less, she'd stay and take her chances, but these people and this town had become far too dear to her.

Ian's name was called by a group that had made a place for him at their table, and she breathed a sigh of relief as that uncomfortable regard transferred from her. She watched him make his way through the crowd, hailed by first one, then another. Sweetgrass might not have an official mayor, but he was certainly the unofficial leader, respected and admired by all.

Life gets hard, but you don't run away. You don't leave everyone who needs you behind.

She wasn't running, not the way he thought. She was sparing them the consequences of her mistakes.

"Ruby just called—or rather, Arnie did," Veronica said, coming up beside her. "She was going to come, but he convinced her to stay. He says she just isn't up to it. I'm worried about her. Ruby is never sick. I don't know what she'd do without you here. Have to close down, I suppose."

Scarlett worried her lower lip. Nana had seemed fine when she left this morning, had even said she'd be back cooking next week.

"Doesn't bother Miss High and Mighty here," Rissa sneered as she approached and filled her plate. "She's got more important things on her mind than her sick grandma."

"Rissa, be nice. Scarlett is doing all she can."

"Yeah?" Rissa gestured with her chin. "Ask her if she's packed yet."

Scarlett glared at Rissa. Rissa glared right back.

"Seriously?" Veronica asked. "You're really leaving? But Ruby—"

"Scarlett, there's something wrong with the cake," called Brenda. "I think it got smushed."

"Excuse me," Scarlett said without bothering to wait for an answer.

She rescued the cake and set out desserts. She'd intended to stay and help with whatever repairs she was capable of performing, but by the expressions she saw, word had spread, probably courtesy of her cousin the cowgirl.

People weren't happy. The earlier affection she'd felt from them withered away as they understood that, just like her mother, she was leaving Sweetgrass.

It couldn't matter, she told herself as she got into her car and drove off. No, she wasn't like her mother in one way. She very much wanted to stay.

But she couldn't. Sure, she could probably eke out a few more days or even weeks here, but what was the point? Like removing a bandage, ripping it off fast was better. She needed to yank Sweetgrass right out of her heart.

Her choices were to run and try to hide, which would have to be forever if she crossed the DA.

Or go back and face the music. Let him put her in a safe place until the trial, then testify and—

And what? What if Kostov won the case? He'd be free, but would he forget her? Just let her go?

She didn't want to be on the run anymore. She didn't understand why her mother had left this place, but Scarlett very much wanted to return if she could ever find a way.

She just didn't know what that way was. Until she did, she should go. She longed to put down roots, and hovering here like a butterfly was no good. They'd get on fine without her. She'd taught Henry how to cook all the main dishes Ruby served, and he was really quite good at it. Ruby wouldn't have to come back to work if she didn't feel up to it—

Oh, Nana. I want you to be well. I want more time with you.

Her grandmother's life had been hard enough, though.

Scarlett would not make it worse by involving Nana in her mistakes.

She would go back, and tonight she would cook ahead as much food as she could manage, then she would go talk to her grandmother and—

And what? Nana had waited all those years for Scarlett's mother to return, kept a faithful vigil every night and every day.

What was it going to do to her if Scarlett left?

Maybe she could be evasive. Tell Nana she wasn't sure how soon she'd be back, but it wouldn't be long. Once she was away from here, she'd stay in touch and she'd do everything she could from a distance. She'd lay out plans for that event center and restaurant she'd conceptualized for the courthouse, start looking for investors. Find a chef for it.

It should be mine. Mine and Ian's. She longed to help him put his ideas into practice. Work side by side with him to help save Sweetgrass.

Scarlett pulled up next to the cafe, her mind a whirlwind of longing and misery, of faint hope and bitter disappointment, of guilt and—

She opened the back door of the cafe and flipped the light switch, but nothing happened. Oh, great. She turned to go to the storeroom for a light bulb—

"Well, now," said a heavily-accented voice that was only too familiar. "A long way you have made me travel, Miss Ross." One gloved hand covered her mouth, and she started to struggle.

"I wouldn't, if I were you. The old lady next door will suffer if you do. Her fate is tied directly to yours."

Scarlett froze.

Not Nana. No.

The glitter of a knife blade darted past her vision.

And came to rest against her throat.

Ian saw her leave alone, and the temper he'd been keeping barely in check boiled over. He rose and excused himself to the group he'd been sitting with, only half-hearing what they said.

She's leaving now, his gut told him. Right now—skating away while the town was busy.

Unless something had happened to Ruby.

No. She would have said something to someone. She knew how important Ruby was to all of them.

"Good riddance," Rissa said, coming up behind him. She snorted. "Forget that hoohah about trouble coming if she stays. She's just like her mom, eager to run away."

He frowned. "What do you mean, trouble?"

"I don't know. Who cares? She tried to play it like she'd prefer to stay, like she had no choice but to go." Rissa snorted. "Yeah, right."

"Rissa, don't be so hard on her," Veronica said. "What exactly did she say?"

"I am sick to death of people in my family leaving." Rissa's chin jutted.

"Rissa…"

She sighed. "All right, all right, let me think." She scrunched up her forehead. "I told her she didn't have to run away. She said it wasn't that simple, that trouble would come if she didn't leave."

Ian puzzled over what she could mean about trouble.

Screw it. Whatever the hell was going on, he was not going to simply let Scarlett go, not without a fight. "Veronica, I'll be back to finish—"

His dad hobbled up. "If you're thinking about going after that little girl, don't you worry about what you were working on. Plenty of us here to fix what needs doing." He nodded toward town. "But I'm thinking you're the only one capable of fixing this."

Ian hesitated. He belonged here, helping out. This had been his idea.

Veronica nudged him. "Ruby will be devastated if she leaves, and I don't think she's the only one. You go on."

"I'll be back," he said.

"Take your time," Veronica responded.

Ian saw her car at the back of the cafe as he passed down Main Street. He wondered if he'd find her there or over at Ruby's and decided to start with the cafe. He parked his truck across the street from Ruby's and headed for her door. As he passed the cafe, he glanced in the side window—

He stopped dead in his tracks. Everything inside him froze.

She was in there, but she wasn't alone. Some big, ugly brute had her in a chair, her mouth taped shut, her wrists bound. He was talking on the phone.

Scarlett was pale as death.

Trouble will come if I don't leave.

What the hell?

His instinct was to charge inside and beat the living hell out of that bastard. Who was he? What did he want? If he only wanted to rob the cash register, he'd be sorely disappointed. Everybody knew the cash register was left empty when Ruby closed.

But he didn't look like a simple thief. As Ian listened, he could hear a foreign accent. Was that…Russian or something? Definitely not a familiar language around here, and the guy was more than pissed.

Just then Scarlett saw him, and her eyes went wide. She

shook her head at him.

Yeah, right. I'm just going to walk away like a good boy.

Ian held up a finger and pointed back toward the street. *I'll be back*, he mouthed. He needed his rifle from the gun rack in his truck. She looked so terrified that it was hard to leave her, but he was too far away, and the guy was too close to her. His best chance was to take the guy down before he knew Ian was there.

He rounded the corner.

The bore of a Glock pointed straight at him. "Where are you going, cowboy?" A second beefy guy. The same accent.

Two thugs with Slavic accents, here in Sweetgrass? What was going on? Even if he could manage to wrestle this guy to the ground, the other one would hear. However inconceivable this was, it was real, and he was all Scarlett had.

"You go inside, cowboy." The guy shoved his shoulder, and Ian had to force himself not to react.

Stay alert. Look for any advantage. He would not let them hurt her, whatever he had to do to prevent it.

They stepped inside, and the one holding Scarlett whirled to face them. His heavy brows snapped together at the sight of Ian. He kept talking in that foreign language but jerked his head in Scarlett's direction before turning away again.

Are you hurt? Ian asked her silently.

One quick shake of the head.

"No talking." The one behind Ian pushed him toward Scarlett. "Be silent, cowboy."

The other one glanced at Ian as he ended his call. "Are there more of you?"

He had no idea what the right answer was, so he went on his gut. "Yeah. More will be here soon."

The two traded glances. The guy next to Ian spoke in English again. "Killing her is one thing. She is stranger here. But this one…I don't know, Ilya. I don't think—"

"You are not paid to think. Shut your mouth and go

outside. Bring me more zip ties for him, then watch for the others."

"What about—"

"I have the gun. They are unarmed. She is small woman, though much trouble. I am waiting for call back, then we will take her and go. There is much empty land in this Texas. She will not be found soon."

The second guy left.

Ian cut a glance at Scarlett. What the hell kind of trouble was she in?

Her eyes met his, dark with sorrow.

He made his expression as reassuring as possible.

Damn it, he wasn't giving up. He needed to act now, while the other one was outside. He scanned covertly for possible weapons. Her knife rack was only a few feet away. If he could somehow distract this guy before the other returned with restraints…

The first brute was watching him. Ian did his best to look unthreatening.

"Who are you to her?"

Instinct told him to disavow any relationship. "Just a customer."

"The place is closed."

"It's a small town. Sometimes we just wander in."

"In small towns, people notice too much." The guy leaned toward Ian. "Do you notice too much, cowboy?"

Ian held his gaze, looking for his opportunity. He hadn't been in all those boyhood brawls for nothing. Mackey had taught the Four Horsemen everything he knew about martial arts and fighting dirty. Ian wasn't sure how much he remembered, but he had motivation, for sure.

"Answer me. Or are you Texas cowboys not so tough, maybe?" The blank eyes gloated.

He did remember one move Mackey had said was too deadly to try out on each other, one that would immobilize a grown man.

It wasn't like he had a lot of options. No telling when anyone would come back into town.

Scarlett made a noise.

The guy glanced over at her.

Ian launched himself forward, knuckles extended. He caught the guy right in the throat.

The guy gurgled. Dropped like a rock.

Ian crouched over him but kept alert for the second man's return. He flipped this guy over, searching the area for anything to bind his hands. He spotted an apron nearby and used the strings to tie the guy's hands. Found another one and restrained the guy's ankles.

He turned to Scarlett and crouched before her, keeping his voice low. "Leave the tape on so the other guy doesn't suspect anything. Keep your hands behind your back. Are there others?"

She shook her head.

"All right."

She made a sound behind the tape, but there was no time for talking. He grabbed the biggest knife and carefully slit her bonds, then moved past her toward the door, plastering himself against the wall behind it.

The second guy clomped up the steps. "I see no one anywhere around. Perhaps he is lying—" His eyes widened as he took in Ian's absence, already drawing his weapon.

Ian sliced at his gun hand. The man yelled, and the gun clattered to the floor. He rounded on Ian, and Ian's boot connected with the side of the man's knee. The man fell away, crying out again. Ian glanced around quickly for the gun, but before he could locate it, the man regained his feet and charged Ian, aiming a vicious chop at Ian's wrist, forcing his knife hand to let go.

Then he rammed his shoulder into Ian's chest, and they both fell to the ground.

The guy outweighed Ian by at least fifty pounds, but much of that was blubber. He might be more accustomed to violence, but Ian worked at hard physical tasks every day of his life.

Still, he couldn't overpower the guy, and they rolled over the floor, delivering punches and struggling for an advantage. Ian's back slammed into a table and sent pots flying.

"Stop!" Scarlett yelled. "I'll shoot!"

Ian glanced over to see her with the man's pistol held in shaking hands.

The guy caught Ian in the side of the head, and he saw stars.

"She said stop," came a voice from the doorway. "She may not know how to shoot, but I do."

The guy wheeled toward the voice.

Ruby stood in the doorway, a shotgun in her hand.

The man roared. Ian took advantage of the distraction to land a punch to the guy's temple.

He slumped to the floor.

"Thanks, Ruby," Ian said. Then he glanced at Scarlett's shaking hands. "If you wouldn't mind pointing that toward the floor, I'd be grateful."

She set it on the table, then charged toward Ian, nearly knocking him back down. "I'm so sorry, so sorry. I never meant to bring my trouble to you."

She felt so good in his arms he held on tight for a moment.

She spoke into his chest. "Now you see why I have to go. He'll just send more."

"Who will send more?" But he didn't wait for her to answer. "Never mind. You're not going anywhere until we talk." He looked at Ruby. "You got this one?"

Ruby nodded fiercely.

Ian let Scarlett go and searched the guy's pockets for the zip ties he'd been sent for. When he found them, he quickly restrained the man.

Finally Ruby lowered her shotgun and swayed on her feet.

"Nana!" Scarlett raced to her, and they clung together. "I'm sorry, Nana," she sobbed. "I didn't know how to tell you. But he won't give up. That's why I can't stay."

"Hush now, sweetheart," Ruby soothed. "Let's go home and talk about this."

"No. I have to pack."

She still meant to go. After all this— "Are they from New York?" Ian asked, his voice harsh.

Scarlett's head whipped toward him. Her eyes looked devastated as she nodded.

He couldn't let himself soften. He forced himself back to the needs of the moment. "Then they're not going to stroll in right away. No one knows we have the upper hand yet. At the very least, you owe your grandmother an explanation."

Her expression was stricken. "And you," she said quietly.

"Later," he said, wondering who the hell this woman really was. "Right now I'm going to call the law. Take her home, Ruby."

Except it wasn't home to Scarlett, was it?

He walked out the door.

Chapter Seventeen

She'd wanted to go to Ian again, but he'd gone remote and cold.

Of course he would be upset. She'd nearly gotten him killed, hadn't she? Lied to him, over and over, never mind that she was trying to save him. Trying to save all of them.

"I'm so sorry, Nana," she said after they'd reached the house and stood in the kitchen. She kept her arms around her grandmother's shoulders. "I should never have come."

"Don't be foolish, child. Where else would you come when you're in trouble? We're family." But Ruby's frame trembled. Though her core was iron-strong, she wasn't young by any means. And Sweetgrass wasn't a big, bad city where violence was an everyday occurrence.

The kitchen door swung open, and Mrs. Oldham stood there, the Judge right behind. "What's going on?"

"Let's go into the living room. This girl needs to sit down, and so do I," Ruby ordered. "Would you mind starting some tea, Mrs. Oldham?"

"I'd be happy to."

She and Nana made their way down the hall. "Nana, I can't sit. I have to leave, the sooner the better."

"Scarlett Ross, I am ashamed of you."

Scarlett's heart broke. "I understand why you would be, but I'm not a criminal, I swear."

"Well, of course you're not," Ruby huffed. "The very

idea!" She led Scarlett inside and settled her on the sofa, then took a seat beside her. "Now first of all, you're not going anywhere. We take care of our own, Scarlett, and you belong here."

You belong here. Had she ever heard anything more beautiful? She'd never belonged anywhere.

"You'd better wait until you hear the whole story, Nana. It's not pretty. I messed up so badly."

Ruby stroked her hair. "Honey, everybody makes mistakes. Not a one of us is perfect."

"You are," she said fervently. "I love you so much. Maybe I can come back one day if only—"

Just then Ian appeared in the doorway, his face grave. "The sheriff needs to talk to you, Scarlett. He has some questions."

Her heart sank. "Am I under arrest?"

An older man in his fifties stepped into the room. "Ms. Ross, I'm Sheriff Collier. Why don't you and I talk alone?"

She glanced at Ruby, then at Ian's stony face. "Are you going to read me my rights?"

"Is there a reason I should? I thought you were the victim in this."

"I—it's complicated. I was arrested in New York. The DA wants me back there."

"Scarlett," Ian warned. "Don't say anything else."

The sheriff's brows rose. "Perhaps I'd better recite them to you, then. And everyone else should go."

"We're going nowhere, Alton," Ruby said crisply. "Now you say what you need to."

She glanced at Ian, but not a trace of emotion was on his face. No telling what he was thinking of her now, but it probably wasn't good, and no wonder. She'd stonewalled him whenever he'd asked her to explain why she couldn't stay.

The sheriff recited the Miranda warning. "Would you like an attorney, Ms. Ross?"

She started to shake her head, but Ruby spoke first. "I'm not sure you should be saying anything, Scarlett. At a minimum, I think we should have the Judge present. Ian, would you call him in here, please?"

"Nana, I—"

"It can't hurt," Ruby interrupted. "Old fool is in the kitchen, probably listening at the door anyway."

Scarlett nearly smiled. Then found her eyes awash with tears.

"Here—" A bandanna appeared before her, held in Ian's strong hands.

She looked up at him. "I'm really sorry, Ian. I thought I'd lost them."

A quick frown, then he left the room.

Soon the Judge made his way in and settled beside her. "Scarlett, I don't want you to answer anything hastily. Perhaps you and I should confer first. You don't have to say anything at all."

"I've already been through this in New York, Judge." She couldn't meet anyone's gaze. "I was arrested and held in jail, but no charges were filed. I want to help however I can. I don't want these men hurting anyone else in Sweetgrass." Ian had already been hurt, defending her. That was too much.

Judge Porter studied her gravely, then nodded. "All right, but I'll call a halt to this the first instant you start badgering this little girl, Alton."

"How the hell am I going to badger her, Judge? I don't have a clue what's going on. Exactly who are these men, Ms. Ross?"

"I think…" She cleared her throat. "I think they're some sort of Bulgarian Mafia. They were sent by a drug dealer named Kostov."

The Judge's eyes widened, as did the sheriff's. "Bulgarian Mafia? Here? Are you serious?"

"I am." Scarlett told her tale as best she could, with the

sheriff asking a question here and there but mostly letting her tell the story the way she needed to.

When she finished, Judge Porter spoke first. "Sounds to me like this DA can't really make his case from your testimony. He's just hedging his bets."

"Do you think so? He told me he could still press charges if I didn't cooperate, but I don't really know anything. Andre handled all the finances and took care of the business details. I just cooked. That's what's so humiliating, that I could be that blind when it was going on right under my nose. What frightens me most is that I have no idea how they found me here. I told no one about Sweetgrass. I didn't even know it existed until two weeks before I got here."

The Judge and the sheriff traded glances. "You thinking what I am, Alton?"

The sheriff nodded grimly. "The DA has a leak in his office. Bet your bottom dollar that's how they found her, through someone there."

"You mean if I hadn't called in…?"

"Quite likely," the sheriff said.

"So what does that mean for me?"

"Both men, this Kostov and the DA, seem to be playing a high-stakes chess match, and you're only a pawn." The sheriff's expression was grim. "I don't like it one bit. DA's an ambitious man, I suppose?"

"Sucker's bet," said the Judge.

"He is up for reelection," she remembered.

The sheriff rose. "Well, little lady, I'll be calling that DA's office first thing in the morning to have a little chat with him."

"And I'll be calling the Texas Attorney General," Judge Porter said. "He's a personal friend of mine, as is our congresswoman. Let's see what pressures they can bring to bear."

"To do what?" Scarlett asked.

"All the DA needs to do is to clear you publicly and say

you had no helpful information, then take you off his witness list. Dollars to donuts, this Kostov loses interest fast."

Could it possibly be that easy? A flutter of hope rose.

"But what happens between now and then?" Ian asked.

Of course it wouldn't be that easy. Panic replaced the hope, and Scarlett stood. "More could come. I'd better just go. I can disappear again. I won't call anyone this time."

Ian's gaze went hard. Ruby grabbed her hand. "You most certainly will not. We protect our own. You think any hoodlum can get into town without us noticing, now that we've been alerted? You've been here long enough to know how word spreads. Every person in Sweetgrass has a stake in keeping you here, Scarlett."

"Ian," the sheriff said. "I know you're not in law enforcement, but you're the closest thing this town has to a man in charge. I don't have the manpower, but I'm betting you can have some folks organized to keep a watch over Ms. Ross here."

A muscle in Ian's jaw jumped. "I can."

But he looked so unhappy about it. She couldn't bear being in Sweetgrass if Ian didn't want her here.

She wouldn't argue about leaving right now, though. They clearly had their minds made up. She would wait until she was alone to make her plan.

"You don't worry now, Ms. Ross. I'll be reporting back to you after I talk to that sorry DA. Daniel, you let me know what results you get, too, all right?"

"Absolutely."

The sheriff tipped his hat brim. "Ruby, Ms. Ross, I'll be getting along now. Got a couple of fellas to lock up nice and tight in my jail."

He left, and Ian quickly followed without even a glance toward Scarlett.

She wished she knew what he was thinking. Wondered if anyone had taken a look at his injuries. He'd been through a lot on her account, and that after having asked her more than once to confide in him. His life had been endangered because she hadn't trusted him.

But what could he have done? He was a rancher—albeit one who had proven himself to be quite a fighter. Still, those men were hardened criminals. If Ian had been one iota less smart or tough…

A shudder ripped through her. He could have been killed. She could have lost him tonight. In trying to protect him, she'd endangered him instead.

Why should he be eager to talk to her?

"Come on now, Scarlett," Ruby said. "Let's get you to bed. You've had quite a day. And don't you give one thought to the cafe. I'll be cooking breakfast in the morning. Henry can help me, and Jeanette can handle whatever else needs doing."

"Jeanette hates me," Scarlett mumbled. "So does Claris—Rissa."

"They're just protective of Ian. They're both good girls."

Ian… Her heart hurt at the wall he'd thrown up between them.

But she couldn't think about him now, or she'd fall apart. Her bones seemed to have turned into molasses. She could barely put one foot in front of the other, dogged by exhaustion and despair. She believed the sheriff and Judge Porter meant well, but she'd met the DA. They hadn't. He wouldn't give up so easily. He'd send the US Marshals after her as he'd threatened.

She'd have to run again.

The thought made her weary to her marrow.

Ruby and Mrs. Oldham hustled Scarlett upstairs and put her to bed like a child.

Sorrow made her compliant. She welcomed the oblivion of sleep. In sleep she could dream of the life she wouldn't get the chance to experience, the sweet pleasure of living in

Sweetgrass, of loving Ian. Of building a life with a grand-mother and cousins to cherish…

Stay, The Lady had pleaded.

Don't leave, Ian had asked.

Gentle hands covered her with a quilt. "Snuggle up," said Nana.

Sweet dreams, she tried to answer, but her throat was clogged with tears.

Ian drove back to Veronica's to finish up, but everyone was long gone. Rather than inflict his foul mood on Veronica, he vowed to check in with her tomorrow and see how everything had worked out and what was left to be done.

When he slammed on his brakes outside the ranch house, he realized he still couldn't talk to anyone. Blue came wagging out to meet him, but even the dog's enthusiasm couldn't put much of a dent into his mood.

But that wasn't Blue's fault. He sank to a crouch and gave the dog a good rub. "Sorry, buddy. Not much company tonight."

The lights were on inside, so his dad was still up. Ian was about to wheel around and escape to the barn when the front door opened and his dad came out on the porch.

"Is Scarlett okay? How about Ruby?"

"Fine."

"What happened? Been getting calls ever since I got home. Bulgarian Mafia in Sweetgrass? How can that be? Did you know she was in trouble?"

That tore it. Ian yanked off his cap and beat it against his thigh, wincing at his sore shoulder. "No."

His dad studied him. "What's wrong with you?"

What's wrong? Ingrained respect kept him from yelling at

his dad, but only barely. "Nothing," he said through gritted teeth.

"Doesn't look like nothing. You sure she's okay?"

"How the hell would I know?" Ian finally exploded. "Think she ever bothered to say one word to me about being in trouble? I knew something was wrong, but would she trust me? Hell, no. She's probably packing right now to leave me—" Barely, only barely, Ian made himself stop.

She's leaving me. That's the problem, isn't it? "She was going to leave, Dad. Likely still will. Just like—"

"Scarlett is nothing like your ma, Ian."

"She's city, through and through. She's been to all kinds of places I'll never—" He shook his head. "Even if she can get clear of all this, she has no reason to stay."

"Think not?" his dad challenged. "You give her any kind of reason?"

She made love to me. I made love to her.

It's just sex, she'd insisted.

Maybe that's all it really had been to her, Ian realized, and a hollow opened up in his chest. Once again, a woman was choosing to go and leave him behind. He glanced up at his dad. "I tried. It wasn't enough."

"Did you tell her you love her?"

"I don't—" *Love her,* he started to say, but his mind filled with images of Scarlett reverently running her hands over the marble slab in his kitchen, of her staring out at the view from his hideaway. Of her laughing and teasing at the cafe and threatening him with her spatula, eyes sparkling with mischief.

Of her in the cupola looking out so wistfully over Sweet-grass, of her grand ideas for what the courthouse could become.

Of her gaze, soft in moonlight as their bodies loved.

Loved.

I never meant to bring my trouble to you, she'd said.

When he thought again of that brute holding her hostage

and what might have happened…

She was convinced they'd try again.

"I don't know if it would help." But was he going to just give up without trying?

What if that made no difference, though? What if she still insisted on going away?

"You can't know without trying."

"But—" Could he really have this discussion? His next words would break his father's heart.

"But what? Isn't it worth finding out? Isn't she worth it?"

"Of course she is, but—" *Just say it.* "What if she can't stay, Dad? I want to be with her, but if she really has to go…" He met his father's eyes. "I can't do that to you."

"You have to." His father shook his head. "It's just land, son. I should have done the same when your ma was so desperate to go. There was a compromise, and I wouldn't make it. I thought these acres were everything."

"They're in your blood," Ian said. "Mine, too." And for the first time in his life, he viewed this place without resentment, feeling the truth of his words. This ground he was standing on had been built with blood and tears and the sweat of generations. His roots went a mile deep. This land defined him as surely as his name. "I can't leave here."

"You can't stay with half a heart, either. I speak from experience."

Ian looked at his dad with new eyes. He'd always thought his dad hadn't missed his mother. "Why did you stay? Was it my fault?"

"No." His dad's voice was resolute. "Not your fault, not one bit. I could have bent, but I didn't. It hurt me that I wasn't enough for her, and I let that hurt harden until it was a big rock that took up all the space inside my chest where my heart should have been." His gaze pierced Ian. "A boulder made up mostly of pride and stubbornness. Learn from me, Ian. Maybe that little girl's got to go, maybe not. But don't you cling to this land so hard that your heart hardens, too. This began as a dream. Be a pity if it turned into a prison instead."

"But what would you do, Dad? How would you get along? The ranch is in trouble. We can't keep going like we have been. Every hand is needed, and still, it's not enough."

"Then maybe we have to sell," his dad answered. "Maybe that's just how things are."

Even though Ian had entertained the possibility, even longed a little for the money and what it would make possible, he found himself shocked to his marrow at the very idea. "No. I can't do that. I can't walk away from all the sacrifices."

"So you'll sacrifice your chance at love instead?"

"What am I supposed to do, Dad? You've put your whole life into this place. Generations before you did, too."

"I think," his dad said slowly, "that no amount of dirt is worth living without the woman you love. My advice to you, son, is to talk to her first. Figure out what's between you. My sense is that she wants to stay, but she needs a reason. Needs to know she has a place to sink roots of her own." He pinned Ian with his gaze. "But that place can be anywhere—being together is what matters. You might want to travel together to scratch that itch you think I don't know you've had all your life. Or maybe you do both—settle here but do some traveling, too. Point is, you and she belong together, and that comes first. If you two decide to stick around, then—" He grinned. "Then, God help me, we'd best talk about how to put some of your newfangled notions into practice so we can make this place thrive again."

Ian's eyebrows rose nearly as fast as his heart. "You'd consider it? Really, Dad?"

"Come on inside, son. This place didn't get built by folks too afraid to take a risk. I just sorta forgot that when I was trying so hard to cling to my belief that I'd made the right choice to stay and let your ma go." As he followed his son inside, he chuckled. "But right now, I'm thinking you'd better get some sleep so you can give that girl your best presentation."

Ian halted. "She might leave during the night."

"Then call Ruby and tell her to lock her in her bedroom if need be."

The image of spitfire Scarlett finding herself a prisoner in her bedroom brought a smile to Ian's face. Shoot, she'd probably climb out the second story window and shimmy down a drainpipe, God help them all.

"Better yet," his dad said with a slap on Ian's back. "You go get your beauty rest, and I'll call Ruby. I'll take guard duty myself, if need be."

The sun was high when Scarlett awoke. She started to stretch, then bolted up in bed, the events of the night before racing scattershot through her brain.

She raced to the door and yanked it open, then charged down the stairs. "Nana!" Her heart thudded as she pondered what might have happened while she was sleeping. "Nana!"

A figure stirred in the entry hall. "She's at the cafe. Everything's fine."

She froze on the bottom step. "Ian." All she could think of was how angry he'd been the night before, how distant. "Why are you here?"

His posture was relaxed. His gaze, no longer cold, scanned her from head to foot. "Tweety Bird boxers, huh?" He grinned, and something inside her eased.

Abruptly she registered her wild mane, her unbrushed teeth. "Um…wait here, all right?" She didn't linger for him to answer but instead raced back up the stairs. She'd showered off the feel of Kostov's man last night, but—

Kostov.

She shuddered. She should be packing. She should already be gone, regardless of what Judge and the sheriff intended. She raced through brushing her teeth and snagged her hair back in a scrunchie. She'd dress and get rid of Ian, then slip out before anyone noticed.

She yanked open the bathroom door.

Ian loomed there. "In case you had any idea of sneaking out, just thought you'd want to know that you're not only being watched over, you're being watched, period."

"What?" She frowned. "You can't imprison me here."

"I can try. Ruby lost the key or she'd have locked you inside the bedroom last night. Instead, folks just took turns on sentry duty."

Her eyes popped. "You cannot be serious."

He closed the distance between them. "As a heart attack. You're not leaving without me."

Her jaw dropped open. "Without...how can you say that? You can't go. Everyone depends on you here."

"Lots of folks depend on you, too, but that doesn't seem to matter."

"I've taught Henry how to cook everything on the menu, and Nana's better now, too."

"You think she's gonna stay better with you gone? She's seventy-one, Scarlett, and tough as nails, yes, but not immortal."

Her heart squeezed. "I know that. I wish..."

"Seems to me you should give folks a chance to weigh in on how much protection they want you to provide them. You might find that everyone here is pretty set on keeping you and taking their chances."

"Rissa's not. Jeanette sure won't be."

He snorted. "Jeanette recognizes what you mean to Ruby, and Rissa...well, she makes a career out of being ornery, but she doesn't mean it."

"So you say. She was pretty clear with me."

"Rissa's been left by more folks than I have. She's just…cautious."

"Cautious, maybe. Bull-stubborn and cranky, if you ask me."

A smile played over his lips. "She'll grow on you." Then his eyes went solemn and intent. "Hasn't this place grown on you some already?"

"Of course it has, but—"

"But nothing." His gaze sharpened. "Have I grown on you?"

You're not leaving without me. She remembered all the books, the longing, but… "Ian, you wouldn't seriously leave here. What would your dad do without you?"

"What I want to know is what would you do without me. Would you miss me, Scarlett?"

Only with every breath. But she couldn't let herself think of that. "It doesn't matter."

"It matters to me." His eyes got the look she'd seen on them before when they were making love, only this time it was deeper and more intense.

"You were furious at me," she pointed out. "You barely spoke to me last night."

His jaw clenched. "Because you nearly got killed trying to be noble!"

"So did you! He held a gun on you! He would have shot you!"

"He didn't. I won."

"But next time you might not—" she cried. "I can't take the chance, Ian—I can't have you dying for me!"

"So you'll just kill me instead by leaving?"

She fell silent. "I—it's not that I don't wish—"

"Wish what, Scarlett? Tell me."

"I wish I could stay!" she exploded. "I wish I could be here forever and ever, that I could be here with Nana and you and make a life and a home and—" She pressed her lips together. "But I can't." Her voice dropped. "I'm afraid to."

His eyes went chocolate warm. "I'm afraid, too, sweetheart. Only I'm afraid of what I'll become without you. My dad told me that he should have compromised, that my mother didn't really want to go, she just needed him to meet her halfway. I'll meet you more than halfway, Scarlett. If Judge and the sheriff can't work their magic, I'll leave here with you, but I am not living the rest of my life without you."

"But...what will happen to everyone without you?"

"It's a problem, isn't it? My dad's actually started talking about putting my concept into practice. Then we'd be able to supply beef for your snazzy events center and restaurant. Sweetgrass might get its second chance to live, and your grandmother might be able to see her dream come true."

"You don't play fair, Ian McLaren."

"Fair doesn't get me the win, Scarlett Ross. What's your middle name, by the way?" He leaned into her, so close she could feel the heat of his broad chest.

"I'm not telling you." She tried to take a step back, but that put her against the sink, and the bathroom shrank to half its size with him in there with her. "And winning isn't everything."

"It is when we're talking about winning you. I'm gonna win you, Scarlett Henrietta Ross."

"Henrietta?"

"Okay, Eloise?" His boots bumped her bare toes. He lifted her with ease and set her on the sink. Bent and pressed his lips to her throat.

Her head fell back. "Not even close."

"I'll just have to keep guessing." He nibbled his way up to her ear.

She moaned. "Ian...this is serious."

"Ethel." His mouth hovered over hers. "That's a serious name."

She tried to shake her head, but he was kissing the corner

of her mouth. "I can't think when you do that."

"I have no intention of stopping for the next fifty or so years."

Her hands clutched at his shoulders. She shoved him back. "Ian…" She gnawed at her lower lip. "Do you honestly believe this can work? Us?"

"I honestly believe I am going to spend the rest of my life making sure it does. Come on, Scarlett. I'd just have to follow you around the country like a stray pup. It would embarrass Blue."

She wanted to laugh. Instead, tears sprang to her eyes. She buried her face in her hands.

"Sweetheart? What did I do?"

Oh, her heart was going to explode with terror and longing and…joy.

Ian peeled her hands from her face and held them. "Tell me what's wrong." His brown eyes were so earnest.

"I want it, all of it. The marble slab and the wood cookstove and the courthouse and my grandmother and…you. I want you, Ian, so badly I can't think, but—"

"You took one hell of a chance coming to Sweetgrass, honey," he said gently. "You didn't know what would happen or what you would find."

She watched him. Nodded.

"Can't you take a chance on me, too? Have faith that we will find a way out of this tangle you're in?"

She could hardly see through the sheen of her tears. "Even if I did, what do I know about staying anywhere?"

"You just start with one day. Today." He bent and kissed the drops from her lashes. "Let us take care of you, Scarlett. Believe we'll fight like hell to defend you—believe that I will do whatever it takes to keep you safe. To make you happy."

His voice was a low, seductive murmur that called to her heart's deepest longing. "Come home to Sweetgrass, darlin'. Sink some roots right here in Texas. Make a home with me."

If she'd ever heard sweeter words, she couldn't recall them.

I don't know why you left, Mama, but I'm closing the circle. Regardless of what I might have to do to make it happen, I'm coming back to stay.

And the place in her heart that had been lonely for so long filled with a warmth that felt like her mother's blessing.

"Magnolia," she whispered.

Ian blinked.

"It's my middle name." She smiled at him.

A slow, answering smile spread over his beloved face. "Welcome home, Scarlett Magnolia Ross." Then he scooped her up, walked out into the hall and swung her in a circle while she laughed for sheer joy.

"Let's go tell Ruby," he said as he bent to kiss her. "Honey, we have got ourselves some big plans to make."

Epilogue

At halftime a few days later, Ruby stood in her accustomed spot in the courthouse cupola, looking out over the town she loved. She no longer kept watch for her daughter, but this time of peace and reflection was a hard habit to break.

Peace. Her job wasn't done yet, but for the first time in many years, she had a peaceful heart and she had hope.

Scarlett had been released from any obligation in New York. The DA, it seemed, had located the sorry excuse for a man who'd taken such advantage of her granddaughter, and he was singing like a little bird, telling all he knew about Kostov in exchange for a lighter sentence.

And Sweetgrass would have a chance to live again. Scarlett and Ian's plans would take money none of them had, but Scarlett swore she could find investors.

Ruby already knew one, however, whose help she might finally relent and accept.

It's time, Jackson. Time you came back home. Veronica needs you. Sweetgrass needs you.

Just then, the cafe's back door opened, and Ruby spotted Ian drawing Scarlett outside, stealing a kiss under the benevolent light of the evening star. She could hear Scarlett's delighted giggle.

Ruby didn't need to make a wish on a star this night. She didn't have her daughter, would always grieve for her absence…but she had Georgia's child to treasure, to surround with years of pent-up love.

*Love…*sighed a soft voice, barely audible.

A faint light shimmered off to Ruby's right.

She turned, but as always, the shape vanished, leaving a palpable sense of sorrow in its wake.

"Scarlett stayed for love," Ruby said to The Lady. "That's not enough?"

Only silence greeted her.

Ruby shook her head and turned back to stare out into the growing night. What would it take for The Lady to find her peace? Who was she waiting for? Maybe The Lady would always grieve, always mourn. Maybe there was nothing Ruby could do to help her, sad as the thought was.

But tonight she wouldn't worry over that. Tonight was for celebrating the living. The hope. The love.

Love strong enough to stay.

~THE END~

Thank you for letting me share my stories with you! If this is your first Sweetgrass Springs book, there are other stories:

TEXAS ROOTS (Book 1 – Ian and Scarlett)

TEXAS WILD (Book 2 – Mackey and Rissa)

TEXAS DREAMS (Book 3 – a reunion of all the Texas Heroes characters at the surprise wedding)

TEXAS REBEL (Book 4 – Jackson and Veronica)

TEXAS BLAZE (Book 5 – Bridger and Penny)

TEXAS CHRISTMAS BRIDE (Book 6 – a Sweetgrass Springs reunion with the Marshalls and the Gallaghers of Morning Star)

There are also three more connected Texas Heroes series (books listed below):

The Gallaghers of Morning Star
The Marshalls
The Book Babes

If you enjoyed TEXAS ROOTS, I would be very grateful if you would help others find this book by recommending it to your friends on Goodreads or by writing a review on the website of the retailer where you purchased this book. If you would like to be informed when my next release is available, please sign up for my newsletter by visiting my website at www.jeanbrashear.com

It's always a joy to hear from you! You can contact me through any of the options listed on the last page of this book.

All my best,
Jean

The Gallaghers of Sweetgrass Springs Series

Texas Roots

When scandal and an ambitious prosecutor wreck talented chef Scarlett Ross's life and she learns of a grandmother she never knew she had, she flees the notoriety to pay an anonymous visit to Sweetgrass Springs, Texas, a town kept alive only by her grandmother's determination and carried on the strong shoulders of sexy cowboy Ian McLaren. There she is surprised to discover a yearning to sink roots deep in the Texas Hill Country—but she is terrified that the secrets she's hiding will endanger everyone she's come to love.

Texas Wild

Hollywood's hot playboy stuntman Randall Mackey replaced the adrenaline rush of his career in the SEAL Teams with another life courting danger, but that existence is jeopardized by injury. The sexy bad boy of Sweetgrass Springs returns to the town where his teenage exploits made him a legend, only to find that his buddy's tomboy little sister has grown up in very interesting ways. If he thinks, however, that gifted horse trainer Rissa Gallagher will simply fall into his arms and help him dodge dealing with a haunting past and a future that looks grim, Mackey might want to think again.

Rissa Gallagher has been abandoned by everyone in her family except the hard-hearted father who is physically present but cold and critical. She is the last hope for the land that has been in her family for six generations, and though Mackey is pure temptation incarnated in one very sexy package, he can never be more than a fling when the only thing he does better than make love is…leave.

Texas Dreams

Take two reluctant brides and two frustrated grooms, mix with both clans of Gallaghers and season with a SEAL or three, a movie star, a Hollywood Barbie and a country music giant—and you get a recipe for family mayhem, laughter and a tear or two. Watch as Sweetgrass Springs matriarch Ruby Gallagher and her granddaughter Scarlett, aided and abetted by the irrepressible Maddie Rose Gallagher, try to pull off surprise wedding plans for each other in the worst-kept secret in Texas.

Texas Rebel

The story of the Gallagher heir who disappeared after a tragedy seventeen years ago...

Jackson Gallagher's teenage rebellion cost him everything: his home, his family and the girl who could only love him in secret. Seventeen years later, a wildly successful multi-millionaire, he is drawn back to Sweetgrass Springs to confront his past: the father who banished him, the town that turned its back on him...and the woman he has never been able to forget.

The last person Veronica Butler is ready to see is the man who made her believe they'd be together forever, then vanished and broke her heart. Widowed and struggling to hold onto her children's heritage, she refuses his help but has trouble resisting the way he makes her remember how deeply she once loved him...except that when he learns the secret she's been keeping all these years, she'll lose him all over again.

Texas Blaze

Stilettos and pencil skirts are more successful, ambitious Pen Gallagher's style than the jeans and boots of the ranch where she was raised. She's fought hard for her success and spared no time for love, certain that marriage and family are not her lot. Now everything she's worked for is jeopardized as scandal brews around her after she got involved with a man who prizes his own ambitions more. Forced to flee D.C. before her identity is revealed and she can never regain the life she battled to build, she reluctantly returns to Sweetgrass.

Former SEAL turned firefighter Bridger Calhoun, on the other hand, visits Sweetgrass every chance he gets. After a recent tragic fire in which he nearly sacrificed his own life, he is ordered to take time off—and Sweetgrass calls to him. After a lifetime spent rootless and fueled by adrenaline, Bridger wants a quiet life, a home and family of his own with a sweet, soft woman as eager for children as he is.

Then a long-legged, sharp-tongued lawyer crosses his path—and flames ignite. While he's waiting to find Ms. Right and she's waiting for the coast to clear…what's the harm in a little fun? It's only temporary, both agree—they have nothing in common except the heat that blazes high between them, and their goals could not be more opposed. Soon the fire will burn down to embers, and they'll go on with their lives. Easy-peasy, right?

Except love may have other plans…

Texas Christmas Bride

It's the first Christmas in Sweetgrass Springs, Texas for several newcomers who have found a real home for the first time—or found home again. As Jackson Gallagher works to save his hometown from withering away by relocating his business empire there, the only gift he really wants is to marry the teenage sweetheart he thought he'd lost forever—but Veronica Patton Butler has other hearts to care for, however much she loves Jackson.

Bridger Calhoun is more than ready to make Penelope Gallagher his bride, but however much she adores him, Shark Girl is dragging her heels on tying the knot—which seems to be a maddening tradition among Gallagher women.

Come join the fun...the heartache...the sweetness, as Sweetgrass prepares for a community celebration that will bring the Morning Star Gallaghers and the Marshalls to town, along with several of Jackson's Seattle geeks and more than one lost soul about to find a place to belong—

In eccentric, lovable, unforgettable Sweetgrass Springs...where hope never fades and love never dies.

The Book Babes

The Book Babes reading group began as five women wanting to talk books—but now they've become family. There's romance author Ava Sinclair, organizer and backbone; happily-married mother of five Ellie Preston, the group's heart; patrician art gallery owner Sylvie Everett; single mom and sociology professor Luisa Martinez; and ambitious attorney Laken Foster, the wild child of the bunch. For several years now, they've met monthly and discussed the current book a little—and dissected their lives and loves far more often.

But now change is rippling through the group, begun by Laken's restlessness with her freewheeling life of serial hookups and sent into hyperdrive by Ava's suddenly-hot career, while Luisa's abusive ex tries to reclaim their teenage son and Sylvie faces her mother's decline. But it's when Ellie takes her first step into life after her children fly the nest and falls under the spell of the sexy artist who's teaching her to paint that the group's orbit begins to wobble on its axis, and life—for all of them and the men they love—will never be the same.

And then there's the Sweetgrass Springs connection that arises…

Get the entire **TEXAS HEROES** series:

The Gallaghers of Morning Star

TEXAS SECRETS (Boone and Maddie)

TEXAS LONELY (Mitch and Perrie)

TEXAS BAD BOY (Dev and Lacey)

The Marshalls

TEXAS REFUGE (Quinn and Lorie)

TEXAS STAR (Josh and Elena)

TEXAS DANGER (Case and Samantha)

The Gallaghers of Sweetgrass Springs

TEXAS ROOTS (Ian and Scarlett)

TEXAS WILD (Mackey and Rissa)

TEXAS DREAMS (Both branches of Gallaghers plus the Marshalls)

TEXAS REBEL (Jackson and Veronica)

TEXAS BLAZE (Bridger and Penny)

TEXAS CHRISTMAS BRIDE (a Sweetgrass Springs reunion with the Marshalls and the Gallaghers of Morning Star)

The Book Babes boxed set

Texas Ties/Texas Troubles/Texas Together

About the Author

New York Times and *USAToday* bestselling author of the popular TEXAS HEROES series and an additional 30 novels in romance and women's fiction, a five-time RITA finalist and RT BOOKReviews Career Achievement Award winner, Jean Brashear knows a lot about taking crazy chances. A lifelong avid reader, at the age of forty-five with no experience and no training, she decided to see if she could write a book. It was a wild leap that turned her whole life upside down, but she would tell you that though she's never been more terrified, she's never felt more exhilarated or more alive. She's an ardent proponent of not putting off your dreams until that elusive 'someday'—take that leap now.

Connect With Jean

Visit Jean's website: www.jeanbrashear.com
Facebook: www.facebook.com/AuthorJeanBrashear
Twitter: www.twitter.com/@JeanBrashear

To be notified of new releases, sign up for Jean's newsletter on her website

51402752R00158

Made in the USA
San Bernardino, CA
21 July 2017